AN
AFRICAN
AFFAIR

NINA DARNTON

℗

A PLUME BOOK

PLUME
Published by the Penguin Group
Penguin Group (USA) Inc., 375 Hudson Street, New York, New York 10014, U.S.A. • Penguin Group (Canada), 90
Eglinton Avenue East, Suite 700, Toronto, Ontario, Canada M4P 2Y3 (a division of Pearson Penguin Canada Inc.) •
Penguin Books Ltd., 80 Strand, London WC2R 0RL, England • Penguin Ireland, 25 St. Stephen's Green, Dublin 2,
Ireland (a division of Penguin Books Ltd.) • Penguin Group (Australia), 250 Camberwell Road, Camberwell, Victoria
3124, Australia (a division of Pearson Australia Group Pty. Ltd.) • Penguin Books India Pvt. Ltd., 11 Community
Centre, Panchsheel Park, New Delhi – 110 017, India • Penguin Group (NZ), 67 Apollo Drive, Rosedale, Auckland
0632, New Zealand (a division of Pearson New Zealand Ltd.) • Penguin Books (South Africa) (Pty.) Ltd., 24 Sturdee
Avenue, Rosebank, Johannesburg 2196, South Africa

Penguin Books Ltd., Registered Offices: 80 Strand, London WC2R 0RL, England

Published by Plume, a member of Penguin Group (USA) Inc. Previously published in a Viking edition.

First Plume Printing, June 2012
10 9 8 7 6 5 4 3 2 1

 REGISTERED TRADEMARK—MARCA REGISTRADA

The Library of Congress has catalogued the Viking edition as follows:
Darnton, Nina.
    An African affair : a novel / Nina Darnton.
      p. cm.
    ISBN 978-0-670-02288-5 (hc.)
    ISBN 978-0-452-29802-6 (pbk.)
    1. Women journalists—Fiction. 2. Americans—Nigeria—Fiction.
    3. Assassination—Nigeria—Fiction. 4. Organized crime—Nigeria—Fiction.
    5. Lagos (Nigeria)—Fiction. I. Title.
    PS3604.A749A69 2011
    813'.6—dc22   2011001507

Printed in the United States of America
Original hardcover design by Carla Bolte

PUBLISHER'S NOTE
This is a work of fiction. Names, characters, places, and incidents are either the product of the author's imagination
or are used fictitiously, and any resemblance to actual persons, living or dead, business establishments, events, or
locales is entirely coincidental.

BOOKS ARE AVAILABLE AT QUANTITY DISCOUNTS WHEN USED TO PROMOTE PRODUCTS OR SERVICES. FOR INFORMATION PLEASE WRITE TO
PREMIUM MARKETING DIVISION, PENGUIN GROUP (USA) INC., 375 HUDSON STREET, NEW YORK, NEW YORK 10014.

FOR JOHN, WITH LOVE

Beware, beware the Bight of Benin
For few come out though many go in.

—Old sailor's rhyme

AN
AFRICAN
AFFAIR

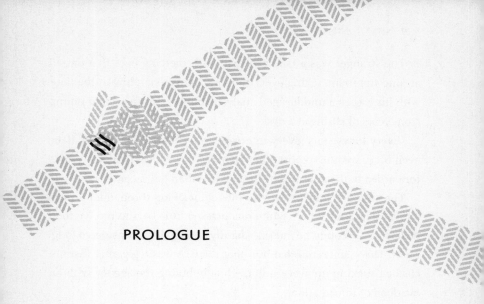

PROLOGUE

The operations room at Langley was unusually busy for a Thursday morning.

Even in the slowest of times, the windowless chamber—the nerve center of the CIA, where all reports and rumors were gathered—was frantically active. The operatives remained vigilant, ready to mobilize at the first sign of trouble anywhere in the world. And today, April 15, 1994, problems were brewing in all the usual places: Serbia continued its attacks on Bosnia, the Hutus escalated their slaughter of the Tutsis, and Moscow and Chechnya were growing increasingly hostile.

The operations room seemed small considering its importance, measuring only thirty by forty feet. In the middle, four computers divided the space into quadrants. An operator sat in front of each monitor scanning the incoming reams of words, then forwarding each report to the correct department as more information streamed in. The operators—two men and two women—were too preoccupied to talk to one another.

A light hanging from the center of the ceiling suddenly flashed, bathing the walls in an eerie yellow glow. It alerted the operatives that someone not cleared to receive classified information had entered.

The stranger was a tall, lean man with piercing eyes that darted around the room, taking everything in. He was standing at the door with his escort, a middle-aged analyst from the Africa section plump from years of sitting at a desk.

"Every news story, every intercept, every piece of economic data, even every weather report pours in here," the analyst bragged, "and is forwarded to the appropriate desk in less than ten seconds."

The stranger smiled. He remembered walking through an experimental psych lab where white rats pressed little bars to receive food pellets. Ten seconds, he mused—hardly enough for a considered judgment. The scene reminded him that the CIA was a gigantic vacuum cleaner, sucking up every tidbit, while hobbling the agency with an overload of information.

One of the operators seemed particularly busy. The computers—set back to back—allowed no one else to see the screen.

"That man," the escort said, pointing, "handles all the field reports. Obviously they get top priority."

The young man suddenly sat upright.

"My God!" he exclaimed before hunching over and hitting some keys.

"What happened?" one of the women yelled.

The young man started to speak, then looked nervously at the two men by the door.

"We'd better leave," whispered the escort, touching the stranger on the elbow.

The coded message was forwarded directly to the deputy director for operations, who immediately summoned an emergency meeting. Within ten minutes, a small group of highly placed analysts and operatives dropped what they were doing and made their way to a secure conference room on the fourth floor. Word had spread throughout the building: William Agapo, their most valuable agent in Nigeria, had been assassinated.

Fortunately, the top experts on Nigeria were already at Langley to discuss what was euphemistically called "the Nigerian landscape," a volatile mix of corruption and drug smuggling with an overlay of politics.

As the analysts and agents filed into the room, there was none of the usual banter. They arranged themselves around an oval mahogany table. James Woolsey, the soft-spoken director, took his seat at the head of the table. Dave Goren, the station chief in Lagos, sat next to him. Goren's pale blue eyes searched the room, then focused on the doorway as Peter Bresson, the elegant ambassador to Nigeria, entered with Bob Albright, the deputy director, a short, scruffy man with crumbs from breakfast still caught in his beard. Albright paused for a moment, staring hard at Goren, who got the message, sighing theatrically as he gave up his seat next to the director.

The last to arrive was Vickie Grebow. Being inconspicuous was not one of her talents. No one could help but notice this thirty-five-year-old Amazon with her platinum blond curly hair and five-foot-ten-inch frame. Everything about Vickie was big—her throaty voice, her exaggerated New York accent, her expansive gestures. She seemed exactly the wrong person to work for an undercover agency, but although she was always noticed, she was never seen.

She plopped her large black shoulder bag on a chair next to Dave Goren and sat down next to it.

"Jesus, I'm sorry," she said to no one in particular. "How did it happen? What do we know?"

"Not much," Goren said. "The message said he and his wife were found in bed with their throats cut. The house was ransacked. The police are calling it a robbery."

"No surprise there," said Vickie.

"Anything taken?" Bob Albright asked.

"We just contacted his secretary," Goren replied. "She said he had taken home all his private papers a few days ago. His safe there was blown. Whatever was in there is gone."

Vickie leaned forward. "Just papers? What about jewelry, cash, electronics?"

"We only know about the safe. There may have been jewelry in it, but the expensive rings and bracelets on the dresser weren't touched."

"Well, that's practically a signed confession, isn't it?" Vickie blurted. "They found out he was working for us and killed him."

Goren raised his eyebrows condescendingly. "Just like that, Vickie, you solved it. It's so easy, we don't even need trained analysts to figure it out."

Vickie shot him an angry look.

"You just heard from a trained analyst. Am I going too fast for you?"

Bob Albright suppressed a smile. "Hold on," he said. "We don't know what happened. But Vickie's right, Dave, it's probably not just a simple robbery."

"Besides, he lived in Ikoyi," Vickie broke in, "home to foreign diplomats and rich Nigerians. It's well patrolled. Most of the houses are surrounded by cement walls and protected by security guards."

Goren snorted. "Right. He had two. They ran away."

"Question them," Albright ordered. "Were they paid to disappear? Did they recognize anyone?"

"If they know who did this they'll be afraid to talk," Vickie said.

"It's our job to make them afraid not to talk," Goren shot back.

"That's where we differ, Dave. I think it's our job to help them feel safe to talk."

Albright nodded his head slowly up and down, a personal tic they all knew well. It meant he had reached a decision.

"We need another asset on the ground. Vickie, I want you to go to Lagos as soon as possible," he said. "Your cover will be as the new deputy political officer. Bill, your office can take care of the details. Nose around, Vickie. I know you're good at that. We want information on this killing, of course, but without Agapo, we've lost our eyes and ears. We need to know what that tin-pot dictator is up to and get a fix on his opposition. So far, we've remained neutral—at least officially. You'll report to Peter on paper, as Dave does. But be sure to keep me up to speed."

"I'll need to be brought up to date on the details," Vickie said. "Are you thinking it's the work of local operatives or are we looking at Solutions, Incorporated? A mercenary operation that assassinates people who can't be bought off would suit Olumide perfectly."

"The point is, we don't know," Goren said, "but that group seems too sophisticated for overt assassination. Why not hire some local to do it?"

He turned to Albright with an air of exasperation. "My apologies if I'm out of line here, but we know that Vickie's strengths—great as they are—are intuitive, not intellectual. Don't we need more mature analysis for this situation?"

The director impatiently pushed back his chair and rose.

"I think we'll go with Bob's plan. If you have a problem with it, Dave, get over it." He turned to the deputy director. "And keep me apprised of whatever they find."

He walked out of the room.

Vickie turned to Goren. "This is just the kind of thing Solutions, Incorporated does—acts of sabotage for a political goal. It's not a wild idea at all, especially if the hit was ordered by the top guy."

"That's enough," Albright said, standing up. "You'll know more when you're on the scene. I'd like to leave this meeting confident you and Dave will work well together."

"Yes, sir," Vickie boomed. "We'll get along fine, won't we, Dave?"

"Sure," he replied. He looked Albright straight in the eye. "You have my word on that, sir."

The ambassador stood up to leave.

"Don't worry," Albright said. "They always settle into a professional relationship. They challenge each other, but it generates results."

Looking skeptical, the ambassador picked up his papers and withdrew. Dave Goren shook Albright's hand and nodded at Vickie.

"Well, welcome aboard. See you in Lagos."

"Thank you. Looking forward to it." Vickie grinned.

Albright walked to the door, then turned to face her.

"I want to stay on top of this. I don't have to tell you how important it is. You'll report through regular channels. But feel free to contact me directly if there are any serious problems."

"I will, sir. I have some ideas about where to start," she began intently.

She was about to elaborate but he had left, his mind already on the next problem.

"You can count on me, sir," she said to the empty space.

≋

Downstairs, as his escort guided him through the front lobby, the stranger stopped to browse through a souvenir shop, much to the annoyance of his guide. The stranger picked up one of the coffee mugs for sale, turning it over in his hand.

It was meant as a joke. CIA was scrawled across the top. Below, large block letters proclaimed: "**SPECIAL AGINT.**" Acknowledging the misspelling, a thick black line was drawn through them. Below, a second attempt read: "**SECRIT OPERATIVE.**" That too was crossed out. The final line was a single word: "**SPY.**"

The stranger smiled and bought the mug. He carried it in his left hand as he shook hands with the little bureaucrat and turned toward the security check. Passing the wall of memorial plaques to the agents who had died in the line of duty, he wondered where the newest one would go.

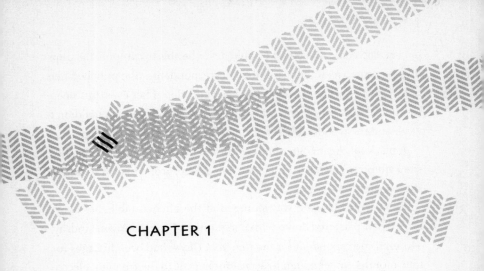

CHAPTER 1

A phone was ringing somewhere. Its shrill, insistent screech broke through Lindsay's sleep, but she was sure it wasn't her phone—that hadn't worked in days. She sat up and threw off her sheets, which were damp with perspiration. There was that sound again. It *was* her phone. She scrambled to lift up the receiver.

"Lindsay," a voice shouted. "What the hell's going on? I haven't heard a word from you in over a week."

Joe Rainey, the foreign editor, sounded far away through the scratchy connection.

"The line's been out," she yelled back.

"Why the hell do you think we gave you a sat phone?" he asked.

"It's broken. No one here can fix it. And the power keeps failing so I often can't use my computer. It's lucky I have an old manual typewriter, but I need a generator," she said. "I'm waiting for the business side to approve it. Can you put some pressure on—" but before she could say another word, the connection was severed. The landline had expired as mysteriously as it had sprung to life.

She glared at the ticking clock: 3:00 A.M. There must be some unwritten law decreeing that editors would never be able to compute the time difference between them and their correspondents. She punched her pillow into a soft lump under her head and closed her eyes. But sleep wouldn't come. The air was thick and muggy. The air conditioner didn't work and the wooden blades of the ceiling fan weren't moving.

A blackout. Again. She fumbled for a candle, lit it with the matches she kept on the bedside table and, half-asleep, groped her way downstairs to get some water.

Her friend Maureen was slumped at the kitchen table, her short brown hair plastered down with perspiration. Poor Maureen. Lindsay, a foreign correspondent for the *New York Globe*, had been in Lagos for four months, long enough to accustom herself to the frequent electrical disruption and the relentless heat. But Maureen, an AP reporter, had arrived only yesterday for a brief assignment.

Both had been based in London and specialized in West Africa. Half a year ago Lindsay began hearing stories about the corruption and cruelty of General Michael Olumide, Nigeria's military dictator. Exiles said he made millions from drug dealing, that he used the country as his private ATM, and that the walls of his underground jails were stained with blood. When she learned that the paper was planning to open a full-time bureau in Nigeria, she had lobbied hard for the job. Rainey had been reluctant to assign her—she suspected that he thought it too dangerous for a woman but didn't dare say so. Then, one of Olumide's advisers, widely rumored to be working for the Americans, was found murdered. Olumide claimed that there was evidence pointing to The Next Step, an anticorruption movement that was an unlikely culprit since it believed in change by counting votes rather than cutting throats. The dissidents pointed to Olumide as the more obvious suspect. Others said it was the work of northern fundamentalists who had been agitating for Islamic law. Lindsay told her bosses that she had already developed a network of sources among dissidents. She insisted this could be a very big story, with international repercussions, a Pulitzer contender. Rainey relented. Pulitzer talk always brought editors around.

Maureen's brief was more specific—a story on the main opposition leader, Femi Fakai, who had promised an interview with the Western press. Since the AP had no resident correspondent, she had also been assigned to write some features on the Nigerian economy and oil production.

The two women had been close friends since high school. They chose the same college—the University of Wisconsin at Madison—and joined the school paper together. In their senior year, both wanted the job of editor, and the board, finding it impossible to choose, split the job between them. Though different in many ways, they worked well as a team. Maureen, barely five feet tall, with curly brown hair and striking blue eyes, was feisty, outspoken, and honest to a fault. She could hone in on the holes in a reporter's story but needed Lindsay's diplomatic talents to communicate her criticisms. Lindsay, whose parents had changed their name from Kaminsky to Cameron, was lively, witty, flirtatious, and pretty. She had a tall, graceful body, long, straight auburn hair, and hazel eyes, qualities which made her popular in spite of her ambition and academic success.

After college, they went into journalism and became indefatigable reporters, but at thirty-six, Maureen had achieved a more well-rounded life. As Lindsay's mother never tired of pointing out, Maureen was married—to Mark, an American diplomat she met in Warsaw. Her mother might have changed her name, but she still had Kaminsky values. Even after her divorce from Lindsay's father, she had absolute faith that marriage and babies defined success for a woman.

"Hi," Lindsay said, coming into the kitchen. "You just get up?"

Maureen shook her head. "I couldn't sleep. Any tricks for dealing with this heat?"

"Yeah," Lindsay answered. "Go back to London."

It wasn't really funny, and Maureen was too tired to pretend.

"The only thing I've found that helps is a bath," Lindsay said. "The water isn't cold, but if you don't dry off, the evaporation cools you off."

"I'll try it," Maureen said, obediently trudging upstairs. "They never told me about this in journalism school," she added over her shoulder.

Lindsay started to laugh. "No? Jesus, I had a whole course in it. It was called 'Resourcefulness in tight spots.' Go back to bed as soon as you can," Lindsay called after her. "You'll need all the sleep you can get. You're in West Africa. You never know what this place is going to throw at you."

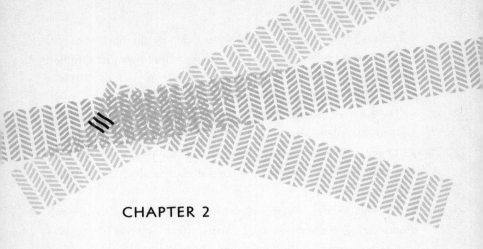

CHAPTER 2

Lindsay awoke at 7 A.M., hot and sweaty. She showered and dressed in a pair of cotton drawstring pants and a white linen shirt and pulled her long hair back into a ponytail.

Walking down the hall, she quietly peeked into the guest bedroom. Maureen was still asleep, her face damp with perspiration. Sensing her friend's presence, Maureen opened her eyes and immediately shielded them from the bright sunlight streaming in through the window.

"I'll make some coffee," Lindsay said.

In the kitchen, she boiled the water and poured it into a large four-quart tin filter to eliminate the silt. Maureen staggered in and sat at the table.

Lindsay poured two cups and handed one to Maureen.

"I'm impressed," Maureen mumbled, her voice still thick with sleep. "And just think—I used to say that you couldn't even boil water."

"Yeah, well, next time check your facts. I happen to be a gourmet water boiler."

They moved to the living room. The power had come on and the ceiling fan was slowly turning, moving the torpid air without cooling it. Lindsay sat on a rattan couch surrounded by plump brown and orange tie-dyed pillows, resting her feet on a brown leather ottoman decorated with gold-stitched geometric designs. A stack of clips was piled before her and she began reading them.

"I've got a lot of background material here," she said. "You're welcome to read whatever you want."

"Thanks, Linds," Maureen answered. "I'll look through it, but I did a lot of research in London." She paused, then smiled. "You seem as cool as a cucumber."

"You should have seen me when I first arrived. I stared out the cab window at the open sewers and crowded streets and thought, 'This is terrible, but soon I'll be in Ikoyi, where the foreigners live.' As we kept driving, the houses got bigger and nicer, but the smell never changed and the garbage mounds were just as high. And then the driver pulled into our driveway and I realized that this was as good as it gets."

"Well, you can't really complain," Maureen said, gesturing to take in the spacious room. "You live better than ninety-five percent of the locals."

"More like ninety-nine percent. When I saw the servants' quarters, where our steward Martin lives with his family, I actually cried. Two small rooms off a dark hallway running along the outside of the house. There was no electricity and the outhouse was just a hole in the ground. I tried to imagine what the British colonialists were thinking when they housed the people who worked for them, what it said about how they viewed them.

"So I had Martin's quarters painted and wired for electricity. They have the right to the same blackouts we have, right? I put in fans, installed a bathroom, and paid some local guys to cart away the garbage. I felt great for about a week. Then one day I was standing in the garden and I saw a huge pile of garbage floating right past the house. Those guys had just dumped it all in the creek. Soon the garbage was piled as high as before. Only now I don't notice it so much."

Martin came into the room as they were talking. A slight man of forty-two, he was dressed neatly in his customary brown trousers and white shirt. He had the slightly self-effacing manner of someone who had worked as a servant for most of his life. Though not formally educated past sixth grade, he had learned Western customs and had almost erased the pidgin English he'd grow up with.

"Good morning, madam," he said, tilting the blinds to protect the furniture from the sun.

"Good morning," she answered cheerily. "Martin, this is my best friend, Maureen. Maureen, this is my savior, Martin. Not only does he cook and shop and make my life here possible, he's also my best source of information on everything from politics to local events."

Martin looked abashed. "I know nuttin' about politics," he said uncomfortably. "Welcome to Lagos, madam," he said, raising his eyes to look at Maureen. "You arrive okay? No big palaver at the airport?"

"Yes, yes, it was fine," Maureen said, trying to shake his hand, but he ducked his head and quickly withdrew into the kitchen.

"Actually, it was horrible," Maureen said to Lindsay. "The immigration guy sits up so high you strain your neck while being interrogated."

"They do that to make you feel like a supplicant. So what did you say?"

"I didn't. I just quietly showed my passport and answered their questions in a matter-of-fact way," Maureen said. "Unfortunately, that seemed to work, because here I am."

"Sometimes I get through it by imagining I'm in a movie," Lindsay said. "And it is kind of like that, isn't it? The guards, with their eyes curtained by dark shades, the demand for papers and visas, the long delays while they wait for the bribe you end up fumbling for."

"They make you show your return ticket to be sure you plan to leave, like it's so wonderful here, you might want to stay forever."

"Once I was in, I knew what to do because I was prepared by Jimmy Garner. Remember him?" Lindsay asked.

"Remember him? Are you kidding? We talked about him at lunch for six months."

"I apologize. But he was the one who gave me the three rules of survival for entering Nigeria." Lindsay held up a finger and enumerated each point. "Fight off the people swarming around like sand flies trying to do something for you. Don't let anyone take your bag; you'll never see it again. Bribe—or 'dash' as they say here—anyone who can get you a taxi into town. Unfortunately, there are no rules for how to survive after that."

They both laughed. Lindsay glanced down at her articles and said she'd secured the promise of an interview with Olumide himself.

"That's amazing. What have you found out about him so far?" Maureen asked.

"That he is certainly one of Africa's gangster heads of state, steadily bleeding the country while transfusing his own Swiss bank accounts. His control is so tight it's hard to imagine the drug trade flourishing without him. The problem is, it's very hard to prove this, or even get anyone to accuse him on the record," she said. "Most people are afraid to talk openly. After the assassination even the dissidents seem to have gone to ground, at least for now. I've cultivated some sources who might talk off the record, but that's about it."

"When is your interview with him?"

"Tomorrow."

"I don't have to tell you to be careful, do I?"

"No, of course not. And don't worry." She paused a beat. "I'm not expecting him to be honest. But he wants something from me—a public forum to reach Washington—and I want to ask him if he's serious about holding elections and ending military rule. Of course he'll lie, but at least I'll have him on the record."

Maureen nodded.

Lindsay checked the clock—the 9 A.M. BBC broadcast was about to begin. She turned on the radio in time to catch the familiar opening strains of the Queen's March. She listened, but the broadcast ended without mentioning Nigeria.

Lindsay had tried to sound confident, but in actual fact she was struggling against frustration. She knew that even if she got a good story, she would have problems filing. With no reliable phone or electrical line, she couldn't count on using her computer, and while some hotels had modems for the Internet, the connections were dicey. That left the public communications office with a single telex and long lines. Friends suggested she might be able to use the private telex of the Agence France-Presse man, who had paid a huge bribe to get it. But he was on home leave for a few more days.

Lindsay decided to focus on small, obtainable goals. Today, she'd simply prepare for the interview with Olumide. She'd read the clips and talk to the American ambassador, Peter Bresson, an old friend. On the way to the embassy, she'd stop at the public communications office and send a message to the foreign desk alerting them to expect the interview.

She looked up to see Maureen fiddling with the telephone.

"It doesn't work," Lindsay said. "You know that, right?"

"Yes. But you never can tell. Maybe a miracle happened while we slept."

"Yeah, right. Maybe you'll have better luck at the AP office."

"Let's hope so. I need to call Mark to tell him I arrived safely and I'll have to contact the London bureau. In the meantime, I'm hungry. What's for breakfast?"

In the kitchen, Martin was setting the table.

"What would madam like?" he asked.

"The usual, please. And the same for my friend."

Maureen leaned over and whispered in Lindsay's ear. "What would *madam* like?"

"I know," Lindsay said softly. "I've tried but I can't get him to stop calling me that—let alone convince him to use my first name." She smiled at Martin. "Can you explain to my friend why you insist on being so formal?"

"Because you are my employer, madam," Martin said softly. "It's not good to forget who we are in Lagos." He turned back to his work.

"This will be good for you today," he said, as he served eggs with pan-fried toast. "For driving in this place you need be strong." Then, almost talking to himself, he murmured, "I will look for a driver for you tomorrow. It is no good you always drive yourself."

"Okay. That would be a help. Thanks."

The women wolfed down their breakfasts.

"Would it be all right with you if I stopped by after work to read to Eduke?" Lindsay asked, referring to Martin's three-year-old son, a favorite of hers. "I have a new book for him."

"He will be very happy, madam. Thank you."

Lindsay nodded, drained another cup of coffee, waved good-bye and stepped outside into the wall of hot, humid air.

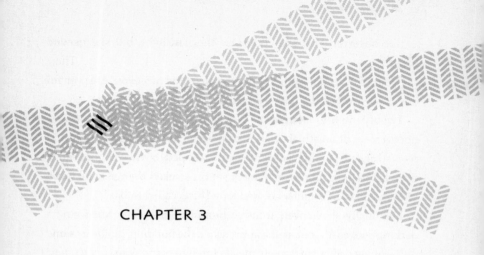

CHAPTER 3

She made her way through the crowded street as if on an obstacle course, careful not to step into the open sewers, trying to adjust to the jumble of smells, a combination of human excrement, perspiration, garbage, and gas fumes. Vendors were already hawking their wares. A man in a blue and gold cotton print dashiki implausibly carrying a couch on his head snaked past a group of women selling cigarettes, candles, and beer. The women wore tie-dyed kaftans with bright head ties. Some had strapped their babies to their backs with wide swaths of matching fabric. They walked easily, swaying only slightly, though they carried their wares in bulky baskets balanced on their heads.

Once in her car, Lindsay entered the mammoth traffic jam that Nigerians, with magnificent understatement, called a "go-slow." More like a "no go," she thought, as she edged along narrow, crowded roads pockmarked with potholes the size of manhole covers. Vendors ran alongside, poking their heads into her open windows.

"You go buy flashlight, madam," shouted a man dressed in a loose-fitting dashiki. "Dis be good flashlight. You no go buy?"

She observed that she could use the flashlight, but she needed batteries.

"Wait," the vendor said. "I go for buy dem and meet you." He pointed one block away at the next traffic light.

Twenty minutes later, as she pulled up to the light, there he was—not even out of breath, the batteries in his hand. She paid for them and plowed ahead, passing legless beggars strapped to wheeled platforms, open-air barbers whose customers sat on stacked orange crates, and bicyclists clad in brightly colored long shirts called Bubas.

Eventually, she arrived at the communications office. She found a parking spot easily, but as she approached the building, her heart sank. A line of harried businessmen, mostly foreigners trying to contact their home offices, snaked around the block. She joined them and waited close to an hour. Finally, she walked up front to see what the problem was. She discovered that no one was in the booth. Finding a clerk, she asked, "Excuse me, where is the man on duty?"

"He not on seat."

"Yes. I can see he's not on his seat. I am not asking where he is not, I am asking where he is," she said. "I have been waiting for an hour." Her voice was rising.

"Don't get hot," the clerk advised her, his face a mask of indifference. "He go come back soon."

After two hours, she took her place at an old telex machine. She quickly typed her message onto the telex keyboard. On her right the machine spewed out the yellow tape whose perforations coded her words. When she finished, she threaded the tape into the transmission slot, dialed the international routing number for her newspaper, and sat back while the machine sent the message.

Getting back into her car, she set out for the embassy. Turning right, she found the road blocked by a large mob. About a hundred people, mostly young men, were shouting in unison, "Olumide Must Go!" The traffic was at a standstill—the driver of the car directly in front of her had disappeared—so she left her car and pushed her way through the crowd. A thin young man appeared to be the leader. He had an angular face and distinct Yoruba tribal scars—three deep, slanted lines on each cheek. Wearing a T-shirt proclaiming THE NEXT STEP, he was pumping his fist into the air and screaming "Fakai First, Fakai Forever, Fakai, Yeah, Fakai, Yeah."

In the distance, Lindsay noticed a group of uniformed soldiers approaching ominously, swinging their clubs. When they reached the demonstrators, they began slamming people in the ribs, the back, the legs. Some protesters tried to run, others started to look for a way out of the tightly packed streets. A teenaged boy fell and screamed as the crowd panicked and trampled him. But the young man in THE NEXT STEP shirt kept chanting, even as two of the soldiers moved toward him. "Fakai First," he spat out, "Fakai Forever." His comrades backed off and he seemed about to follow when he noticed Lindsay and paused, as if wondering who this white woman scribbling in a notebook was. As he reached out to hand her a leaflet, she saw a soldier moving behind him, his club raised. "Run!" she screamed, but her warning was lost in the noise of the crowd. He was still chanting when they grabbed him. Horrified, Lindsay saw the soldier raise his club and bring it down hard on the protester's head. The man crumpled and they threw him into a black van, the infamous Black Maria of the military police.

Lindsay continued writing down everything she saw as she navigated her way through the fleeing crowd. She had just found a place to stand when a hand reached from behind her and grabbed her notebook. She turned and looked up at a tall and angry soldier.

"What you tink you do?" he asked.

"Nothing, Officer," Lindsay answered, realizing this was the same man who had clubbed the protester. "I'm a reporter. I'm just doing my job."

"What you be? You be English?"

"No. I'm American," she answered, "from New York."

"So maybe you be American spy, yes? Maybe you be CIA?"

This alarmed her. Nigerians were paranoid about the CIA.

"No, Officer. I'm an accredited correspondent whose papers have been approved by the highest authorities. I have an interview tomorrow with General Olumide himself." She removed her papers from her handbag and offered them to him.

The soldier glanced at them.

"They be expire," he lied, staring straight at her.

She paused for a fraction of a second.

"Oh, Officer, I am so sorry. I know there is a fine for that," she said, taking a one-hundred-naira note out of her wallet. "Would it be possible for me to pay it right now?"

He grabbed the bill from her hand and pocketed it.

"Be sure you go for fix it," he said, handing back her notebook.

Lindsay retreated as fast as she could. Looking back, she thought she saw the officer point another soldier in her direction. She started to run and when she reached her car, she didn't see anyone following. Her heart was beating wildly. Had she imagined that he was coming after her?

The traffic began to move and the people stuck behind her car were leaning on their horns, so she climbed in quickly and started the engine. Driving to the embassy, she kept checking over her shoulder, but saw nothing suspicious. She was just beginning to relax when she noticed a black car turning after her. She parked a few doors from the embassy's main entrance, looked back and saw the same black car stop at the end of the street. Two men in army uniforms, one in the driver's seat, one in the back, did not move. They just sat. Waiting.

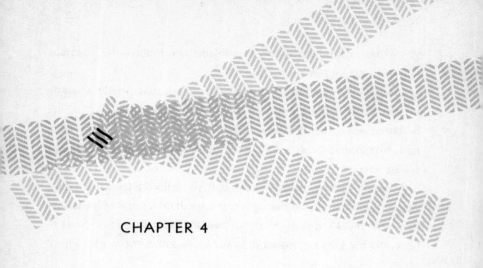

CHAPTER 4

A marine guard led Lindsay into the ambassador's waiting room. Hot and sticky, her clothes moist with perspiration, she luxuriated in the air-conditioning. Linda, a perky blond secretary, offered her a soft drink. When she returned with an icy Coca-Cola, Lindsay downed it gratefully.

"I love America," Lindsay said as she flopped back on a green tweed upholstered sofa under a large print of New York harbor in the nineteenth century.

Linda looked pleased.

"Yes," she said. "Isn't it wonderful? We're very lucky."

Lindsay had meant the air-conditioning, but she smiled politely. After checking that the ambassador was ready, Linda ushered Lindsay through a set of double doors.

"The ambassador will see you in the secure room," she said.

Lindsay was puzzled. She knew that in certain countries, especially in the Eastern bloc, U.S. embassies guarded against electronic eavesdropping, but she couldn't conceive of such a need in Lagos. In fact, given their telephone and power problems, she doubted the Nigerians had the necessary infrastructure.

Lindsay had dated Peter Bresson, the ambassador, briefly when he was on the Africa desk in Washington. She had liked him, but then he had been reassigned to Kenya, and she too moved on to London. They had corresponded only a few times, but she was looking forward to seeing him.

Running her fingers through her hair, she followed Linda up a staircase to the top floor. On the right was a small door with a plaque saying: "TOP SECRET. ANY MENTION OF THE EXISTENCE OF THIS ROOM IS GROUNDS FOR PROSECUTION UNDER ACT 831 OF THE NATIONAL SECURITY CODE."

The room was windowless with white noise pumped in to drown out all other sound. Lindsay saw another small room within, made of transparent plastic. Wires suspended this room so it didn't directly touch the outside wall or the floor. Peter Bresson was sitting inside.

"Pete," she said, kissing him on both cheeks. "Is all this really necessary? Because if you're just trying to impress me, you've succeeded."

He was a big man, tall and broad-shouldered, with an athletic frame that had softened slightly around his middle in the years since she'd last seen him. He charged toward her awkwardly, pulling her into a bear hug.

"Hey, Lindsay. It's great to see you. I'm sorry about all this cloak-and-dagger stuff, but we do really need to be careful about what gets back to the Nigerian government. This room is totally secure."

"It's not the room I'm worried about," Lindsay answered. "I just had a really disturbing experience." She told him about the demonstration, the brutal arrest, and her own brush with the military police. He nodded thoughtfully.

"I'm sorry that happened, but maybe it's a good thing you saw first-hand exactly what we are dealing with here," he said. "I wanted you to come in anyway, partly to warn you."

"Warn me about what?" Lindsay asked, startled.

"I hear you have an interview with Olumide tomorrow."

Lindsay nodded. Of course he would know.

"I wanted to talk to you before you go. First of all, everything I say is completely off the record."

Lindsay understood perfectly. She could use the information as background, but couldn't say anything that would allow it to be traced to him or the embassy. She hesitated for a second, then said, "Okay."

"Well, the situation here is heating up. Our information indicates that things will get very tough in the next few weeks, tough for everyone. By all means do your interview tomorrow—you're lucky to get it. But afterward, you should leave. If you file any story from here that is critical of Olumide, you'll be in serious personal danger."

"You mean like William Agapo?" she asked.

Bresson flinched. "Terrible business. Him and his wife—throats slashed. That's one more reason you should leave."

Lindsay sat quietly, watching her old friend's face. Then she leaned forward and spoke slowly.

"Now wait a minute. Let me get this straight. You're telling me that something really big and newsworthy is about to happen. And you decide that, good reporter that I am, I should get out of town, leaving my colleagues to hit the front page day after day? Did I get that right or did I leave something out?"

The ambassador smiled ruefully and stood up.

"Yeah, well, I knew this was a long shot."

He poured himself a glass of orange juice, offering her one. She shook her head no.

"You're the one with the Olumide exclusive. I don't think you should be here when it comes out. You can always come back later."

"Right. If whatever it is you think is going to happen is so potentially dangerous, they'll never let me back in and you know it."

Bresson looked crestfallen, so she softened for a moment.

"Pete, thanks for your concern. Really. But you know I can't leave. This is the kind of situation a reporter dreams of. I wouldn't be much good if I left the country because I knew that some big story was about to break. Anyway, you don't really know for certain."

Bresson paused for a few seconds. Then, lowering his voice, he repeated, "This is off the record."

"I understand."

"We have information that sometime in the next few weeks Fakai will be arrested."

Lindsay leaned forward.

"Arrested? For what?"

"He'll be charged with plotting a coup. They are going to pin the Agapo murder on him."

"Jesus. Is there any truth to this?"

"Not likely. We think the charge is trumped up."

"But if they arrest him, there'll almost certainly be demonstrations."

"Exactly. That's the idea. Olumide will then use the chaos as an excuse to call off the elections and continue military rule."

"And Fakai will be effectively out of the way since he'd have been sure to beat Olumide in the elections," said Lindsay. She paused, then added, "Well, frankly, that doesn't sound like a scenario that would upset our government. American oil companies can't be too happy about Fakai. He's been hinting at more local controls, even partial nationalization."

"It's complicated. I'm not going to say more on that." He poured himself another orange juice.

"I'm grateful you said what you did, Pete. Thank you."

"Lindsay, I can't force you to leave, but I am asking, as your friend, for you to be careful. I'm not going to lie to you. Of course the U.S. doesn't want an incident. You know as well as I do that Olumide is dangerous. And I'm sure you realize that there are factions in our government who will tolerate anything to get rid of Fakai. I don't know how much I can protect you."

"I guess we'll find out," Lindsay answered. "But I do promise to be careful, and I thank you for the warning. I'll see you tonight."

"Before you go, I'd like you to meet our new political officer. Since you are obviously going to be here for a while, she will be your main contact."

He picked up the phone.

"Ask Vickie to drop by, please."

A few minutes later, Vickie bounded into the room and shook Lindsay's hand.

"Welcome to the Bat Cave," she said. "Is this your first time?"

"Well, yes," Lindsay said. "At least the first time in Lagos. But I should be welcoming you. When did you arrive?"

"Just a few weeks ago, but I did a tour here five years ago. Things were even worse then, if you can imagine that."

"So how badly did you mess up for them to send you back?"

Vickie laughed and looked at Peter. "Hey—you told me it was a reward for a job well done. . . ." She looked at her watch and then turned to Lindsay. "I'm really sorry, but I've got to run to a meeting. I'm sure we'll be seeing a lot of each other." She walked out, wiggling her fingers in a wave.

"I really ought to be going too," Lindsay said. She thanked Peter, and caught up with Vickie in the hallway.

"Are you coming to the ambassador's party tonight?" Vickie asked.

"Yes, I'm planning to."

"Well, good. I'll see you there."

Vickie had reached her office and was about to enter when she turned back toward Lindsay.

"What are you wearing?"

Lindsay was taken aback, but only for a moment.

"A silk dress. Bright orange, wraparound skirt. What about you?"

"I'm not sure. I was thinking of a black cotton sheath. I read in some fashion magazine that it doesn't matter what you wear, as long as it's black. Bye."

Lindsay smiled, watching her disappear behind the closed door.

As she was leaving the building, she bumped into Dave Goren, the embassy's chief political officer.

"Hey, Lindsay, how's it going?"

"Pretty well," she answered, guardedly.

Goren was thirty-two, a total straight arrow, growing up in Racine, Wisconsin, graduating Georgetown, followed by an orderly climb up the State Department ladder. His blond hair was cut very short, like a marine's.

He was good-looking in a clean-cut midwestern way, but she'd never trusted him. He moved around a lot and it was unclear exactly what his duties were, but he dropped in at most of the hot spots. In fact, he turned up in a lot of the same places as Lindsay, which was natural for a journalist, but for a government man it suggested one thing and one thing only: CIA.

"You do your Olumide interview yet?" he asked.

Of course, thought Lindsay. He knows too.

"No," she said. "Tomorrow."

"So, who you been talking to?" Dave asked casually.

"Peter," she answered.

Dave snorted. "Did he say anything helpful?"

"Nothing much," Lindsay answered. "Just background."

"Well, just between us, and off the record," Dave said, leaning closer to her, "I'd take his briefings with a grain of salt if I were you."

"Really? Why?"

"I don't mean to criticize Peter, but he can be a little naïve. You should talk to me before the interview."

"Naïve how?"

"He sees things in black and white—forgive the pun."

Lindsay waited.

"He doesn't realize how important Olumide is to our interests," Dave continued. "We have a lot of influence as long as he's in power. He deserves our support."

They were standing on the steps of the embassy and, looking out, Lindsay noticed the black car still waiting at the end of the street.

"Well, see if you can use your influence to get those guys to stop following me," she said.

Dave glanced at the car. His expression didn't change.

"It might be better if you left the country after your interview," he said.

"Ah," Lindsay answered. "There's something you and Peter agree on. Why do I get the feeling you're all trying to get rid of me?"

He shrugged.

"What have you been doing lately?" she prodded.

"Nothing much."

"I heard you were out of town when William Agapo was killed."

"Really? Who told you that?"

"I hear things. Any idea who's responsible?"

"No."

She was about to ask more but stopped when she noticed him staring at her, his eyes icy blue.

"Coming to the party tonight?" she asked.

"Wouldn't miss it."

"Well, I'll see you there," she said, walking toward her car.

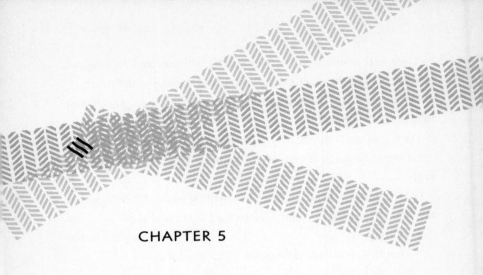

CHAPTER 5

Lindsay made her way to the bar and ordered a scotch, hoping the liquor would steady her. It burned going down but had a soothing effect. It had been a trying day. The black car had followed her home. She hadn't seen it again when she left for the party, but she remained on edge throughout the drive, nervously checking the rearview mirror.

She looked around the room, spotting a few of the local hacks who turned up regularly at these events for the free booze and the hope of loose tongues among the diplomats and occasional government officials. She saw a man she didn't recognize chatting with some journalists and, assuming it was the new man from the *Observer*, made her way over to meet him. She stood at the edge of the group, listening to the end of a tense exchange between the stranger and Dave Goren. When Goren left, the newcomer muttered under his breath, "Stupid shit."

Lindsay moved forward. "Well, I can't think of a better moment to introduce myself," she said. "We already have so much in common." She put out her hand. "I'm Lindsay Cameron with the *Globe*."

He turned toward her, his expression still angry.

"Mike Vale," he said, reflexively taking her hand. "*Observer*."

His face took on the engaging expression she sensed he used for pretty women.

He was tall and thin with black hair, hazel eyes, and a complexion dark enough to make her wonder about his ethnicity. He was dressed in the classic safari suit of light cotton pants and a matching shirt. He was handsome, Lindsay thought, a filmmaker's idea of a foreign correspondent.

"Welcome to Lagos," she said. "I knew your predecessor. I'm surprised we haven't run into each other before."

"I just arrived. My last assignment was Washington and I had to go back to settle my family and tie up some loose ends for the move."

"When does your family come?"

"They don't. My wife's decided to stay in D.C. with the kids."

"Oh. I'm sorry."

"No. Don't be. This is no place for children."

Ken Abbot of the *Telegraph* chimed in: "I'll drink to that." He sidled up and put his arm around Lindsay's shoulder.

"You'll drink to anything." She laughed. "What's going on?"

"Goren just finished his 'we ought to love Olumide' speech," Ken said. "He thinks he's the best Africa hand in the business but he doesn't know jackshit."

"He did some time in the Congo before he came here," Mike said.

"Yeah, that's true. That makes him the only one in Nigeria who thinks he's come up in the world," Lindsay remarked.

"He's a spook," Ken said. "Who knows what he's thinking? All you can be sure of is that whatever he does tell us is a lie."

A veteran reporter who had worked for the *Telegraph* in posts from China to South Africa, Ken had been stationed in Lagos for five years. He was so burned out he rarely covered anything more than government releases.

Lindsay spotted Maureen across the room standing next to Vickie, who, true to her word, was decked out in a sexy black dress adorned with large amber beads. They were in an intense conversation with a man Lindsay didn't know. Vickie caught her eye and gave a friendly wave, gesturing in the direction of the bar. Lindsay was about to join her but was stopped by Maureen, who was leading the stranger over to meet her. He was about forty, with sandy hair that touched his collar. As they approached, the man smiled at Lindsay with an easy grace. She smiled back. His intense brown eyes never left her face.

"Lindsay," Maureen said, "I'd like to present an old friend, James Duncan. James, this is Lindsay Cameron, an even older friend."

"Such an old friend, in fact, that I can't believe Maureen has a friend that I don't know," Lindsay said.

"Well, he's really an old friend of Mark's," Maureen admitted. "But we've both seen him several times in London. I had no idea he was coming to Lagos."

Lindsay extended her hand.

He took it and held it just a fraction of a second longer than necessary. "It's a pleasure to meet you," he said. "I know and admire your work, but I've mostly seen a London byline. What are you doing here?"

"I'm here for the paper. And you?"

"I own an art gallery with branches in London and New York. One of my New York clients has developed a passion for West African art—ibejis. I'm looking for some good ones."

"What are ibejis?" she asked.

"Now you've done it," said Mike Vale, who was still standing at the edge of their little group. "James loves to impart information. Should have been a teacher, really."

Lindsay smiled. She'd have been happy to listen to him. She liked the way he looked directly at her when he spoke, as though no one else was in the room.

"I see you are old friends too," she said. "Am I the only one here who doesn't know you?"

"Luckily that's a loss that can be remedied very easily," James replied with a smile.

"I did a piece on art fraud a few years ago and James was one of my expert sources," Mike chimed in. "He really knows his field, so actually, you could do worse than listen to him lecture."

James gave a half smile and turned toward Mike. "How was D.C.?" he asked.

"The same."

Ed Courvet, the *Guardian* correspondent, ambled over. This was it—an assemblage of most of the local hacks. Much as James was distracting her, Lindsay couldn't squander the opportunity to find out if they knew anything new about Olumide and Fakai.

She leaned over and greeted Ed with a peck on the cheek.

"I intend to listen," she said, "but first I need to talk business." She turned to James. "I hope you don't mind."

"Not at all." He smiled.

"So, what do you hear?" she asked. "Anything happening?"

"Nothing new," said Ed. "We just got back from Zaire. Incredible. Kinshasa is still the same scary place. You remember Gabe Weston from the L.A. *Times*? He hid in the hotel the whole time. He kept coming up with phony reasons not to come with us. Wrote his piece from the bar at the Continental. The rest of us tried to get by the military blockades and talk to villagers about that Australian stringer who disappeared."

Interesting, Lindsay thought, but an old story. Still, she couldn't seem too eager to get back to Olumide, or they'd know she was on to something.

"Oh, right. Did you find out anything?"

"No. Nothing but rumors. One story is that the stringer stupidly went into the barracks to interview the soldiers about torture. They say he never came out. Word is the bastards tortured him to death, but you can't get anyone to say so."

"I wish you guys didn't despise Gabe so much," Maureen said. "I know he's cautious, but he's also idealistic. He really believes his work can do some good."

"It's not his doing good that we despise. It's his riding on our coattails," Ed responded.

"Come on, let's get something to eat," Lindsay said, trying to guide Maureen toward the buffet table.

"It just makes me mad," Maureen confided, ignoring her friend. "This macho guy thing. Next thing they'll be bragging about their sexual exploits."

Ken overheard her. "Not this time," he said. "Zaire was pretty much a nonevent on that score. We were all on our best behavior. No sneaking around to get an exclusive and no sneaking in and out of bedrooms."

"Well," said Ed. "There's always Vale, the great swordsman."

"I thought Vale was in D.C., packing the last of his meager possessions," said James.

"I was, but I met up with everyone in Kinshasa after."

"Bragging about sex on the road." Maureen laughed. "That's right up there with cheating on your expense account."

"That we managed to do," said Ken.

Lindsay burst out laughing and Maureen couldn't resist joining in. "Touché," she said.

Ed put his arm around Maureen and gave her a hug. "What would we do without our very own Jiminy Cricket?"

Maureen rolled her eyes and drifted away. Lindsay turned back to Mike.

"You know a lot of people here for someone who spent the last few years posted in D.C."

"Yeah, well, I spent the five years before that posted right here."

"I didn't know. How do you feel about being back?"

"Resigned. I got a stint in D.C. basically for R and R. But my beat is West Africa. You can't cover it from the cocktail circuit there."

"I see. Your piece on art fraud—was that about African art?"

"Mostly African. That's why I needed to know this guy." He gestured to James.

"I'd really like to know about the ibejis," she said. "I hope all this shop talk didn't put you off."

"Not at all."

"Please—go on," said Lindsay.

James guided her toward the garden. "Ibejis are twin sculptures," he said. "They're related to religious ceremonies—like the best of African art."

"I don't know anything about African art," Lindsay admitted. "How does the religion come into it?"

"Twins have a special value. Some tribes consider them a blessing, like the Yoruba. The Ibos think of them as a curse."

"Which tribe makes the ibejis?"

"The Yoruba. They have them made to honor the birth. Then, if one twin dies, the family makes a shrine to the ibeji representing that twin. They bring him flowers, shower him with gifts on his birthday. The idea is to prevent the dead twin from being jealous of his living brother. Otherwise he might take the boy to the land of the dead. The good ibejis—by that I mean the real ones—are very old. There are hundreds of imitations, but when you find an authentic one, you know it immediately."

"And what about the Ibos? What do they do?"

James took a canapé off a passing tray.

"Their custom is brutal, I'm afraid. They take one twin into the forest and leave it there to die."

"Really?" Lindsay said, shocked. "Even now? This still goes on today?"

"Sometimes. It was a custom the English tried to stop, of course. They were somewhat successful, but it still goes on in the bush."

"How fascinating," Lindsay said. "Do you think it would be possible to meet someone who is familiar with the practice? It would make a great story."

"No. It's against the law and very hard to even get anyone to talk about it."

Lindsay and James walked a bit closer to the lagoon. It looked mysterious in the twilight. Lindsay watched a lizard the size of a small squirrel pause on a stone wall. Its skin shimmered in the floodlit garden, an iridescent aqua. It hovered for a moment, tilting its head and leaning forward as though searching for something to eat, flicking its tongue in and out of its mouth. A city girl at heart, Lindsay was squeamish about its proximity. She tried not to show it, but she was relieved when it scurried off.

"I wish I knew more about Nigeria," Lindsay said. "I fly in and out writing about politics, coups, and corruption. It's easy to get cynical and forget that there is a powerful ancient culture here."

"Well, much of that is disappearing. There are still some remnants, but they're not easy to find."

"I've seen some of the modern artists," Lindsay said. "I thought they were amazing. Would you say they're any good?"

"Yes. But their work isn't the kind I deal with; it's closer to folk art." She smiled. "I told you I didn't know anything about African art."

He shrugged. "Just because I don't have any clients who want to buy it doesn't mean it's not good. Anyway, I don't know anything about African politics."

"You're not missing much," she said.

"Why don't you meet me for lunch tomorrow and fill me in?"

She was silent for a moment, pretending to think about it. The sun had set and the garden was lit with tiny colored lights. The moon was only a sliver but the lagoon appeared to be bathed in its light. The water flowed lazily downstream, toward the British high commissioner's residence. In the distance she made out a large mass, probably twigs and moss, carried by the water, pushed along by the gentle current. Lindsay watched it as they spoke.

"I'd be happy to meet you," she said at last. "It will have to be the day after, though. I've got a morning interview at the president's office and I don't know how long he'll keep me waiting or how much time he'll give me. I'll want to write the piece right after, while it's fresh in my mind."

"That's fine. Can you meet me on Awolowo Road, by the Motorboat Club?"

"Well, yes. I'll find it. I thought that was members only. Do you belong?"

"Don't worry about that," he said. "I've got a surprise for you. Just meet me there between one and two. And bring your swimsuit."

"My swimsuit?" she asked, puzzled. She saw Ed and Ken watching her from across the garden. They were horsing around, giving her a thumbs-up as a sign of approval. Maureen had a big know-it-all smile on her face as well. What a bunch of goons, Lindsay thought, but not without affection. She turned back toward the water so as not to encourage them.

Her eyes focused on the debris, floating down the river. It was now close enough to see that the twigs and moss were attached to some large, bulky object. Lindsay leaned forward, as did James and a few other people. Suddenly a woman screamed, "Oh my God, that's a body." Now, everyone in the garden started moving to the water's edge for a better view. Lindsay could make out a man, facedown, his arms and legs splayed wide, tangled in algae and bits of rubbish. The body drifted past them, slowly pulled by the current, and finally washed up on the British high commissioner's lawn.

The American diplomats began circulating through the crowd, trying to calm everyone down and move them inside. As Lindsay slipped away, she saw James looking for her, going inside to see if she was among the reporters who had regrouped at the bar.

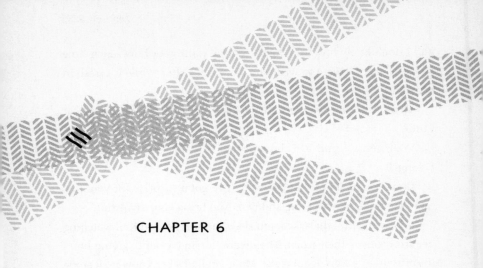

CHAPTER 6

Lindsay walked along a narrow side road that led to the rear entrance of the British high commissioner's residence. Two uniformed guards stood on either side of a white gate leading to the garden. As she approached, they pointed their weapons and brusquely told her to move along. She thought of trying to charm her way in, but they looked as if they were nervous enough to shoot. She walked around a hedge to the front of the house, where she spotted two more guards.

She knew there was only a slim chance of gaining entry. Still, she put on an innocent face and, summoning an air of assurance, approached the guards. One put his hand on his weapon.

"I'm a reporter for an American newspaper," she said calmly. "I'd like to go in if I could."

The guards stared at her in silence. She knew she had to tread a delicate line—polite but not supplicating, assured but not bullying. "I need to go in to get information for my story."

"That's not my lookout," said the guard.

"Look, I've got official identification," she said, hoping that this time her papers would help. She rifled through her purse for her pass to interview President Olumide and held it out. It was impressive: her photo, three signatures, and two stamps marked "ENTRY APPROVED" under the seal of Dodan Barracks, seat of the military government.

She waved it so that the plastic reflected back the light over the doorway.

"Surely this entitles me to enter," she pronounced.

One of the guards seemed less sure of himself. He looked at the pass for a long time and then handed it to his partner, who did the same.

"Wait here," he said, walking off—undoubtedly in search of a supervisor.

Fifteen minutes passed. Lindsay saw activity at the gate as a group of policemen entered along with some other men whose identity she either didn't know or couldn't make out. Her chances of getting in were diminishing with each passing minute. Finally the guard returned.

He handed back her pass and waved her through. Apparently Dodan Barracks trumped orders from the local authorities.

"Be quick," he said, nervously.

Inside she was met by one of the high commissioner's house staff, who ushered her through the house to the back door. A flood of light from the second floor blazed over the garden, elongating the shadows. A few policemen and some British diplomats were grouped near the lagoon, standing by the body.

No one seemed to take any notice of her as she approached. The body was lying in an unnatural position, covered in algae and mud. But the face was visible and she gasped when she saw the Yoruba scars, three horizontal lines on each cheek. Even before she noticed his sodden T-shirt proclaiming THE NEXT STEP, she recognized him. His neck was circled with a purple mark and bits of refuse clung to his hair and body. She saw a gash on his forehead where the club had landed. Feeling sick, she turned away when something caught her eye.

A contingent of military police was arriving. The leader was the officer she had encountered at the demonstration, the very man who had followed her. Could she pretend not to recognize him or the body?—he just might believe that a woman could be that stupid. She began to walk away from the corpse, just as the MPs swarmed into the garden.

The officer strode purposefully toward her. He spoke sharply, dropping the pidgin he had used earlier.

"You!" he barked. "What are you doing here?"

"I was at a party at the American ambassador's next door," she said. "I was hoping to get some details, but I didn't want to go near the body." She pretended to shudder at the thought. She took out her notebook. "I was told he's been hanged, right?" The officer just stared at her. "I wonder if this is the guy who's been doing all those robberies in Ikoyi and Victoria Island?"

The officer nodded slowly.

"Maybe," he said, less threateningly. "We don't know anything yet. There will be an official statement tomorrow."

Lindsay jotted a few words in her notebook. "Thank you," she said evenly, moving a little nearer to the house. "I better get back to the ambassador's party now." He continued to stare at her, but he allowed her to leave.

She walked as fast as she could, trying to look inconspicuous, which was impossible under the circumstances. She just needed to get out of there before he changed his mind. Her sense that her identity as an American journalist would shield her had evaporated. The images were burned into her memory: the purple gash on the young man's bludgeoned head, the red wound circling his neck. The authorities were undoubtedly trying to make it look as if he were just another victim of street justice, but she knew he was a protester, possibly a leader of the dissidents. She wondered just how big a triumph this murder was for the government.

As she passed through the house, the steward came over to show her out. As they walked, he mumbled something she could hardly hear. She looked at him. He appeared angry, in contrast with his officious manner. He glanced around, then raised his voice ever so slightly.

"That man no be robber. He be Babatunde Oladayo," he said softly. He pronounced the name with emphasis, as though it were someone who might be known to her. Before she could respond, they reached the door and he said in a loud voice, "Good night, madam."

Babatunde Oladayo. Lindsay stopped to write the name in her notebook. As she passed the guards at the door, she saw Maureen trying to talk her way in. Lindsay caught her eye, shrugging her shoulders in mock sympathy.

She had to return to the American ambassador's to fetch her car. When she reached the house, the party was breaking up. Her colleagues had disappeared, except for Mike Vale, who was sitting at the bar. He offered her a drink and when she refused, he flipped open his notebook and asked her what she'd found. Talk about riding on other people's coattails, she thought, but she filled him in with a few facts, though not The Next Step or the name of the man who had been killed. He asked how the victim had died. When she mentioned the burn marks on his throat, he quickly closed his notebook and went back to his drink.

Lindsay moved outside, realizing she was scanning the stragglers for James. She spotted him across the parking lot, chatting up a pretty young secretary. She watched as he held the car door open for her, then she turned away. Dave Goren was in the driveway, his car keys in his hand.

"Let me ask you something," she said, catching up to him. "Does the name Babatunde Oladayo mean anything to you?"

He raised his eyebrows. "You're always all business, aren't you?"

"Right now—yes."

"Oladayo," he said thoughtfully. "He's a student opposition leader. They support Fakai, hate Olumide, and organize demonstrations. They make a lot of noise but they're harmless, and Olumide lets them operate pretty freely. Why the sudden interest?"

"Maybe Olumide's changed his mind. I think that was the boy's body that just floated up."

Goren shrugged. "Sorry, Lindsay. That guy was just a local thief hanged by the crowd. Hardly of interest to your readers in New York."

"How do you know that?" Lindsay asked. "I didn't see you over there."

"But I saw you—just as I was leaving."

"Are you sure it wasn't Oladayo?"

"It's my job to be sure."

"Mine too," she answered, and turned to go.

But she wondered if the steward had made a mistake. She waited until all the guests had left, then retraced her steps along the side road. The lights were all out in the high commissioner's compound.

As she approached the back entrance, one of the guards stepped out of the darkness and ordered her away. She replied indignantly that she had lost her purse. Perhaps it was in the residence. She wanted to ask the steward if he had seen it. She looked distressed—which was not difficult under the circumstances—and after much back and forth, the man relented. He got the steward, who came out looking confused and scared. Out of hearing range of the guard, she whispered, "I told them I thought I left my purse at the house."

"No, madam," he answered in a loud voice. "I no find madam's purse. I very sorry."

"I want to be sure," she murmured. "Are you absolutely sure that man is the student leader, Babatunde Oladayo?"

"I sorry, madam. But it not be dere. I sure. I know dat purse. I see it before."

Lindsay thanked him loudly, and left. She found her car, climbed into the front seat, and looked behind her; she didn't see any signs of a tail. They probably had more important things to do. She drove home, pondering how to file this piece without getting thrown out of the country. The story of the murdered dissident was significant—it demonstrated the resistance to Olumide and the ruthlessness of his regime—but it was not worth missing the crackdown against Fakai and the cancellation of the long-anticipated elections.

Finally she thought of a way to get the story into the paper. She'd mark it "hold for orders" so that the desk would not print it without her okay. The first plane to London was at 6 A.M. Her interview with Olumide was at 11 A.M. That would give her time to go the airport and search for a pigeon, someone who would be willing to smuggle her report out of the country and then call it in to the *Globe*.

Luckily, Maureen was in her room with the door closed—she didn't know how much of her scoop she would share with her friend. She sat at her desk and began to type. When she finished, she pondered where to put her notes. What if the government decided to search the house? She hesitated a moment and then ripped the pages out of her notebook, tearing them into still smaller pieces and, finally, flushed them down the toilet. As she got into bed, she allowed herself one final thought about James. What was he doing with that secretary?

CHAPTER 7

Lindsay's alarm went off at four the next morning. The British Air flight to London would leave in two hours. The early hour meant that traffic was not a problem, and in the terminal she found a young American tourist who was eager for an adventure. He promised to carry her story out and to call the phone number she gave him.

She got back in plenty of time to prepare for her interview with General Olumide. She was sitting at the kitchen table going over her notes for the last time when Martin came in. It was only 7 A.M.

"Good morning," she said. "Why are you here so early?"

"I am sorry, madam. There was no time for you meet the new driver. He here now."

Eager to get back to her notes, Lindsay said, "Not today, Martin. I have too much on my mind."

Martin refused to be put off. "Sorry, madam," he said, looking uncomfortable. "You cannot go to Dodan Barracks by yourself. You need a driver."

Usually deferential, his insistence gave Lindsay pause.

"Where did you find him?"

"He once work for my first employer at the British embassy. He is very good driver. He know the ropes. Believe me, madam. He will help. They take you more serious if you come with driver."

She waited, still unsure.

"He has four children, madam. He need work."

She sighed. "Okay. But I can't meet him now. Just give him the keys and ask him to wait for me in the car."

"Very good, madam. "

When Lindsay walked out of the house, a young man with closely cropped hair jumped out to open the door of the Peugeot.

"I be call John, madam," he said.

"Okay, John. I'm glad to meet you." She settled back in her seat. "We are going to Dodan Military Barracks."

"I know, madam," he said grimly. It took them an hour to get there. When they arrived at the gate, Lindsay gave John her pass. He showed it to the guard, who scrutinized it for what seemed a very long time. Still unconvinced, the guard peered in the window at Lindsay without saying a word. Finally satisfied, he waved them through. John looked nervous as he got out of the car and opened her door.

"Please, madam," he said. "Be careful."

"Don't worry," she said. "I'll come back as soon as the interview is over."

Lindsay made her way to the squat brick building that housed the general's private office. The first thing she noticed in the waiting room was that it was almost bare. There was no attempt to evoke authority with the solid mahogany British colonial furniture she had expected; the room was furnished only with a few modern, inelegant chairs and four cheap metal desks. Behind each was a secretary. Two were on the phone, engaged in what appeared to be personal conversations, and two were polishing their nails and chatting to each other in Yoruba. When Lindsay finally succeeded in getting one of the women to look up, she encountered an expressionless stare. The woman rudely gestured for Lindsay to sit down, while continuing to talk on the phone.

Lindsay chose one of the hard-backed chairs and settled in to wait. In addition to the stock portrait of the dictator that hung in every government office and private shop, the walls bore photographs of him shaking hands with various African leaders. Some of the photos hung crookedly, and she had to suppress the urge to straighten them. After about twenty minutes, a phone rang. The secretary picked it up and rose, gesturing for Lindsay to follow her. In all that time, she realized, not a word had been spoken to her.

The president's office was more imposing. General Olumide sat behind a vast ebony desk, flanked by green and white Nigerian flags bearing the country's seal (a unicorn holding a crest) and next to a life-sized oil portrait of himself in a uniform glittering with medals. He faced three separate black dial telephones as well as an important-looking red one, which she surmised gave instant access to his troops.

He got up and crossed the office in two great steps and thrust out a large hand. His grip was hard.

"Well, well, we meet at last," he said, his voice deep and mellow, his gaze direct and warm.

He ushered her to a comfortable chair, taking an easy chair across from her for himself.

"So, Lindsay—I hope you don't mind my using your first name, we tend to overlook formalities in Africa—how are you enjoying our country?"

"Oh, it's fascinating," she said.

He smiled. "Oh, I know some of our problems are difficult for you Westerners to get used to," he said kindly, "the crowds, the heat, the communication and electrical problems, but we are working on improving conditions as much as possible. That is one reason we need help from a great, developed country like your own."

She smiled, surprised. Although she had seen photographs, nothing had prepared her for his stature and magnetism. His ebony skin was so smooth she had a momentary urge to reach out and touch it; his posture was proud but not rigid, and his manner was friendly, even gracious. An upper-class English accent reflected his Sandhurst education. He was, moreover, undeniably attractive.

"Have you been out of the central city?" he asked. "Have you been to our forests, our beaches, our villages? Have you seen the real Nigeria?"

"Not yet," she replied. "But I hope to do a lot of traveling around the country soon."

"Well, look around," he said, waving his long arms at his office walls. "I have had photographs of some of our finest attractions hung right here to remind me what I am working for on those days when I wonder whether it's worth the struggle."

Lindsay obediently turned to examine half a dozen poster-sized pictures of banana plantations, wide-gapped rivers, offshore oil wells, and even some modern-looking factories. Her eyes stopped at a photograph of an isolated beach, palm trees nearly up to the shoreline.

"That's Bar Beach," he said softly. "One of our most beautiful."

She stared at the wild surf, lulled by the resonance of his voice.

The site, she reflected, could be any one of a multitude of beautiful beaches around the world, but the longer she looked at it, the more she had the feeling she had seen it before. Then she suddenly remembered that Bar Beach was the place where the young Olumide, who had seized power in a coup some ten years ago, had ordered his predecessor executed by firing squad, to musical accompaniment no less. Journalists had joked that despite the brutal coup and sadistic execution, he was nonetheless a man of culture. After all, they pointed out, he chose Mozart.

She turned back and found him staring straight at her, his eyes now suddenly appraising, reminding her of her initial wariness.

If you met him at a party, she thought, you'd guess he was the director of a prestigious media company. He didn't wear Ray-Bans, long the trademark of African dictators, or, on this occasion, his military uniform. Since he was never seen publicly without it, Lindsay realized, his decision to appear for the interview in a business suit was obviously calculated. For Nigerians, he wrapped himself in the accoutrements of power. For the Western press, he cultivated a corporate image.

"Did the pictures displease you?" he asked, something menacing in his smooth demeanor.

"Oh, no," she answered. "I just realized how busy you must be and that I should conduct our interview before you are called away."

"No one will call me away until I want to go," he said.

She detected an implied threat, a flash of danger. Despite his charm, she could not forget the stories about him she knew to be true—about his deceitfulness, his violence, his cruelty. Critics were routinely arrested, several had vanished. She had personally witnessed what had happened to one of them. Others had "accidents" that removed them from the political scene. She remembered the private words of Kofi Ransom, the dissident reporter arrested last year who had not been seen since: "If you are walking in the forest and you see Olumide and a python, kill Olumide first."

She reached into her bag and removed her tape recorder.

"Would you mind if I record our interview?"

"No, not at all," he replied graciously. "We are doing the same of course."

She pressed the record button and double-checked that the machine was running.

After a few obligatory softball questions about his goals and accomplishments, Lindsay worked the conversation around to his politics and the likelihood of his sponsoring a return to civilian rule.

"Do you believe democracy is a workable option for Nigeria?"

"Yes, of course," he said, smiling benignly. "You know, Lindsay, I was educated in the West. I have a deep faith in democracy. But I want to be sure the country is ready for it." He leaned forward in his chair. "I cannot express how deeply I regret some of the excesses that have occurred under military rule, but they were necessary to ensure order. Stability is the first step in our march toward freedom."

Lindsay wrote down the quote and then looked up.

"In fact, you have announced a return to free elections, haven't you?" she asked, her pen poised to scribble his reply.

"Yes, of course."

"But you haven't set a date yet," she pressed.

His eyes quickly registered his irritation. "They will take place any time from now," he said, slapping his desk for emphasis. The election process would be aided enormously by increased U.S. aid, he added, "and a most favored nation trading status that the U.S. government currently refuses to allow because of false allegations of so-called human rights violations.

"You see, Lindsay," he continued, reverting to his amiable mode, lecturing her as though he were an avuncular professor, "it is circular. When the lives of our people improve, we will be able to trust the nation to democracy. By slowing down our economic growth, your government keeps us from holding free elections."

This, clearly, was the message he wanted conveyed to the West. He leaned back in his chair, conspicuously looking at his watch.

"I am so sorry," he said, "but I have an appointment with the French ambassador and I have some papers to look over before he arrives." He dismissed her with a disingenuous smile.

Her fears had been realized. The interview was practically worthless. Olumide had given away nothing and was about to send her off with a bromide sound bite and a pitch for American aid. Irritated, Lindsay decided to take a chance. "General Olumide," she said, a little nervously, "there are rumors that Fakai is going to be arrested before the end of the week. Can you confirm or deny them?"

There was a brief pause. It was so slight that someone less observant might not have noticed that his grip tightened on a pencil he'd been casually holding in his right hand. Abruptly, he snapped it between his fingers, as though he were imitating a thug in a gangster movie. Then he reached over, so abruptly Lindsay jumped, and turned off her tape recorder. When he spoke again, it was clear that the interview was concluded.

"There are rumors of every kind in this city," he said. "It never fails to amaze me what people will say. Now, if you will excuse me, I must go."

Stubbornly, she pressed further. "So I can quote you, sir, as denying the rumors? My sources said your government would use the chaos such an act would provoke as a pretext to postpone elections."

Knowing she was crossing a line, she added: "I wonder if the death of Babatunde Oladayo, when it is announced, will also provoke demonstrations among the students."

He froze. She had obviously taken him by surprise. Before he could speak, the phone rang. He picked up the receiver and shouted into it.

"I told you to hold calls."

He listened for a moment and then, sputtering in rage, answered in Yoruba so Lindsay wouldn't understand, but there was no mistaking the menacing tone as he gave an order and hung up. His gaze fell back to Lindsay, and he seemed to be making an effort to control himself. She turned to look at the door and sat quietly.

"Babatunde Oladayo." He spat out the name like a curse. "I talk to you of progress, of democracy, and you talk of Babatunde Oladayo. People like him, they are nothing. They are bugs. Did you say someone swatted one bug? That is not my lookout."

She watched his hands clench and unclench and finally, with relief, she saw he was regaining his composure. She hurried to gather up her belongings, stuffing her tape recorder into her bag, and rose to leave. As he walked her to the door, he said, "I'd love to find out who your sources are." Then, more ominously, "Perhaps I will one day. But I'm sure, as a professional, you will be sure to check them very well and not publish anything that is not substantiated. We believe in a responsible press. We have laws that encourage it—and penalties that ensure it." He took her hand as if to shake good-bye and gripped it so tightly that her ring dug into her finger and broke the skin.

"Do you understand?"

She nodded. "Yes." She understood all too well.

"Good day," he said.

"Good day," she answered. "Thank you."

The general turned to the window. He didn't turn back as she left.

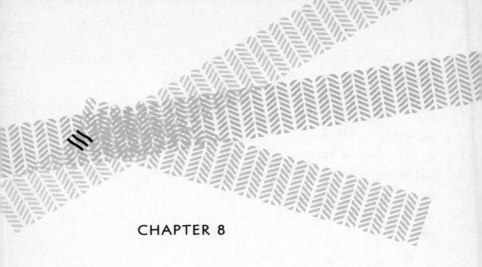

CHAPTER 8

Hunkered down in the rear seat of her car while John started the engine, she willed her heartbeat to return to normal. A chorus of Olumide's threats played over and over in her head: "I'd love to find out who your sources are. Perhaps I will one day. . . ." "We have laws that encourage it and penalties that ensure it." The intimidation came not just from his voice but also from his abrupt movements. She thought of the lizard in the ambassador's garden—heavy-lidded and scarcely moving, darting its lethal tongue to snatch a bug.

John pulled out into the street. Were they being followed? She turned to look out the back window. Not a single Black Maria in sight.

She decided to file her story immediately. She looked at her watch: 12:30 P.M. It was five hours earlier in New York, giving her plenty of time. Interviews with African heads of state were customarily relegated to the back pages of the paper, but this one might just make it onto the front page. Oil-rich Nigeria was important, and Olumide, who rarely spoke to the press, was a figure of mystery to the West.

She wrote the piece in an hour and a half, then tried to figure out the best way to file. Tentatively, almost on impulse, she picked up her phone, fully expecting it to be dead. But by some miracle, her landline was working.

Perhaps Olumide wanted the story printed. She didn't waste time trying to figure it out but dialed the *Globe*'s recording room and began the tedious job of reading her story to a machine, which necessitated including all punctuation, and spelling out every name. ("Olumide: O for orange, L for London, U for ukulele . . .") She finished without being cut off. Relieved, she decided to place another call. The connection was weaker this time, but on the fifth try, she was delighted to hear a secretary say, "Foreign desk."

"This is Lindsay Cameron," she said. "Is Joe Rainey around? I'm calling from Lagos and I don't know how long the line will hold."

Joe picked up. He's in early, she thought, probably didn't go home last night. Once again his wife, Janine, would be furious.

"Jesus, Lindsay. We were wondering when you'd check in. What's going on?"

"It's been hell getting through and now that I've got a line, I'm going to talk fast. I just filed twelve hundred words on my interview with Olumide. He didn't say much, but I'm using it as a peg for some background on the situation here. There may be a big story coming up. I don't want to talk about it on the phone, but I'm on top of it."

"What kind of time line are we talking about?"

"Not sure. Maybe a week or two."

"Okay. What about the interview? Can we reach you later for questions?"

"Beats me. You can try. If the phone's down, don't send a fax through the public communications office. I'll try my best to reach you."

"There's something else," Rainey said. "You marked a piece 'hold for orders.' What do we do with it?"

She glanced down at her notebook and saw Olumide's only comment about Babatunde Oladayo: "People like him, they are nothing. They are bugs." Her face flushed with anger. It took her less than a minute to make up her mind.

"Run it," she said. "You can pair it with the interview."

"Okay. Good. Listen, we could use some features for page two while you're waiting around for your big story. Maybe some lifestyle pieces. What's Lagos like now? Write about African art, music, food, that kind of thing."

Lindsay rolled her eyes in exasperation. Editors! She was talking about real news, and he wanted a goddamned feature. Still, she could always do something on African art—she'd talk to James.

"I'll see what I can find," she said.

"Right. Good."

There was a slight pause.

"So," said Lindsay, "what's going on there?"

"Same old shit. The big news is that Greenberg's secretary Anna, who as you know is married, just had a baby boy that looks a hell of a lot like Greenberg."

"No kidding."

"Gotta go, kid. Page one meeting's about to start. How you doin'?"

"Not so great. But I'm surviving. Can't wait to finish up, frankly, and go home. It's tough being so cut off, really. . . ." She waited for a response but could hear him talking to someone else on the desk.

"Well, hang in there and keep in touch, Linds," he said hurriedly.

"Right. Wait. Just check with the recording room to see if they got it all, okay?"

"Sure. Hold on."

A long pause.

"They lost you, Lindsay. They got a few graphs but then just static."

"Oh no. I'll try again," she started to say before the line went dead. Her only hope now was the AFP man, whose office, luckily, was just a few blocks away.

She found Georges Pontier, drink in hand, looking at the lagoon behind his house. Introducing herself, she reminded him of their correspondence.

"Ah, yes," he replied graciously. "The telex. I remember."

"How amazing that you've got one working. I heard you paid a big bribe to get it."

"Yes, I did." He smiled and shrugged. "Unfortunately, it seems it was not quite big enough. The line has been dead since I returned from leave."

"But how do you file?"

Pontier smiled laconically. "When the desire to file overtakes me, which isn't often anymore," he said, sipping his scotch, "I usually lie down until the impulse passes." He grinned at his adaptation of the famous quote. "But when I have to file—you know, a coup or something—I do what you will have to do. I wait in line at the government message center. Oh, sorry, can I get you a drink?"

"No." She knew she looked agitated.

"You'll get used to it," he said, chuckling. "We call it WAWA."

"WAWA?"

"West Africa Wins Again." He poured himself another scotch.

"I simply can't let that happen," she said. "Thanks anyway. I've got to go."

As John pulled away, she cast a rueful glance back at the house. A Nigerian man in a dark Western suit sauntered onto the porch. He spoke to Pontier and then fished in his pocket and handed him something. Pointier pocketed it and the two of them broke off their conversation to look at her car.

She wondered if Pontier's phone line was really out or if he'd been bribed to force her to file through official channels. She told John to head for the public communications office, nervously peering through the rear window to see if she was being tailed.

Filing was, as she had anticipated, an ordeal. She didn't trust the slow Internet connection, so she decided to wait for the telex. It was three hours before she got back in her car to go home. Two blocks away, she spotted the yellow and white truck of the Nigerian Telephone

Company, hardly an unusual sight since the technicians were often out and about, climbing telephone poles and busily poking around the bird's nests of tangled wires that constituted the Nigerian telephone system. Inspired, she stopped to talk to one technician who was about to climb the pole outside the Ghanaian embassy. She told him that her phone was dead and she desperately needed it fixed.

"You go call company," the technician said, his back to her.

"Well, actually, I can't call anyone, that's the problem."

The technician shrugged and started his ascent. Halfway up, he yelled down at her: "How much you pay?"

"Whatever it costs."

"You pay dollars. Five hundred. I give you good line." He gestured toward his friend. "He come too. You pay both or no good."

"Yes. Yes. I'll pay both," she answered. "But when?"

The two men consulted in the low tones of Yoruba. Then the first asked her where she lived. She told him and the men resumed their discussion. Finally the first man spoke to her.

"You go for get dollars. Dollars, no naira, den we go give you line."

With a tilt of his head, he indicated that the line would come from the Ghanaian embassy.

She went home and retrieved the money from her bedroom safe. On her way out, she ran into Martin, who asked her where she was rushing off to. Proudly, she told him about her negotiations.

Martin nodded thoughtfully. "Madam, maybe you make a mistake. Don't give them all the money now. Maybe you give them half and tell them you pay more each month the line keeps working," he suggested.

"Martin, you are a genius."

When she returned to the repairmen, she explained that she would pay them a retainer that they could come each month to collect. The men agreed, but demanded the full $500 up front. She nodded and handed over the money. She watched as they climbed the pole again, searching for the wire that connected the working line in the embassy to the central system. She saw them pulling several strands from the tangle of wires and connecting them to a pole near her house.

As soon as she got home, she tried the phone, but it was still dead.

She was concerned. Her encounter with them could have been anything from a government setup aimed at bugging her phone to a con job, but Martin counseled her to be patient and served a strong cup of coffee and some muffins he had baked. She collapsed in the living room, glancing at the Nigerian newspapers. She remembered she had promised Martin she would read to Eduke. Playing with the three-year-old always distracted her, so she roused herself and fetched *The Very Hungry Caterpillar*, which she had asked her mother to send from New York.

As soon as she sat down, he climbed onto her lap. He could identify all the colors in the butterfly and proudly recited them in English. He made himself comfortable, cuddling into her and, when the story ended, put his head sweetly on her chest. He was a special child, she thought, brighter, more sensitive than most. His father had high hopes for him. "He is the one I set my mind on," Martin had told her. She determined she would help Martin with Eduke's school fees when the time came, even when her tour in Nigeria ended.

As it was getting dark, she walked back into the house. Over dinner Lindsay told Maureen about her attempt to bribe the telephone workers. Maureen was skeptical but impressed nonetheless as Lindsay picked up the receiver, willing a dial tone. It was still dead.

As she started upstairs for bed, Lindsay said, "I'm having lunch tomorrow with that guy you introduced me to."

"James?"

"Yeah. How come I never heard about him before?"

"He's really more Mark's friend than mine. He met James freshman year at Yale. When James transferred to Michigan, they kind of lost touch for a while but connected again in London. I don't think they talk too intimately. You know that male thing." She leaned heavily on the banister as she climbed the stairs.

"Are you feeling okay?" Lindsay asked.

"I don't know. I feel a little weird—super exhausted and queasy. I hope I'm not coming down with anything."

"It's probably just the weather and the change in food. And you're probably still jet-lagged. Go to bed. You'll feel better in the morning."

Before turning in herself, Lindsay picked up the phone again, but it was still dead.

In the morning, she was awakened by ringing. She reached to quiet her alarm, but it hadn't gone off yet. It took her a few seconds to realize that it was the phone. She picked up the receiver.

"You go have phone now," a voice said.

Then the caller hung up. But his voice was replaced by a truly beautiful sound: a dial tone.

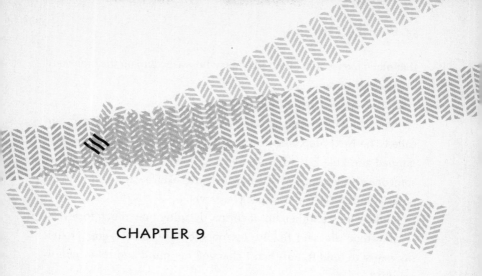

CHAPTER 9

Lindsay got out of bed the next morning, high on the thrill of her new phone line. She was connected, and it was a heady sensation; she could phone the desk and the editors could phone her—well, that wasn't quite as good, but maybe she could dodge those calls. She could also reach her friends and occasionally her mother, a worrier. She doubted that her father, busy with his new family, thought about her often—or, for that matter, that he ever had.

She glanced at the clock: 7:30. She brewed the coffee and opened the door to retrieve the *Nigerian Times* from its usual spot next to the garbage heap, scanning the headlines as she walked back inside. The lead story was "Operation Feed the Nation a Big Success." She knew that wasn't true. There was no mention of the death of Babatunde Oladayo. No surprise there. She calculated how long it would take until the Nigerian authorities read the *Globe* and she pictured Olumide's face when he was told.

Just then, Maureen, her eyes swollen and her hair uncombed, came into the kitchen. She refused coffee, saying her stomach was still upset.

"You know," Maureen said, "I heard something at the office yesterday that made me wonder about the man who washed up on the high com-missioner's garden."

Lindsay sipped her coffee.

"One of our office assistants has a connection with a dissident group called The Next Step. She claimed that one of their people was kid-napped and killed. His family was told he was lynched for stealing someone's wallet, but they all saw him being taken away by the military police. Could that be the corpse you saw?"

Lindsay took another sip of coffee, deciding how much to reveal. "I knew that," she said, finally. "I wrote the story and was going to tell my paper to hold it, but then I changed my mind and told them to print it."

"Why did you do that?"

"I don't know—I hope I didn't make a mistake. I just couldn't let Olumide completely get away with what they did to him."

Maureen was silent.

"I should have known you'd find out," Lindsay said. "I feel bad that you're sharing it and I didn't."

Maureen shrugged. "That's okay," she said. "I told you a rumor. You actually witnessed an exclusive. I don't hold that against you. And don't worry—I'll visit you in jail."

"Very funny." Lindsay hesitated, then continued. "There's more to the story. I was at a demonstration. I saw them club that guy and take him away."

Maureen's eyes widened. "Did you put that in the story? Don't answer—I know you did. Maybe I won't be able to visit you."

Maureen placed two slices of bread in a pan on the stove. "Seriously, what do you think the reaction here will be?"

"Not happy. But I don't think they'll move against me yet. I included all the quotes that mattered to Olumide in my piece on him. It wouldn't look good if they tossed me out so soon just when he wants the West to believe he's moving toward a democracy. But I'm pretty sure they'll be watching me."

"I hope that's all they do," Maureen murmured. She shrugged. "Well, this exclusive's yours. I'm next."

"Not if I can help it."

"Ah, but you can't."

"We'll see."

Lindsay smiled and retrieved some papers from the filing cabinet. "I have to read this before I—"

"Oh yes, I almost forgot," Maureen said. "You have a lunch date."

Shortly after noon Lindsay washed and dried her hair so it hung thick and straight past her shoulders. She slipped into a pair of white cotton pants and a pale yellow V-neck T-shirt. She dabbed on some lemon toilet water, grabbed a sun hat, a bathing suit, and a straw bag and went outside where John was waiting.

The traffic was as bad as ever, and it seemed as though the government's effort to improve it had made it worse. The army had posted red-capped military officers at busy intersections, armed with three-foot-long whips called kabukis. If a motorist ignored any traffic regulation, he was summarily yanked from his car and whipped on the spot. Unfortunately, this only aggravated the problem, as no one could pass until the motorist resumed driving.

Lindsay had heard about this novel approach to traffic control, but had never witnessed it firsthand until John was turning onto Awolowo Road. Cars were at a standstill and a hapless Renault driver in a cotton suit was lying on the ground, shielding his face as a military policeman whipped him furiously.

"Please, sir, I no go do dis no more," he begged, while the crowd watched, adding their own insults.

"Dey no go fix go-slow dis way," John commented under his breath. But there was nothing they could do but wait. Finally, the cars started inching forward.

They pulled up in front of the Lagos Motorboat Club. She got out and looked around, hoping that the police had dropped their tail. There was no sign of James, so she waited in front of the boatyard, facing the road and watching the approaching cars. After a few minutes she heard a low whirring noise and turned toward the water. James was in a speedboat, waving one arm above his head. He pulled up at a jetty.

"So this is your secret," she said as she climbed into the bow.

He smiled conspiratorially and sped off. Looking back, Lindsay saw a black car arrive in front of the club. A man in a military uniform got out and stared at the receding boat. She smiled, imagining the surprise of her pursuer.

James stood in the stern, one hand on the throttle, his dark hair tousled by the breeze. She stood next to him, watching the whitecaps ahead.

"Where are we headed?" Lindsay shouted over the din of the motor.

"We're going to Agaja Beach," he said. It's not too far away, and it's a nice place for a picnic and a swim."

They crossed the harbor and headed west on the lagoon. On the shore to the left were groves of coconut palms and on the right thick mangrove swamps. James docked the boat in a calm inlet and they disembarked on a spit of sand about fifty feet wide. They walked across it to reach the open sea. The beach, a strip that extended all the way from Lagos to Benin, had small palms in the center and half a dozen open-air shelters. Inside were benches and small wooden tables. The sound of the surf was louder now, and stretching before her, as far as she could see in either direction, was endless white sand. Absolutely no one was in sight.

James carried a large wicker picnic basket toward the huts. He handed her a heavy ice cooler.

"Are we expecting company?" she asked.

"No. Just us."

He walked toward the ocean. They reached the water's edge and stood silently, watching the waves that smashed against the shore, sending up a thin haze of spray and hanging tiny rainbows in the air. They kicked off their shoes and waded into the dark green water. Their feet sank into the wet sand.

"It's spectacular," Lindsay said, gazing at the sea.

"It's a special place. A guy named Henry Stewart brought me here when I first came to Nigeria about five years ago. He was the West African rep for Shell Oil. There's a fisherman's village farther up the coast, but otherwise it's pretty much deserted. It's one of those little perks the big companies provide to cushion their people from the problems of daily life in Lagos."

"Well, they can't avoid the go-slows," she said. "That's the great equalizer."

"Oh yeah, they can. Helicopters. Anyway, they all have boats and get away on weekends. You'd be surprised what a difference that little break makes."

"I can imagine. It's the constant frustration that's the worst. This is the first relief from the crowds and smell I've had since I got here. Up till now, my happiest moment was feeling the air-conditioning in the American embassy, which is really a sad statement, when you come to think of it."

She bent to pick up her sandals and started off towards the nearest hut. "I'm going to change into my suit and take a swim."

When she returned, James was already in the water. She noticed the muscles in his legs and his tight, flat stomach.

"Just one thing," he said. "The undertow here can be ferocious. Even if you're a very strong swimmer, I'd advise you not to go far out."

She ventured a few steps into the water as a large wave broke and almost knocked her off her feet. Laughing, she caught herself and stepped back to the shore.

"So this is the dreaded Bight of Benin. It seems to be as wild as they say."

"Yes." He reached out to be sure she was steady and led her back to the water. "These very waves frightened off the early European explorers. Of course they soon found harbors to dock their ships. . . ."

"And Mother Africa was never the same. Imagine their surprise when they finally settled here. All that effort, all those dangerous trips, and what they finally found was heat, disease, and poisonous insects."

"And slaves. That's what they came for. The Portuguese first, then the British. They quickly installed a few governors to run the place and got the hell out. They ended up in Nairobi, with rum punches served under the baobab trees. That's where they brought their families."

"Well," said Lindsay, sitting down so the water ran over her legs, "I suppose the Nigerians go around thanking God for the tsetse fly. It saved them from living with the English."

He laughed, sitting down next to her. "You know that famous quote from Jomo Kenyatta, the first president of Kenya? He said: 'When the British came to Africa, we had the land and they had the Bible. They taught us to pray with our eyes closed. When we opened them, they had the land and we had the Bible.'"

Now it was Lindsay's turn to laugh. "Amazing that so many Africans came to believe in that British God," she said.

"God or black magic. This is a place for powerful juju. It's what makes the artwork I collect great." He paused. "Do you really think the British were so bad?"

"I do, actually. Aside from everything else, I will never forgive them for the mindless bureaucracy. I'd like to know the name of the guy who brought the rubber stamp to Nigeria."

He laughed. "Hey, I swear it wasn't me."

He stood up and started to walk into the water. "Remember to stay close to shore until you get your bearings."

"Don't worry," she said. "It would be embarrassing to drown on a date. Getting shot covering a coup, now that would be different."

His eyes narrowed. "Why?"

"It just would," she replied. James had a way of looking at her with an unnerving intensity. Covering her discomfort, she said, "I mean, it would be in the service of something noble."

He nodded, still looking at her. "You'd be just as dead."

She met his gaze. "Don't you think it matters how and for what you die?"

He reached out his hand to brush a stray lock of hair from her eyes. "No. Not really. Anyway, why would dying covering a story be noble?"

"Because I would be disclosing the truth."

He let that pass, creating an awkward silence.

"That sounds so pretentious, I know," she admitted, embarrassed. "But do you think there is anything worth dying for?"

"I don't know," he said, smiling. "Today I had in mind something less dramatic. A swim. A picnic. Some champagne. Getting to know you. That kind of thing."

He turned, and dove into an oncoming wave. Lindsay inched in slowly, a few steps at a time, getting used to the cold until, with a sigh of pleasure, she dropped into the water. She paddled about putting her head under, then slicking her long hair off her face. James swam farther from the shore, swimming with long, strong strokes, disobeying his own injunction. She watched him for a few minutes. When he returned, he took her hand and they walked back to the hut. They spread a blanket, filled their glasses with champagne and sat down.

"To a great day," Lindsay said.

He clicked his glass against hers. There was that look again, as if he could see right through her. Lindsay believed on some deep level that she fooled people, that her act was so convincing no one ever discovered the real person behind it. When an attractive man made her feel exposed, she felt aroused. Jim Garner, in the early days of their relationship, had had this effect on her.

"To accidental encounters," she said, raising her glass.

"I thought Freud said there were no accidents."

"Indeed he did." He reached forward, put her glass on the ground, and kissed her gently. Then he kissed her again, harder. She responded, pulling him down onto her. They caressed and explored each other with a kind of fever, now one on top, now the other, pushed on by the glare of the sun, the rough texture of the hot sand. The depth of her desire surprised her; she felt herself gasp for breath. But, somehow, she pulled back.

"No," she said. "It's too soon. Please."

He responded almost lazily, raising his thumb and running it across her lips. Then he stood up. He walked back to the water's edge and plunged into a wave.

She lay in the sand, trying to understand why she stopped him when she wanted him so much.

James emerged from the ocean and she handed him a towel.

"What was in that champagne?" she asked lightly.

"The truth." He sat down beside her. "We were just much closer to it than any newspaper story."

She closed her eyes, enjoying the sensation of the sun baking her skin. He fetched the picnic, spread it on a blanket under a thatched umbrella and ordered her to eat—"Before you fry in the sun." There were deviled eggs, pâté, caviar (complete with chopped egg whites and lemon), and cold salmon. Who would have imagined? And in Lagos!

"So, Lindsay, tell me a story."

"A story? About what?"

"Whatever you want. About you. For example, why are you lying on a beach in Nigeria instead of having a picnic with a husband and two kids in . . . where are you from? New York?"

She took a bite of deviled egg followed by a sip of champagne. "Oh, I don't know. That was never my goal. Most of the men in my life didn't like competing with breaking news. I think I was just too independent—I wanted a relationship but on my own terms, and that's a luxury usually reserved for men."

James didn't answer for a moment, as if he were waiting for her to say more. "Is that it, really? It sounds like the kind of prepared response people give when they don't want to talk about the real reasons they do things."

Stung, Lindsay met his eyes. "And that sounds like the kind of psychobabble people use when they want to sound smarter than they are."

He grinned disarmingly. "Whoa. I'm sorry. Have I hit a nerve?"

"No. Maybe you've simply met your match."

"I don't doubt it."

He reached forward and put his hand over hers. "Hey, I'm sorry. I didn't mean that the way it sounded. I like you and I guess I was hoping for something more intimate than the story you probably tell anyone who asks."

She shrugged. "Most people don't ask. Besides, we don't know each other well enough yet."

"I hope we will."

She was quiet for a while, sipping her drink.

"Maybe you're right," she said finally. "Maybe that isn't the reason. Maybe I just say that to make me feel like it's not my fault."

"I don't think it's about fault. I just meant it's better to start by being honest with each other."

"You don't have some kind of copyright on honesty, you know."

"I know. But I try. I've learned it's the only way."

After a while, she turned to him and said, "I don't know why I never married. Of course, it is partly the work and my reluctance to give up my independence. That's the truth. But it's not the whole truth. Lately, I've wanted some connection I haven't ever made, some overpowering passion, something like I've heard about all my life and seen in the movies. But I've never seen it work that well in real life. My parents divorced when I was fifteen—my father left and my mother never really got over it. And I'm just not so sure love and marriage is all it's cracked up to be. Some of my friends' husbands come on to me when their wives aren't around. Is that what I want?"

He reached over and, once again, brushed her hair out of her eyes.

"No," she continued. "But it's easier to know what you don't want than what you do, don't you think?"

She was genuinely interested in what he thought, but he didn't answer. He refilled both their glasses. "You know, there's another possibility. A much simpler one."

"What's that?"

"Maybe you just haven't met the right man."

She met his eyes. "Maybe not." She dug her hand into the sand, running it through her fingers. "What about you?" she asked. "Is there a wife and a child or two in . . . where are you living . . . London?"

"New York, mostly, but I have a flat in London too. And no—no wife—anymore. No children either."

"I'm sorry," she lied.

"No, you're not. And you shouldn't be, at least not for my sake. It was a relatively amicable divorce."

Lindsay couldn't help smiling. She picked up her champagne glass, drained it, and held it out to him to pour another.

In the background, she heard again a faint, persistent drumbeat. "What is that?" she asked. "What are they doing?"

"Juju. African magic. Someone is casting a spell."

"I think someone is doing that here too," she said.

"But you don't believe in spells, do you?"

"I'm not so sure. There are all kinds of spells."

"I believe juju is powerful stuff." He paused, handed her the champagne glass. "You will believe in it, you know, before we're through."

"Before we're through with what?" She laughed.

"With each other. Before we're through with each other."

CHAPTER 10

James was late and Lindsay was restless. She had seen him a few times since their date at the beach, and he had urged her to join him on an art-buying trip up-country to the village of Oshogbo, outside of Ibadan. He promised she would find an arresting story. At first she demurred. What if she were away when Olumide made his move? Then she remembered Joe Rainey's request for features. Besides, she liked the idea of spending a weekend with James.

Martin knocked on her bedroom door to tell her that Mike Vale, her new colleague from the *Observer*, was at the door. Surprised, she went downstairs. He was dressed in the ubiquitous safari suit that male reporters favored in Africa and, she had to admit, looked dashing. She offered him a cup of coffee, but he had not come for idle chatter.

"I'm sorry to barge in, but I've got a good reason," he said. She gave him a quizzical look.

"The murder. At the ambassador's party. The guy you told me was probably killed by an angry crowd."

"I think I said he had a rope mark on his neck."

"It's what you didn't say. But then, maybe you didn't know. In which case, I am here to enlighten you—for a price."

"Why don't you give me the merchandise and then I'll tell you how much it's worth."

"Now why would I do that? But, in the interest of our future relationship, I'll bite. Apparently the victim was a popular student dissident. This student, Babatunde Oladayo, has been missing since that night." He waited for her to look impressed, but her expression didn't change.

"So how much do you think it's worth?"

She shrugged. "Not much. I filed that story and a lot more and it ran in the *Globe*. Have you been asked to match it?"

He was quiet for a moment, looking at her. "Shit. My line is dead and no messages have arrived. They'll be going crazy in London." He accepted the cup of coffee she offered. "It just proves I was right in coming here. Listen, Lindsay. You're good. You were on the spot minutes after you saw the body and you got inside. I know I blew that, but I've developed some great sources here and in Washington that you don't have. You write for an American paper, I'm at a British one. We could work together, feed each other information."

"I don't think so, Mike. I don't think my editor would like that. And besides, I'm not really a team player. I like beating the competition."

"I'll admit you beat me this time. But you also risked expulsion—or worse. Sure you don't want a partner to cover your back?"

"Not yet. Thanks anyway."

He turned to go. "Well, if you won't be my partner, how about joining me for lunch?"

"I can't today. Maybe next week."

"I'll count on it." He walked toward his car. Halfway down the driveway, he turned and winked. She smiled, wondering whether his studied efforts at seduction worked on other women.

She went back to her room to pack a few clothes, a notebook, a pen, her tape recorder, extra batteries and cassettes, and a camera. She started downstairs, then turned back and pulled a black silk nightgown out of a drawer, stuffing it into her bag. When she returned to the kitchen, Martin was busily mopping the floor.

"Good morning, madam," he said. "You go for see traders?"

"Why? Are they here?"

Local itinerant merchants stopped at Lindsay's door almost every day, but she had never had time to look at their wares.

"I send dem way?"

She looked at her watch and saw that she had some time to kill.

"No. Please tell them to come in."

Martin admitted two traders. Both had huge raffia baskets on their heads, filled with African artifacts wrapped in brown paper. They placed the baskets on the floor, carefully unwrapping their treasures: horned masks from the Calibar region meant to scare away the evil spirits and graceful antelope masks to bring good luck in the hunt. They showed her calabashes, beaded stools, talking drums, and ibejis dressed in jackets made of cowry shells. She particularly liked a carved wooden staff that was used to worship Shango, the Yoruba god of lightning, and a bronze lion's head, its lifelike mouth opened in a fierce roar. She gazed covetously at a life-sized wooden fertility statue with angular pointed breasts, its stomach protruding into a sharp point.

"How much for the statue?" she asked.

The trader, accustomed to Americans and their currency, bargained directly in dollars.

"Three hundred dollar," he said.

"That's way too much," Lindsay protested. "I'll give you fifty dollars."

He laughed. "Fifty dollar? Oh no, madam. I go for starve." He pulled out a small primitively carved doll from Guinea with a raffia skirt. "Dis be fifty dollar," he said. "For dis," he gestured grandly at the fertility statue, "maybe two hundred fifty, last price."

"I'll give you two hundred fifty if you throw in the lion," Lindsay offered.

"No, madam. The lion be juju. You rub for head and make prayer. It give you power. You need power, madam?"

"Yes." Lindsay laughed. "Everyone needs power, right? I still say two hundred fifty for both, last price."

Looking as though he had been robbed, the trader nodded and started to pack up his belongings. He picked the lion up reverentially, and handed it to her.

"Rub here," he showed her, pointing to a spot on the head worn so it shone brightly, contrasting with the tarnished, nearly black body.

Lindsay also bought the Shango staff for another $75. She was feeling pleased with herself when James appeared at the door. She leaped up to greet him, kissing him quickly on the cheek.

"Don't worry. I just bought a few things but I'm all ready to go."

"So I see."

He looked over the masks and ibejis as the traders rewrapped them. Lindsay noticed he was frowning. He picked up the Shango staff, saying, "What an amazing array of junk. You know how they try to imitate the ancient patina? They bury the fake in the earth for a few months."

"But these aren't pretending to be originals," Lindsay said. "Don't be such a snob. These are clearly reproductions, but I still think they're fun."

"Do you?" He paused and looked at her as if she had said something more profound than she knew.

He picked up the lion.

"See where its head is shiny?" Lindsay asked. "It's magic. Juju. Rub there and make a wish."

He turned it over in his hand, shaking his head. "This is pure commercial tourist fare."

"I thought I was fated to buy it," she said, ignoring his condescending tone. "But this is my favorite," she said, showing him the fertility statue.

He examined it carefully.

"This piece is not exactly a copy, but it's similar, in a very crude way, to a really beautiful statue from Benin that's in the Metropolitan Museum," he said. "Notice the breasts and the stomach. Can you see how Picasso was influenced by this? Did you buy it?"

"Well, I was thinking about it," she said. "Just a minute, I need to pay the traders."

She dashed upstairs to get some cash. When she returned, she saw James looking intently at one of the small statues. He stared at it, turning it upside down and scrutinizing it from every angle. It appeared to be an ibeji, but whoever made it didn't try to make it look authentic; it was very lightweight, and the wood hadn't been aged. James asked the trader in a sharp voice where he had gotten it.

"It be mine," the trader said fearfully. "I buy it."

"Who sold it to you?" James asked, looking troubled.

"Don' know," the trader answered. "Dis come from many place, some boy found me dis. You like it? One hundred naira, you take it, boss."

James extracted a hundred naira from his wallet and, surprising Lindsay, bought the ibeji. Lindsay gave the traders her money and accompanied them to the door. When she returned, James was still inspecting the statue.

"Is something the matter?" Lindsay asked.

James looked up. "I'm not sure," he said. "I ordered a shipment of original artwork from Oshogbo—statues that look surprisingly like this one. I'm exporting them to Europe and I don't know how this one ended up in a trader's sack. Some local thievery, I'd bet."

He was clearly angry. "And I intend to find out," he said. "I won't know how many are missing until I receive my order—if I ever do."

"Is it possible that just a few were pilfered?"

"Yes. Of course. That's what I'm hoping for. I'm sorry," he said, turning to Lindsay. "Now let's talk about your purchases. What did you pay for the fertility statue?"

"Fifty dollars," she lied. "And I get the statue plus the fertility. That's not a bad deal."

He smiled. "And the fertility bit doesn't scare you?"

"I don't know. A bargain's a bargain."

"Well, that's not too bad a price. You wouldn't believe what some of those American oil company wives pay for this shit," he said. "It's obscene. . . ."

He walked to the door, his mood brightening. "Well, are you ready?"

"Yes. I'll get my bag."

He picked up the statue of the lion she had purchased. "Shall we bring him?" he asked, playfully. "For luck?"

"I thought you said he was just 'commercial tourist fare.'"

"I did. And you were right. It was a snobby thing to say. Let's take him. We can both use the extra luck."

"Done," Lindsay said with a smile, taking the lion from him and putting it in her bag. "Now, are we taking your car?"

"Wait a minute. Don't you want to see your present?"

Lindsay was surprised. She smiled at him. "You brought me a present?"

"Yes. I didn't expect the traders to be here." He reached into his pocket and pulled out two small packages, wrapped in brown paper.

Lindsay hesitated.

"Go ahead. Open them."

She opened the paper carefully to reveal two beautiful ibejis, their deep, rich patina reflecting the light coming in through the windows.

"These are stunning," she said. "Truly beautiful."

"They're authentic," James said. "I thought you would like them."

"Oh, James, thank you." She threw her arms around him. "I feel such a fool for having bought the fakes."

"Not at all. Now, why don't you put them somewhere secure and we can get started."

"I'll put them in my safe," she said, and went upstairs.

She was beaming when she came down again.

"Well, what's our route?"

"We drive to Ibadan, about two hours to the north, and then another hour to Oshogbo. There's a studio there run by the Austrian artist I told you about, Roxanne Reinstadler. It's grown into a thriving artistic community. After we meet with her, I'll leave you there to do an interview while I keep an appointment with another dealer. Then I'll come back to pick you up."

"Sounds good." She patted her tape recorder. "Martin's packed us a lunch—it's just sandwiches and warm Cokes. Don't expect it to live up to your beach extravaganza."

"It'll be fine. Let's go."

CHAPTER 11

Even in the best of times, the hot and dusty drive to Ibadan was not easy. Lindsay had heard that it could be downright dangerous, with armed gangs ambushing cars on the open highway, leaving passengers stranded, broke, and lucky to be alive. James, however, was as relaxed as if they were driving through southern France.

Lindsay had insisted on driving the first shift, saying it relaxed her. She did in fact begin to unwind. She hadn't realized how much her reporting had spooked her. She felt an urge to tell James about it, partly to work it out in her own mind and partly to impress him.

"Do you think we'll run into trouble on the road?" Lindsay asked.

"I don't think so. There used to be many more bandits. The government has cut down on a lot of it. That's one good thing they'll say about Olumide, he made the roads safer."

"Mussolini made the trains run on time, but he was still a fascist," Lindsay said. "I found Olumide pretty scary when I interviewed him."

"How so?"

"He tried to charm me, but he tried to scare me too. There was something . . . I don't know . . . sinister about him."

She paused, hesitating for only a moment. "Don't repeat this. But I heard from the American ambassador that Olumide was planning to have Femi Fakai arrested. He's determined to stay in power, and why shouldn't he be? He gets richer and richer every day from his piece of the drug trade."

She tried to reach under the seat for her bag. He beat her to it.

"What are you looking for?" he asked.

"My sunglasses. I can't see a thing."

He fished around, pulling out some bunched-up papers and a bulging Cartier makeup bag before he located the glasses, out of their case and dusty from accumulated debris. He wiped them and handed them to her.

"What good would arresting Fakai do?" he asked.

"Oh." She put on her glasses. "The idea is that the arrest will set off protests that the government can use as a pretext to cancel the elections. He denied it, of course."

James didn't answer, so she looked over at him. He was staring at her in an intimate, suggestive way that, under the circumstances, was almost condescending. She decided to continue.

"Anyway, the ambassador warned me to get out of the country. I can't believe he thought I would."

James grunted skeptically. "But why you, in particular? Aren't there other journalists who would cover the story if you left?"

"There's Maureen, but she's due to fly back to London in a week. The others are all British hacks. Most of them are pretty burned out. They travel a lot and spend as little time in Lagos as they can get away with. It's not hard to pull the wool over their eyes."

"This is too byzantine for me. Who is trying to pull the wool over their eyes?"

"Look, James, I imagine you think I'm paranoid and of course it's possible that the Americans are playing it straight. Maybe they're even the good guys in this situation. But maybe not. Maybe they have a secret agenda. There's a guy here who is listed as political officer, but

I know he's a spook. The other reporters don't want to rock the boat. So it might make sense for the CIA to try to get rid of someone like me who's always asking too many questions."

"A secret agenda? Like what?"

"I don't know." She shifted in her seat. "Maybe they're trying to bolster Olumide? He may be a drug lord, but he doesn't bother the international oil companies. Fakai criticizes U.S. policy and keeps making speeches about redistributing wealth. That kind of talk upsets Washington."

"If the CIA wanted to get rid of Fakai, how would they go about it?"

"I don't know . . . maybe work with Olumide to set Fakai up so Olumide can arrest him. Maybe just assassinate him."

He made a gesture of impatience. "This is sounding a little far-fetched. Why would our government go so far as to assassinate him?"

"I assure you it's not out of the question. The oil companies, which our government represents, hate Fakai. He supports the activists in the east who claim that the local people aren't getting any benefits from the oil. He points out that the pipes are old and bursting and safety measures are lax. There was an explosion last year that killed thirty people. Fakai supported the demonstrators. Instead of making the fields safer, the company hired private security guards."

"That doesn't explain why the CIA would eliminate Fakai."

"Are you kidding?"

"Jesus. I'm glad I'm in the art world. All I have to worry about is fraud." He casually dropped his hand to her thigh, as though he hadn't realized he was touching her. "Politics everywhere is a giant cesspool, Lindsay."

She moved his hand away.

"So what do you do if Fakai is arrested?" he asked.

"Get ready to cover the riots, I guess. What about you?"

"Well, normally, I'd get the hell out as fast as possible. But with you here, I don't know."

Lindsay was touched, but said, "James, if we're going to spend any time together, you can't think that way. This is my job and I'm pretty good at it. I always stay where the trouble is or I fly in looking for it. I want you to care about me. But I don't want you to worry about me."

"Maybe we'd better slow down."

"No, I didn't mean I wanted that. I—"

A police car raced by, its siren blaring.

"That was close," James said. "Getting stopped for speeding is the last thing we need. I can think of better ways to spend my money than on a big dash for him."

Lindsay laughed, relieved.

They drove the next few miles in silence until James took the wheel and pulled onto a bush road he knew. It was unpaved and rutted. Green hemmed them in on all sides—palm fronds, sugarcane, and banana trees. Every so often they came to a small village of rounded mud huts. Naked babies toddled in front yards, chickens ran free, pecking at the ground.

They passed fields where they saw women planting or cutting the tall grass with machetes. The men, as usual, were nowhere to be seen. Some, Lindsay knew, were working in the cities sending money to their families. Others had fled to the slums and did little of anything, trying to scrape by, often getting into trouble.

After driving another ten minutes they came to an even narrower road that led to the outskirts of Oshogbo. They passed a crossroads of fruit and vegetable stalls, drove up a hill, and turned left onto a long driveway surrounded by thick woods. At the end was a modest white European-style house with a slate roof.

James filled her in about Roxanne Reinstadler, how she'd come here some twenty years ago to teach. Slowly, a group of talented Nigerians had formed around her, and together they painted in bold colors, made batiks, and started selling their work, mostly to foreign visitors. Roxanne, as good at marketing as she was at teaching, encouraged her students to depict various Yoruba gods and christened them the "Oshogbo School." For some time now their paintings and sculptures were de rigueur in most expatriate homes in Lagos and Port Harcourt.

"By now, Roxanne believes in the gods she paints and sculpts," James said, parking the car. "She's devoted herself to the goddess Oshun, the Yoruba goddess of water and fertility. Follow me."

He led her into the woods along a dirt path past flowering bushes and scrub trees. Before long they came upon two gigantic stone statues placed side by side: huge, pendulous women-gods with bulging bellies and spreading, thick thighs. Lindsay saw many more of them, rising from the ground, angular, imposing, lifelike. Soon they were surrounded, and the copse looked like a mad Picasso-inspired village. James was right: the place would make a great story. A woman, thousands of miles from the Austrian town of her youth, giving herself over to the creation of a fantastic world in homage to an African deity. In fact, Lindsay could imagine returning with a film crew to do a documentary.

"What do you think?" asked James.

"It's absolutely amazing. I've never seen anything like it."

"Come and meet her."

"Is she expecting us?"

"No. But she's always at home and she loves receiving guests."

They retraced their steps and he knocked on the door. It was opened by a hearty-looking woman, about seventy, with the kind of fair skin that was rosy and smooth in youth but now deeply wrinkled. She wore no makeup except rouge, which she applied too heavily, making her look a bit like a Kabuki doll. Her eyes were pale blue, lively and curious. She was wearing a long shapeless batik dress in a riot of yellows, blues, and oranges, and her long white hair was held back by an ebony comb with a carving of the Yoruba goddess Oshun on the top.

"James," she said, with a thick accent. "Well, well, this is a pleasant surprise. Are you visiting me? Are you buying? And what have you brought me?"

"I've brought you a good friend," he answered, giving her a hug. He introduced the two women. "She's a journalist. She wants to make you even more famous, so be nice to her."

"When am I not nice?" Turning to Lindsay, she added, "Come in, my dear. Would you like some tea?"

James explained that he had an appointment with a dealer and would return shortly. Roxanne led Lindsay to a heavily curtained parlor where she served tea from a clay teapot and even, somehow, produced a plateful of German Bahlsen biscuits. Her voice was surprisingly powerful, considering her age.

"I suppose you think I am a crazy old lady, yes?" she said, smiling. "Many people do. But I believe I was meant to be here. I came on a visit and stayed to teach. Something led me to create these god-figures and through them remind the people of the ancient gods they abandoned. These gods become angry if they are ignored for too long. I believe I am here to prevent that disaster." She stopped and stared at Lindsay. "Do you believe in fate?"

Lindsay hesitated. "No," she finally answered. "Not really. I'm afraid I am too Western, too linear in my thinking. But I am awed by what you've done here."

"Stay in Africa a bit longer, my dear. It is the best cure for linear thinking."

Then she gave Lindsay a tour of the grounds, explaining the symbolism behind each of the statues.

"Think of me as a reverse missionary," she said, her eyes dancing. "I try to help the villagers to abandon Christianity and return to their true gods. Oh, I know that many villagers think I'm crazy—but they tolerate me. A few even believe me."

She grabbed Lindsay's arm. "For them, I am a priestess. They call me the white priestess of Oshogbo. I have twelve converts. Soon we will have a whole community, then a village, and then . . . who knows?"

Lindsay recorded the conversation and shot two rolls of film. Then they walked back to the house, and when James returned he found them still deep in conversation.

Roxanne rose and gave James a peck on the cheek. "Now, my dear," she said, "I must do some business with your friend." She led him into an office. Lindsay wandered around the small gallery stocked with replicas of the giant sculptures outside.

After half an hour, she decided to go for another walk outside. As she opened the screen door, she heard a murmur of voices coming from a small arbor. She was surprised to see Roxanne and James talking with a striking-looking man she hadn't seen before. His skin was almost blue-black, his hair cut close to his head. Although he was probably a Hausa, Lindsay thought, he wasn't wearing traditional dress. He sported a sharply tailored, expensive-looking white linen sports jacket, a pale blue shirt open at the neck, navy blue trousers, and soft black Italian shoes. She noticed that he was holding an impressive black ebony cane. There appeared to be an ivory dragon's head carved at the top.

The three seemed deep in some kind of negotiation, speaking softly, presumably working out details of a sale. She didn't want to disturb them so she walked away, strolling through the woods for another half hour. When she returned, Roxanne and James were in the sitting room waiting for her and the man was nowhere to be seen.

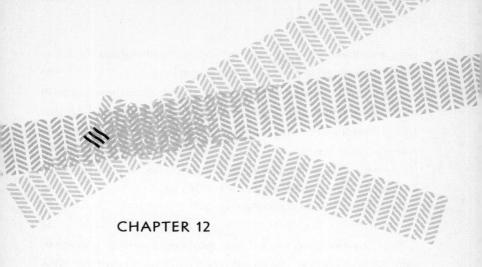

CHAPTER 12

"Who was that snazzy-looking guy you were talking to?" she asked, as they climbed into the car.

"Oh, did you see him?" James looked surprised. "I thought he'd come and gone while you were taking your walk."

"Just a glimpse. Pretty sharp."

He grinned. "He's a local business contact. Did you notice his jacket? A few trips to Italy and now it's nothing but Armani."

They stopped at a hotel James knew on the outskirts of Ibadan. He went to register while she parked the car. She found a space next to a black Mercedes government car, identifiable by a black and white license plate with the number 4 in the upper left corner. The lower the number, the higher the position. She pulled out her overnight bag, locked the car, and went to join James in the lobby. He was talking to a Nigerian man sporting a pair of dark Ray-Bans. As she walked toward them, the man moved on to the elevator bank.

"You certainly know a lot of people," she said amiably, when she reached James.

"He's from the export bureau," James said. "I have to have good relations with these guys if I want to get any really old artifacts out of the country. It's illegal to export antiquities, you know."

She nodded, already having assumed James greased the wheels like every Western businessman. In any case, who was she to talk? If she hadn't done the same, she'd still be waiting on line at the public communications office.

"I wonder if he's the one with the impressive license plate," Lindsay said, filling him in on the car in the parking lot.

"What number did you say was on it?"

"Four."

"No. That's way too low for him. Four would go to an important minister or his deputy." He thought for a moment. "I heard that Billy Anikulo drives number four."

"You mean the health minister?"

"Yeah. I wonder what he's doing here."

She approached the desk and asked the clerk if Billy Anikulo was registered at the hotel. The clerk blinked quickly.

"No, madam."

"Well, have you seen him here? Has he met with someone staying in the hotel?"

"I don't know, madam."

Lindsay smiled at the clerk. "You don't know or you can't say?"

His face showed only the slightest trace of a smile in return. "I don't know, madam. And I can't say."

"What difference does it make?" James asked. "Why do you care if he's here?"

"Just curious."

She asked the reception clerk to book a long distance call—she needed to give her whereabouts to the foreign desk and tell the editors to expect a feature on Roxanne—and was told, to her surprise, that there would be no problem. Then they had to choose a room.

The hotel offered two options. One possibility was relatively modern with air-conditioning (no small consideration). This was where

James usually stayed in Ibadan. The other was what the management called a "Safari cottage"—a round mud hut with thatched roof, part of a simulated African village. Intrigued, they decided to investigate it, and the clerk offered to take them around the back for a look. James started to follow him. Lindsay hesitated a minute and slipped the receptionist fifty naira to let her know if he found out who Billy Anikulo was visiting.

The hut appeared authentic, though it did include some modern amenities—a phone on the bedside table and, to judge by an immobile ceiling fan, possibly electricity. A few shafts of light filtered in through tiny windows. African crafts had been randomly scattered around—a woven rug, reed baskets, soapstone and small thornwood carvings of zebras and giraffes. In the center was the pièce de résistance—a lumpy double bed surrounded by a ragged mosquito net.

Lindsay said she was game, but James was appalled. Only after Lindsay poked fun at his bourgeois heart did he relent. Inside, she picked up the phone and ordered two bottles of Star beer. The air was hot and muggy, the ceiling fan moved too slowly to create a real breeze, and flies buzzed aggressively around their ears, but, for once, none of this bothered Lindsay. Waiting for the drinks, she asked if she could see the statues he bought, but he was reluctant to unwrap them. Then came a moment of awkward silence as she wondered who was going to make the first move.

She glanced at the bed. "It looks pretty uncomfortable."

"Yeah."

She walked over and sat on the edge. The mosquito net had huge holes in it. "Doesn't look like it offers much protection."

"No."

She lay down and bounced a few times. "It manages to be lumpy and hard as a rock at the same time. Why don't you come over here for a minute and try it out?" she invited.

He didn't move. Then, after a long moment, he turned toward the door. "If we want those beers, we'd better go to the bar. They'll never get around to delivering them here. And we should get something to eat before the restaurant closes."

She quickly got up, straightened her shirt, and headed for the door. Suddenly he pulled her back, put his hand under her chin, leaned down and kissed her very lightly on the lips.

"You're irrepressible," he said. "I feel like I've plugged into a private energy source." Then he opened the door for her.

They ordered the only dish the waiter said was available—chicken piri piri, a fiery hot chicken stew served over rice with plantains—and two bottles of beer. When the drinks arrived, Lindsay quickly drained her glass and asked for another. She didn't eat much, but he finished everything on his plate and then ate what she left. She drank a third beer and relaxed, feeling a little light-headed.

"Tell me about your ex-wife," she said abruptly.

He looked up, surprised. "Not much to tell. We met in college, sophomore year, University of Michigan. I transferred to Michigan because the African arts faculty was stronger. I came from Atlanta, she grew up in Ann Arbor. We met the first day of classes and were together all three years. We married the summer we graduated. But we were too young—it lasted for only two years."

"Did you love her?"

He paused, taken aback briefly. "That's a hell of a question to throw out between dinner and the coffee."

She played with her spoon. "I'm sorry. I really didn't mean to interrogate you. I guess I just can't stop acting like a reporter. Don't answer if you don't want to."

He lit a cigarette, inhaled deeply and slowly exhaled. "I certainly thought I loved her at the time. But she was full of complexes. She was extremely attached to her family. Hated change of any kind, couldn't bear traveling, didn't ever want to leave Ann Arbor. It's hard to imagine a worse fit, frankly."

"Did you part as friends?"

"I wouldn't say that. She was pretty angry because I got involved with someone else right away. But now she's remarried with a couple of kids. Still lives in Ann Arbor."

"The someone else—was that the obligatory love affair that follows a divorce? The one that always ends badly?"

"No. The one that ended badly came later."

The waiter brought the coffee and she took a sip to cover the silence.

"Do you want to tell me about that?" she asked.

"Not really."

An uncomfortable pause.

"Well, so after the marriage, then what?"

"Then there were others. Many others. But nothing worked out."

She realized she was pushing kind of hard. "Maybe you just haven't met the right one."

He put out his cigarette. "I thought I had. I'm still recovering from that. Listen, Lindsay, I'm not . . ." His voice trailed off. "I can't seem to make the commitments that most women want—that most women have a right to want."

"Are you warning me?"

"Yes."

"Well, don't. I'm a big girl. I can take care of myself."

"I believe you," he answered. "I think you could do just about anything you wanted to."

"We'll see." She smiled and leaned back. "Don't you want to know about me?"

"I don't think I'll find out what I want to know by asking you questions. Shall we go?"

Walking back to the hut, he reached for her hand. In the room, James busied himself trying to fix the mosquito net by tying knots to close the holes. She lay down and watched, wanting him to make the first move.

He finished working on the net and turned to her. He seemed to be struggling against his own desire.

"Are you tired?" he asked.

"A little. Are you?"

"Yes. But I have some reading to do. Will the light bother you?"

He opened his briefcase and took out a folder. Heading to the bathroom, she murmured just loud enough for him to hear: "It's not the light that's bothering me."

She washed up, wondering what to sleep in; her sexy nightgown no longer felt appropriate. She settled on an oversized T-shirt. She lay down on the bed, feeling ridiculous, angry at him and at herself. Was it possible she had so misunderstood him? Had her reluctance on the beach so easily turned him off?

The bedside phone rang and she picked up the receiver. After a moment she answered: "Listen, that's just not possible. I cannot wait two days for a line to New York. I need to get through by tomorrow morning." She heard her voice rising. "How can you call yourself an international hotel if I can't make a phone call or use the Internet or send a fax? What am I supposed to do, use the talking drum?"

She slammed down the receiver.

James put his work aside and with a sigh walked over to the bed. He sat next to her, brushed the persistent stray hair out of her eyes, and said gently, "That sounded pretty angry."

"Well, I have a right to be."

"Are you sure it was the hotel that made you mad?"

"Yes, of course. What else would it be?"

"I thought it might be me."

She fidgeted, playing with the mosquito netting.

"I think I may have misread our relationship, that's all," she said casually, getting up to unpack.

"This is what I was trying to warn you about," he said.

She shrugged. "I thought you were talking about a commitment. I didn't think that extended to enjoying each other."

He smiled. "Aren't we enjoying each other?"

She put down the shirt she was holding and looked at him.

"You know what I mean."

He met her gaze.

"It usually doesn't. But it does with you."

"James, is this your way of saying you'd like us to just be friends? Because if it is, that's okay."

"No, Lindsay. I'm just being cautious. Trying to build something real before we jump into bed." He saw her stiffen. "Look, if we become lovers too quickly everything changes. It will end sooner. I've been through that so many times."

It was, she thought, an odd perspective—one she had never encountered from a man before.

"Fine," she said, grudgingly. "I don't want to talk about this. Let's go to sleep."

He nodded and put his papers away, then climbed into bed next to her and turned out the light.

They lay silent for a moment.

"What was that about on the beach?" she blurted. "You weren't so cautious then."

"I know. But that was before I realized that this might be more than a few days' diversion."

Silence again.

"Maybe you just think too much," she added. "Don't you ever just follow your impulses?"

"I thought you didn't want to talk about this."

"I don't."

"Good. Good night, Lindsay," he said.

In the morning, she awoke early because she itched all over. She was covered from head to toe with mosquito bites. Her neck, arms, legs, and stomach were blotched with angry red welts. She stared at herself in the bathroom mirror. Oh, God, they were on her face too. The mosquito net had been completely useless.

When he awoke, his expression didn't temper her anxiety. She tried to hide her face. "Move your hands," he ordered gently. He had brought some calamine lotion and tried to apply it with cotton balls, first dabbing lightly at her face, then her arms and legs. Miserable, she looked at him. Miraculously, he had emerged relatively unscathed—just a few bites on his legs and chest. "I guess I'm just not as sweet as you are," he said.

"That's for sure," she said. "But I should have known better."

"Well, you said you wanted an authentic African village."

"Not a really authentic one. I wanted a tourist African village, a sanitized version without snakes and mosquitoes. No wonder the other cottages were all empty."

"Yeah, that was a clue. I warned you about romanticizing Africa."

"I know. You've warned me about all kinds of romance. What about you? Are you itchy?"

"No. But we've got to get you to a doctor. You're having an allergic reaction and you probably need some extra quinine too."

They packed their few belongings. While he went to settle the bill, she waited in the car, too embarrassed to be seen. She looked around the parking lot to see if the number 4 license plate was still there. She found it, and watched three men approach the car. She didn't recognize any of them. One of the men got behind the wheel. Another rode shotgun. The third, probably the health minister himself, climbed into the back. He was tall and heavyset, dressed casually in a pair of khaki pants and a loose-fitting lightweight shirt. When James returned seconds later, she gestured toward the car and asked if he recognized anyone. He too couldn't identify any of its occupants.

She was feverish on the long drive home. She finally fell into a fitful sleep full of dreams in which she narrowly escaped multiple dangers: a crocodile crept up on shore and dragged her underwater, bandits chased her with pangas, and a lion paced up and down, up and down outside her tent, ready to pounce the moment she emerged.

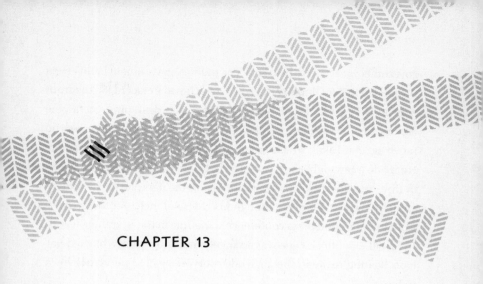

CHAPTER 13

It took nearly a week for the fever to subside and the welts to diminish. James visited every day, bringing lotion and Benadryl to control the maddening itch. He sat on the edge of her bed, telling her stories about his adventures in bush villages trying to locate religious sculptures. He was charming and attentive, but, although he liked to tease Lindsay about her romantic notions about journalism, he resisted mentioning his own emotional state, or their standoff in Ibadan. She began to wonder if he simply wasn't attracted to her. She would have liked to talk more with Maureen, but Maureen was busy following her own stories and, when she was home, spent a lot of time in her room. She seemed to have come down with some kind of low-grade virus that sapped her energy. It worried Lindsay, but Maureen dismissed it as simply a reaction to the heat.

Lindsay used the enforced bed rest to write and file her feature on Roxanne Reinstadler. By the time she was ready to resume her full workload, several weeks had passed since she had identified Babatunde Oladayo's body. There had been no announcement or local coverage of his death—no student uproar, no demonstrations, and, so far, no government reaction to her story. The military government hadn't even responded to her Olumide interview, which had in fact made the front page in New York; the silence, as they say, was deafening. So far, the American ambassador's predictions hadn't come true. There was no move against Fakai, whose campaign seemed increasingly paranoid. He made a few public appearances but didn't announce them ahead of time, in order to keep the authorities in the dark; he gave no interviews to the foreign press, though his aides still held out the promise of an underground press conference sometime in the next three weeks. In fact, the political scene was strangely quiet, like a huge bloated balloon floating eerily in the air while everyone waited nervously for it to burst.

She understood that she had done little to help move the story forward. It was the first time ever she had become so distracted that it affected her work. Since the trip to Ibadan she couldn't stop thinking about James.

Her ambition returned with her health. She determined to follow two loose threads: the killing of Babatunde and the murder of William Agapo and his wife. It was widely believed that Agapo's death was a political assassination—his wife's murder was likely collateral damage. But why was Agapo killed? The most likely reason was that he angered Olumide. Since he was one of Olumide's closest advisers, his crime must have been more than just lining his pockets. She figured that Agapo had been a spy and that Olumide had discovered his betrayal. But if that was true, who was Agapo spying for? Rumor pointed to the CIA, but there was no proof. Still, she thought she'd try talking to the new political officer. Maybe she would point her in the right direction.

She called the American embassy and asked for Vickie Grebow. Vickie was in meetings most of the day, but Lindsay set up a lunch date with her for the next afternoon. In the meantime, she would get to work on her other priority—Babatunde Oladayo. Her first stop was the high commissioner's steward. Driving up to the guard at the gate, she pulled out her press credentials and U.S. passport. "Good morning," she said brightly, handing the papers through the window. "I'm Lindsay Cameron. I left my purse here at a party a few weeks ago and I wanted to check with the high commissioner's steward to see if he found it."

"He gone," the guard answered mechanically, barely glancing at her.

"Well, when is he coming back?"

The guard shrugged.

"Do you mean he is not working here anymore?"

The guard shrugged again.

"Then please tell the high commissioner I'd like to see him," she bluffed.

"He not at home, madam." The guard's eyes danced nervously.

"Oh, what a shame. Could I possibly see his wife? She's a friend of mine." This was more risky, but she counted on a high commissioner's wife having duties that would take her away from home.

"No, madam." The guard was slightly more attentive now. "Madam go out early."

"Well, then I think I'd better have a word with the steward's wife," she said with relief.

The guard hesitated.

"It's important that I find my bag," she said. "I'd really rather not bother the high commissioner with this. He might worry that someone on his staff stole it."

The guard relented. He phoned the house, swung open the gate, and touched his cap as Lindsay drove through and parked. She had just gotten out of the car when a young woman, carrying a small child wrapped in a *kanga* on her back, entered the courtyard and approached her.

"Good morning," said Lindsay.

The woman shifted the baby's weight but didn't look up or answer.

"I came to see your husband. Do you know when he will return?"

Still looking down, the woman spoke with hushed intensity. "He not here, madam. Please no go come here. He in hospital. He very bad."

Lindsay felt her mouth go dry.

"What happened? What's wrong with him?"

"An accident, madam. A car go hit him on de street. Please no go come here. Please no go see him. Leave us be. We no want trouble."

Lindsay didn't speak for a moment. "I'm so sorry," she mumbled at last. "I thought he wanted to tell me about Baba—"

The woman interrupted her.

"What he want no import, madam," she hissed. "Please, madam, for my babies. Go way. Don' come back."

"I understand. I'm very, very sorry." Lindsay reached over and touched the baby's plump arm.

For the first time, the woman looked her in the eye. Lindsay smiled weakly, turned and got in the car. As she started the ignition, the woman poked her head timidly in through the window, seemingly emboldened by the engine's noise. "You want The Next Step. . . . Yes?" she whispered. Lindsay nodded. "Go to de Juju House."

"What Juju House?" Lindsay was whispering too. "Where is it?"

The woman shook her head impatiently. "De *Juju House*. Ask in Surulere." She turned away and walked quickly back to her quarters, her baby swaying as she moved.

Lindsay knew about Surulere, a vast slum on the outskirts of the city.

She drove through the gate, waving at the guard, who stared straight ahead. She worried about the steward, feeling a sharp pang of guilt. She didn't even know his name, she thought, and she had brought him nothing but trouble. It was clear that he didn't end up in the hospital because of an "accident," and equally clear that she could never approach him again. But what had happened to draw attention to him? Was she responsible? She had started to drive home but changed her mind and passed her own house, heading for the residence of Mike Vale. Mike had gotten the Babatunde story on his own. Maybe he'd have heard something about the repercussions.

Like most of the foreign press in Lagos, Mike lived in the same house as his predecessor. It was just a few short blocks from her own. She pulled into the driveway and got out of the car. She knocked at the door, but no one answered so she knocked again, harder. She was just deciding to leave when Mike opened the front door.

"Hello, darling," he greeted her. "I knew you'd reconsider."

"Hi, Mike. Can I come in?"

"Sure." He stepped aside to make room for her to enter. They sat down in his living room.

She told him that a source had been injured and she suspected governmental foul play.

"It's connected to the Babatunde story," she said. "Have you heard anything new on that?"

Mike looked surprised.

"I'd guess that after your story ran, anyone who helped you with it got in trouble. I'd have thought you'd be prepared."

"I was prepared for fallout against me," she snapped, "but I don't know how they found my source."

"They probably went back over your tracks. Maybe they questioned your source and he admitted talking to you."

"I don't think so. I think it's more likely someone at the house or at the party knew I was at the ambassador's and figured out who I talked to. They didn't question you, did they?"

He frowned. "Of course not. You think I'd report you to Olumide's thugs?"

"No. Sorry. I'm just trying to figure this out."

"He'll probably be all right now that they've put a good scare into him. But what about you?"

"If you mean am I scared, yes, of course. I'll have to be more careful."

Mike got up. "I think you could use a drink," he said. "What'll it be?"

She asked for a vodka tonic and he left to prepare it. Restless, she got up and paced around his living room. A sculpture similar to her fertility statue caught her eye and she wondered if it was done by the same artist. Like her, Mike had bought a lot of tourist pieces, including, she noticed, a small statue very like the one that had angered James. She picked it up and studied it. When Mike returned, she put it back on the shelf. He handed her the vodka tonic and she sipped it slowly.

"Did you get that piece from a trader?" she asked, indicating the shelf.

He walked over and adjusted the sculpture so it stood straight.

"Yeah. Don't tell our friend James. He hates this new art."

"He hates when they try to pretend it's old. He doesn't mind the new ones. In fact, he's exporting some. A trader showed me one exactly like this when James was over. Actually, he was upset the traders had gotten hold of it, but that's another story."

"You'd better tell him I've got one too. You know Lagos. They could wind up pilfering his entire order."

"Yeah, I will." She drained her drink. "Thanks. I gotta go."

She got back in her car and drove home. Martin was in the kitchen, cleaning the stove.

"Have you ever heard of a place called the Juju House?" she asked him.

"Yes, madam. But it not safe for you. It is in Surulere."

"What is it? A religious place, for spells?"

Martin smiled. "No, madam. It's a club. It be where Bayo play."

She made the connection. Bayo was a musician. She'd been told he played a mean saxophone and had about thirty "wives" who lived with him in a kind of cult. He'd been described as a flamboyant figure, a rebel artist, but not, as far as she knew, a political dissident. She had thought of him as a subject for a possible feature, if she had the time, but now it appeared he might be something more.

Maureen was working in the living room. Lindsay interrupted her to tell her about Bayo and insist that they must see him perform sometime soon.

"How about tonight?" Maureen replied. "If he's that interesting, we should track him down right away, and I'm finally feeling a little better today."

Lindsay hesitated. "I'm supposed to have dinner with James."

"So what? Invite him. Or have dinner with him tomorrow. Lindsay, it could be important. Aren't you curious?"

"Don't lecture me, Maurie." Her harsh tone surprised herself. Softening, she added, "Of course I'm curious." She paused. "Okay. Let's go tonight. I'll see if James can join us."

"Whatever."

Lindsay got up. "I'm sorry," she said, moving toward the kitchen. "Let's get a cup of coffee."

She poured some lukewarm coffee from the pot she'd brewed earlier. Maureen tasted it and grimaced, so she poured both cups into a small pot to heat on the stove.

"I'm kind of off coffee these days," Maureen said, pouring herself a glass of orange juice. She opened the food pantry, extracted a box of English shortbread, set it on the table between them, and started munching on one. "So, tell me, how are things with James?"

"It's hard to say," Lindsay began. "In some ways, things are really good. I mean, we see each other pretty regularly. . . ." She paused.

"But?" Maureen encouraged.

"What I hate," Lindsay murmured almost to herself, "is that my relationship with him somehow always leaves me hungry. I always seem to want more than he's prepared to give." She paused. "When we went to that hotel in Ibadan, he didn't want to sleep with me. He said he didn't want us to jump into bed so fast—wanted to build a relationship first. Why are you frowning?"

"Because I don't believe men think that way. So I'm wondering why he said that. Maybe it was manipulative, holding off so you'd want him even more. I wouldn't put that past him. Maybe you should think more about what exactly it is you want from him and whether you think this is going to go where you want it to."

Lindsay sat up straight in her chair. "I like the fact that he seems to value the best things about me instead of the superficial trappings. I'd like him to share more of himself with me, want me more. I think he's scared of feeling too much and I think I can help him get over that."

"Maybe that's just who he is. He's a mysterious guy—I've always thought he was pretty closed off. People our age don't really change, not deeply."

"What I know intellectually and what I know in my heart are not the same. This one time, I want to follow my heart."

"Then go for it," Maureen said. "And good luck." She stood up and headed for her room. "If we're going to go out tonight, I've got to take a nap. We can talk more later."

Alone, Lindsay felt a little better, but she hadn't confessed the depth of her obsession. She couldn't look at James, talk to him, listen to him, without feeling a flutter of desire. And there were other feelings she couldn't talk about: How she thought he was beautiful and how her eyes often lingered over the elegant lines of his face and his body. And how it was the pain in his eyes that attracted her; the very mystery that made Maureen distrustful, she found alluring. She wanted to protect and nurture him, and at the same time, she sensed a danger in him. All those qualities made him irresistible. But was that love? If it wasn't, she thought, then beside it, love was a pale thing, uninteresting, irrelevant.

Lindsay was upstairs changing for dinner when James arrived at seven o'clock sharp. She heard Maureen greet him at the door, then heard her singsong shout, "Lindsay, your date is here."

"Coming." Lindsay started chattering as she walked downstairs.

"James, we have a great idea. There's this incredible musician I've heard about. He performs in a club in Surulere. I hear it's amazing and it might make a great story for me. Do you want to go?"

She poured three drinks.

"It seems it's been decided," James said. "But sure, why not? I think you'd enjoy it. You're talking about Bayo. I've seen his show—in fact, I've met him. You'd never guess it, but he's a serious art collector. I've sold him a few pieces."

"And you never told me?" Lindsay asked. "You've got to start looking at the world in terms of what would make a good story, not just a sale."

"It's still a sale. Only it's newspapers instead of art."

Maureen bristled. "Come on, James. Giving people information isn't just for the sales. And selling art isn't just selling soap."

James shrugged. "Isn't it? Well, I guess you're right. It's much more expensive."

Lindsay suggested they go out for dinner first since the show didn't start until midnight. Maureen said she'd skip dinner and take a nap, but asked them to pick her up afterward.

The meal at the local Chinese restaurant went smoothly enough, though James seemed a little out of sorts. Maybe, thought Lindsay, he's annoyed at the change in plans. At one point, as he was preparing his mu shu pork, he mentioned casually that he might be able to finish his affairs here in two weeks and return to London. She noted, with a sinking feeling, that he made no mention of what that would mean for them. She nodded slowly. She was tired of her doubts, tired of wanting more than he could give. She welcomed an unlooked-for moment of resolution. What would be would be; she wouldn't try to force it anymore.

She launched into a litany of complaints about Lagos, concentrating on the electrical blackouts.

"You need a generator."

"I know, but I can't find one. There's a long waiting list."

"A bribe would fix that," he said. "I'll find out who you need to deal with."

"Thanks," she said. "But, you know, I feel bad doing that—I promised myself I wouldn't join in the general corruption and this would be the second time."

He gave her a patronizing glance. "You're just playing by the rules of a different game. If you've learned nothing else about Africa, you should have learned that rules were made to be broken."

"By whom?"

"By those who can." Then, noticing her disapproval, he added: "What I mean is, life is different here. In the United States, in England, a rule is a rule. In Africa, it's an orientation."

They both laughed and for some reason found it hard to stop. Then she asked him to give her some background on Bayo, but he said it would be more fun for her to be surprised.

"Be ready for a scene."

She was. She felt she'd be ready for anything.

CHAPTER 14

At 11 P.M., with James at her side and Maureen in the backseat, Lindsay drove her white Peugeot into the heart of the city. Slowly, the stucco white villas and lush empty gardens gave way to drab wooden shacks and noisy, crowded streets. A group of young men huddled around a radio blaring the upbeat rhythms of high life. A woman swathed in bright yellow and brown fabric sold fruit, cigarettes, and coconuts from behind a makeshift booth illuminated by a row of candles.

Finally, at James's direction, they pulled up to a large ramshackle house on a spacious corner lot. It stood behind three majestic palms in the middle of a neglected plot of gravel, dirt, and litter, fenced in by chicken wire. They had arrived at the home, the compound, the commune of Bayo Awollowa Soti.

They had come early since Lindsay hoped she could arrange a brief meeting with Bayo before showtime. She reasoned that once she made an initial contact, he would be more likely to grant her a longer interview. They knocked at the door and were greeted by a beautiful young woman with elaborately braided hair pinned up in half-moons around her head. Lindsay identified herself as a journalist and asked if she could speak to Bayo for a few moments. The woman hesitated, but James said something to her in Yoruba and she nodded. "Wait," she ordered in English, and disappeared into the house. Lindsay looked at James in surprise.

"I didn't know you spoke Yoruba," she said.

He shrugged it off. "Just a few words," he answered.

After a few minutes, they were joined by a stocky, affable man in his thirties who introduced himself as "J.R." and said he handled Bayo's public relations. He put out his hand to James and told them to accompany him. As they followed him through a maze of corridors, James whispered that although J.R. always deferred to Bayo in public, he was smarter than he seemed.

"He's really a key adviser," James said. "Bayo calls him his 'Minister of Information.'"

"How modest," Maureen answered. "Does Bayo think he's a head of state?"

"That's no joke," James whispered back. "Don't forget he calls this place his own republic."

They stopped talking as they were ushered into the sitting room.

Bayo was ready for them. He was perched on a high-backed wicker chair like a king astride his throne. An image of Yul Brynner in *The King and I* flitted through Lindsay's mind. He was dressed only in white bikini Jockey shorts; his black, bare, muscular chest glistened with oil, as did his taut legs. His stomach was flat, his wiry hair cropped short. He was not handsome, but he emanated power and sensuality, and Lindsay felt drawn to him.

There were about twenty women milling about him. J.R. said they were his "wives," but it seemed clear to Lindsay that their job was simply to service him in whatever way he wanted. The women were beautiful and young, dressed scantily in tight shorts or long African skirts with halter tops. They all had vacant eyes, the look of people perpetually stoned. They seemed more like cult followers than musical groupies.

J.R. nervously ushered them forward for an audience with the great man himself.

Bayo looked appraisingly at Lindsay, slowly moving his gaze upward, over her long legs, her blue paisley sleeveless dress, till he reached her face. The look was so brazen she wasn't even offended. She stared at him, refusing to lower her own gaze. He didn't say a word but shifted his attention to Maureen, whom he looked over in the same way. Lindsay saw him take in her delicate frame, her bright red Chinese silk jacket, and finally her blue-green eyes, which, like Lindsay's, met his without flinching.

James grabbed his hand in a thumbs-up handshake and introduced the women, saying they were there to see the show. "They're reporters," he said. "Maureen is with the Associated Press and Lindsay writes for a big-time New York paper."

"Which one?" Bayo asked quickly.

"The *Globe*," Lindsay answered. Bayo nodded, impressed. He'd lived briefly in California as a student at Berkeley, where he had picked up the rhetoric of the Black Power movement. He knew the *Globe*'s reach.

He turned toward the women with new interest. "Well, let's see what you can tell the Americans about us," he said. He put a cigarette in his mouth and snapped his fingers. Three of the blank-eyed women leapt forward to light it. A slender woman with a high forehead and delicate features got there first with a Zippo, and Bayo bent his head slightly to the lighter. Then he mumbled something and she withdrew, returning a minute later with a box full of joints, each the size of a Cohiba cigar.

"NNG," Bayo announced proudly to the group in a loud voice. "Nigerian Natural Grass, the best there is."

Bayo lit it, inhaled deeply, holding the cigarette in one hand and the joint in the other, and nodded toward his guests. The woman brought the box over to Maureen, who shook her head, and then to Lindsay.

"No, thank you," Lindsay said. "If I smoked that, I'd never make it to the show." James accepted.

"Yeah, smart to take it slow, baby," Bayo said to Lindsay. "It's strong stuff." Lindsay noticed he never looked directly at anyone; he always gazed toward some unseen but ever-present audience.

"When I was in L.A. the first time," he said, "I was at a party and someone brought out this tiny little joint—I mean, it was so thin, in Lagos we'd have been ashamed to light it. And they acted like it was this great thing." He screwed up his face and raised his voice to a higher pitch: "'Ooh, grass, great, man,'" he imitated, laughing derisively. "And then they passed it around to share with about five other people," he continued. "I couldn't believe it."

He curled his lip at the memory. All the women laughed obligingly with him and stopped as soon as he stopped. Then, as abruptly as a cat who after purring on your lap suddenly bites your finger, Bayo looked bored. He got up, shook hands with James, offered his hand limply to Lindsay and Maureen, and walked toward the door.

"Catch you later, man," he said to James over this shoulder.

He exited, followed by his entire retinue, leaving Lindsay, James, and Maureen unsure of what to do next.

"Well," said James. "What do you think?"

"I can't say I like him," Maureen said, "but he's certainly interesting. He'd make a good feature—plenty of local color."

Lindsay nodded. Turning to James, she said: "He seemed to know you pretty well. How come?"

"I met him the first time I came to Nigeria about eight years ago. I had this friend in college, a Nigerian named Fendi Omagbracpaya, who used to play the saxophone, which as you'll see in a minute is Bayo's instrument. When they were students, he and Bayo used to jam together. By my first trip he'd become an executive in the import-export business, but he still loved Bayo's funky music. When Bayo heard that I was an art dealer, we did some business together. He hasn't changed much. I'm still just about the only white face in the crowd."

"Now there are three of us," Lindsay said.

"Yeah. And over the years I've seen a few others, mostly awkward State Department types trying to understand 'the scene,' but it's rare."

As they were talking, J.R. came for them. "Bayo say I take you in. Show go start now." He winked at Lindsay. James whispered that his pidgin was an affectation. "He's been to university in Yorkshire and can speak perfect English."

As they moved outside, they saw that hundreds of people crowded up and down the narrow streets. Bayo was slowly making his entrance on the back of a donkey. He was dressed now in tight black pants and a purple sequined shirt, opened to the waist. The crowd went wild when they caught sight of him, chanting "Ba-yo, Ba-yo, Ba-yo" with mounting frenzy. Lindsay was struck by the power of the man—not just his charisma but also the hold he had on his followers. She thought that he could be a populist force, drawing power from the most disenchanted voters. She'd have liked to watch his triumphal march longer, but J.R. hustled them out of the crowd and toward the Juju House, the ramshackle club just down the street, shepherding them across a foul-smelling open sewer.

Maureen leaned over to Lindsay and whispered in her ear. "This is one helluva story."

The crowd surged around the club, a simple cement house with a tin roof, trying to get in. J.R. waved his charges past four thugs acting as security guards who were frisking arrivals for weapons. As their little group passed through, someone thrust a bunch of yellow printed flyers into their hands. "Brothers and Sisters, Follow Bayo. Take *The Next Step*," Lindsay read. At the bottom was an address and a date later that week for a political meeting where Bayo would speak.

J.R. noticed Lindsay reading the pamphlet. "Watch out for de black boots, man," he said.

"What?" Lindsay asked.

"De black boots. De police wear dem," J.R. answered. Then, losing the pidgin, he said: "The police have spies here. They are hard to spot, but they always wear black boots."

Lindsay looked down.

"You are wearing black boots," she said, looking around. "A lot of people are wearing black boots."

J.R. laughed. His eyes twinkled. "Yeah man, dat's why dem hard to spot." He pushed his way forward and they followed.

Inside, a club that had been built to seat about two hundred people was overrun with more than three times that number—mostly men—crowding in around tables. Above the stage, on either side, were four huge dangling metal cages, each holding a topless woman who gyrated and danced to Bayo's recordings. Their faces wore that same stoned look as the girls in the house. Except for Lindsay's own small group, everyone in the audience was black. Some stared with curiosity, others with what appeared to be open hostility.

J.R. led them to a table and sat down. They waited, transfixed, listening to the loud, throbbing music. Finally the lights dimmed, the recorded music stopped, and Bayo bounded onstage. The place went wild. He picked up his sax and started to play Afro beat—a combination of American jazz, rock and roll, and African percussive rhythms. At intervals, he'd put the sax down and sing, strut, and prance around the stage, pacing like a panther as the caged women danced more and more wildly, contracting their pelvises in rhythmic sharp movements.

It was . . . fabulous, an assault on the senses such as Lindsay had never before experienced. Some people got up and danced to the music. Maureen and Lindsay exchanged looks. It had been many years since they had danced together at high school parties, ignoring their dates and commanding the floor. Now, swept up in the frenzy, they spontaneously got up and began their old, well-practiced routine. James and J.R. stared agape. After a while, laughing and out of breath, Maureen sat down and Lindsay followed.

"You're full of surprises," James said.

In between numbers, Bayo talked politics, attacking the government, Nigerian laws, and specifically Olumide, whom he called a fascist pig, in true American sixties style. "Oink oink," he screamed, as the drums beat accompaniment, and then put his hand to his ear, encouraging audience response. "Oink," they screamed. "Oink oink . . ."

"We go do sometin dis time, brothers and sisters," Bayo shouted. "We go stop dem fuckas. We goin take da NEXT STEP, you heah me brothers, what we goin take?"

"DA NEXT STEP," the crowd roared, "DA NEXT STEP." Lindsay was shocked that the movement was already so brazen in its opposition. She had had no inkling. That is what comes of spending too much time with foreign diplomats and journalists and not enough on the streets, she thought. She scanned the crowd and saw that in addition to the usual Lagos working-class men there were also a sprinkling of visitors wearing the long cloaks of the north.

"These be Hausa," J.R. said. "Members of the Hausa Radical Union."

This was unusual—crossing tribal and religious lines for a protest movement.

It was getting late, after two o'clock in the morning. J.R. had drifted off to visit other tables. Lindsay had drunk too many beers and was beginning to feel the Afro beat like a hammer in the back of her head. She wanted to go home, but there was no sign of the show's coming to an end. She looked over at Maureen, who had been furiously taking notes but now signaled that she was ready to go. Lindsay leaned over so James could hear her above the music.

"Shall we go?"

They were sitting up front. To leave meant getting up and pushing through the crowd.

"I don't think that's a good idea just yet," James said. "Can you wait a bit?"

"I guess. But my head is killing me."

"Try to hang on a little longer," James said.

Maureen asked Lindsay what was happening.

"Nothing," Lindsay said. "I think it's time to go, but we're a little worried about walking out in the middle of the show. This crowd might not take it well."

Maureen looked around at the adulating audience.

"Maybe J.R. can help," she said.

Lindsay scanned the room and saw J.R. talking to some people a few tables away. She made her way over to him, whispered in his ear and then returned to the table.

"J.R. is going to try to arrange something," she said to James. Then, to Maureen, "How are you doing?"

"I'm okay. Whatever happens, it will beat trying to use the bathroom in this place."

Ten minutes later, as Bayo finished one song and started talking to the audience, J.R. came over and said "Let's go." Bayo noticed them from the stage as they stood. J.R. made a sign and suddenly it seemed as if every eye in the place was on them. They nervously moved in the direction of the door. "Excuse me," Lindsay said as they wriggled past the tightly crammed tables. There was an irritated murmur, and hard stares. Then Bayo said: "Hey, man, we got some friends for here, some REPORTERS. Dey come all de way from New York City for see us. Dey goin' spread de word, man . . . dey goin' spread de word." He started applauding from the stage. There was a pause and then everyone joined him, banging the table and grinning as Lindsay, James, and Maureen made it to the door.

"Whoa," Lindsay said when they were outside. "That was truly incredible. Thanks for coming with me. Really. It was a great night."

"And a great story?" asked James.

"Absolutely. More than one, I think."

"Anytime you want a job as an art smuggler, let me know. You've got nerves of steel. Both of you."

"Don't believe it—they feel like rubber, just now," Maureen said. "And I could really use a bathroom."

They stopped at Bayo's place. The door was open, so they went in, found the bathroom, which was surprisingly middle class, containing a toilet with a seat, a wash basin, and soap in a small dish. Maureen hurried in first.

"When are you going to write your piece?" James asked Lindsay.

"Pretty soon. I want to get it out of the way before the group inter-view with Fakai. But I need to get more information. I'm going to ask J.R. for a real interview with Bayo, this time away from the Juju House."

"Good luck," James said skeptically.

He spotted J.R., who had just entered the house.

"I'm going to thank him," James said. "I'll be back in a minute."

When he returned, Maureen and Lindsay were ready to go. Maureen looked tired. She told them she needed to get home and go to bed. Lindsay noticed that the grinding music, the rawness of the sexuality had affected James. He put his arm around her and pulled her close as they walked to the car. She felt so much electricity between them that when James suggested he come in for another drink, Lindsay assumed that his self-imposed abstention was probably over. She was relieved when Maureen quickly excused herself and went upstairs to bed.

But James had something else on his mind.

"J.R. told me something I think you should know," he said. "Please sit down."

She went over to the sofa.

"He said he saw a guy he recognized at the Juju House, someone high up in the security service who reports directly to Olumide."

Lindsay shrugged. "So?"

"His point was that the guy only shows up when Olumide sends him. He was probably there because of you."

"That's paranoid. How would he know I was going? We decided at the last minute."

James looked impatient. He stood up and sat next to her on the couch.

"Lindsay, we were there for hours. Someone could have seen you and notified them. Or more likely, we were followed."

Lindsay took James's hand. "James, I've been followed almost every-where I go, including when I met you at the motorboat club. So what? I'm not doing anything illegal. I can't stop them from keeping tabs on me."

"If Olumide is telling his top guy to watch you, then something more serious is happening. I think you should keep a low profile for a while. And if I were you, I'd hold off on Bayo as a political story for now."

She nodded thoughtfully. "I'll think about it."

He smiled at her and squeezed her hand.

"That sounds smart. Look, I just care about you, that's all. I don't want to see you hurt."

She felt a rush of gratitude.

"James," she confided. "After the party, I tried to investigate that body that washed up at the high commissioner's house. I spoke to a steward who gave me some information. When I went to see that person again, his wife said he was in the hospital. I'm afraid Olumide's men got to him. The wife won't let him talk to me now and I don't blame her. I have to protect my sources, but I can't stop talking to people. If I do that, then why am I here?"

"You might want to ask yourself what good you are doing if you do write about the protests. It will just force the government to crack down. In this case, they could close the Juju House."

Her head was spinning. All those drinks, she thought. "Let's not talk about it now," she said, pulling him toward her and kissing him on the lips. He responded, pressing his hand into her lower back and pulling her closer. Then he gripped her hair, tilting her face upward to meet his eyes, and smiled regretfully.

"I've got to leave," he said. "I take off for Ibadan very early tomorrow. I'll be back in a few days."

And he was gone.

Before going upstairs, Lindsay noticed the light blinking on her answering machine and pressed the button to hear her message. It was Joe Rainey in New York. "Hey kid, just wanted to let you know there's been some fallout from your story about that murdered kid. The Nigerian ambassador made a formal complaint. We're supporting you. But watch your back."

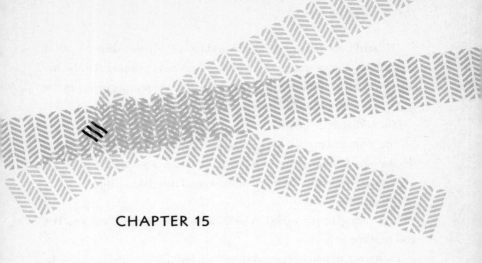

CHAPTER 15

After Joe Rainey's warning, Lindsay was on the alert for trouble as John drove her to lunch with Vickie at the Chinese restaurant on Ikoyi Island. She was actually relieved she would be with an American diplomat. She left early and was the first to arrive. John dropped her off in front and showed her where he would meet her when she was ready to leave.

It was unusual for Lindsay to wait for someone else and, after fifteen minutes, she saw how irritating it was. She looked around the nearly empty restaurant, at its gray Formica tables and soiled white walls. Finally, Vickie came charging in, a heavy bag slung over her shoulder, looking sweaty and frazzled.

"I'm so sorry," Vickie said, in a voice everyone could hear. "I expected traffic but nothing like this. It took an hour to get here from the embassy. I finally got out and ran."

"It's fine, really, Vickie. I know how you feel. Relax. I'll order you a drink."

Lindsay beckoned the waiter and ordered a gin and tonic for Vickie and a Diet Coke with lemon for herself.

"How did you know I drink gin and tonic?" Vickie asked.

"I didn't. Lucky guess on a hot day. But that's supposed to be my line. You're the political officer so you're the one with contacts in the CIA. You're supposed to know what I drink."

"Diet Coke with lemon."

The women laughed and relaxed a little. The waiter brought the drinks—both without ice—and Vickie raised her glass for a toast:

"Cheers," she said. "To new solutions and new friendships."

"I'll drink to that."

"I'm very glad you called," Vickie said. "I was about to call you but you beat me to it."

Each woman had her agenda and each felt that she had to play soft-ball for a few minutes before embarking upon it, so the first twenty minutes were spent commiserating about the petty irritations of life in Lagos. Finally, Lindsay asked if there was any new information about the Agapo murder.

"Nothing hard. I'll tell you, off the record, that is one of the reasons I'm here—to investigate those murders."

"Would you call them murders or assassinations?" Lindsay asked.

Vickie looked up quickly. She seemed to be weighing what to say.

"I'd call them, very much off the record, assassinations."

"Some local thug hired to do the dirty work for a higher-up we both know?"

"That I can't say. But I'm not sure it was a local thug. I'd say the evidence points away from that."

"What do you mean?"

"I mean it might well have been an SI operation."

Lindsay looked blank. "I'm sorry. I don't know what that is."

"Solutions, Incorporated. They're a private mercenary group that is hired to do everyone's dirty work because their operatives are hard to trace."

"I've heard rumors about something like that, but never from any-one I could trust."

"You can trust me."

"But why are you leaking this?"

"Because I want you to use it, obviously—but not for attribution. This group has operated in the shadows for too long. It's time to shine a little light on their actions. See if they react."

"Yeah. If we're really lucky they'll react by eliminating the source of the light. Should I be worried?"

"No. Not unless Olumide takes a contract out on you."

"How likely is that?"

"I wish I knew."

"I heard there were complaints about my piece on Babatunde Oladayo."

"Yeah. I'd go slow for a while. You might hold off on this Agapo story until you're out of the country."

"It seems like someone is telling me to hold almost every story I get. I'll have to think about it. In the meantime, I can't leave because I'm waiting to learn what Olumide plans to do next. I've heard he wants to arrest Fakai, provoke riots, and then call off the elections."

Vickie smiled. "Where did you hear that?"

"Oh, I have sources . . ."

"And I hear you also have sources in The Next Step. What do they say?"

Lindsay stiffened. Ah, she thought, the other shoe drops. "If they say anything worth knowing, you can be sure I'll include it in my articles."

Vickie beckoned the waiter to order another round of drinks. After a brief, uncomfortable silence, she changed the topic completely. Two drinks later—by now Lindsay had switched to gin and tonic too—they were talking like old friends.

"So, Lindsay," Vickie said, "what do you do when you aren't talking to sources and writing stories? Is there someone back home you're involved with?"

Lindsay smiled and took a sip of her drink.

"Not at home. Here, believe it or not."

"That's lucky. Who?"

"This guy I met at the ambassador's party, actually. He's an art dealer—name of James Duncan. He lives in London, but he's an American, and I've been seeing a lot of him. What about you?"

"I've been pretty seriously involved with a guy—Hal Bodkin," Vickie enunciated his name with care—"but I'm not sure where it's going. He didn't want me to take this assignment, but he didn't make me a better offer either."

"I know how that is," Lindsay said. "James is right here, but he never talks about what might happen when one of us leaves."

"Well, maybe you should just tell him how you feel."

"It sounds like I could say the same to you." Though she warmed to Vickie, Lindsay still didn't completely trust her. But it felt good to confide, however carefully, in someone with a fresh point of view.

"I don't know if I did the right thing coming here," Vickie said. "This posting could last a year. I hoped it would force him into making a commitment, but what if he just finds someone else?"

"I don't know what to tell you," Lindsay answered. "I don't even know what I think about these things anymore, since James. Before I met him I would have said that you have to live your life independently and if he's right for you he will understand."

"Well, what would you do if James was ready to leave right now, tomorrow, and you had to stay to follow this story?"

"I don't know. If he asked me, I might go with him. You know," she continued slowly, "I wanted to be a journalist since I was in high school and being a foreign correspondent was my dream. And I've done it. But lately I've been feeling that whatever it was that sustained me no longer does."

"Do you ever feel you want to be part of the solution instead of just observing and recording the problem?"

"Sometimes. James saw my doubts even before I did. He helped me recognize them."

"So, if he asked you, would you leave your job?"

Lindsay laughed. "Somehow, I don't think I'm going to have that problem."

"But if you did?"

"Maybe. Maybe I'd leave the job if it meant we'd stay together. I could get another assignment. I guess I could even get another job, if it came to that. I don't see how I could risk letting him go."

It was the first time Lindsay had articulated that thought, even to herself.

Vickie nodded her head thoughtfully. "You've got it bad."

"Tell me something I don't know."

The food arrived and they both served themselves in silence. Then Vickie looked up.

"How much longer do you think James will stay?" Vickie asked, finishing a spring roll.

"I don't know. He said he might be leaving soon. He's here for a wealthy client who collects Nigerian art and artifacts. He says it's a big deal for him."

"What kind of artifacts?"

"Oh, local paintings and sculpture. Have you been to Oshogbo? He has an Austrian friend there, this incredible character named Roxanne Reinstadler whom the locals call the white witch. She carves huge sandstone sculptures as well as small statues. He buys the statues by the crate to sell in the U.S. and in England."

"Really? Are they good?"

"Yes. They look crude at first, but there is a kind of rough beauty to them. You know Mike Vale, don't you?"

Vickie nodded. "I know who he is."

"I'm sure you'll meet him for a briefing pretty soon. He's with the *Observer* and he's a pretty aggressive reporter. He'll want to get to know you. Anyway, he has one he bought from a trader. You could ask him to show it to you. If you like it, maybe you could get one from James. It's got to be a lot cheaper here than in the U.S."

Vickie looked at her watch. "Maybe I will, but right now I have to run. I've got to meet with the ambassador in an hour."

Lindsay nodded and signaled the waiter for the check. When the bill came, they split it, promising to get together again soon.

CHAPTER 16

Lindsay walked to the spot where she expected John to meet her. She felt a little tipsy, and so was surprised, but not alarmed, when she reached her car and saw that John was not in it and that all four tires were flat. John was nowhere in sight. She surveyed the damage and crouched down to see what had happened. All the tires had wide nails driven deep into the seams. As she checked the back, she felt someone approach from behind, a shadow falling across the fender. Strong hands lifted her up and threw her into the backseat of a nearby car. The last thing she saw before the door closed was a pair of black boots.

They drove in silence out of Ikoyi, through the crowded streets, down back alleyways, into a neighborhood she had never seen before. There were two of them, one driving and one in the passenger seat. They didn't blindfold her, which was scary because they didn't seem to care if she could identify them. She struggled to think clearly—her fear had sobered her up pretty quickly.

The driver was a large, muscular man with a shaved head. She looked at his face in the rearview mirror. He had small eyes set wide apart. He was wearing a black nylon sleeveless T-shirt with a scooped neck. Rising from his smooth, black skin was a thick white keloid scar that ran around the back of his neck and ducked under his collar. When he raised his left arm on the steering wheel, she saw that the scar reemerged on his shoulder, extended down his arm and ended at his wrist. The scar mesmerized her; she could barely take her eyes off it. She hardly noticed the second man, who wore a dashiki and a heavy gold chain around his neck. She didn't know if these men were thugs looking for money or secret police intent on hurting her. When she finally asked them, they ignored her, laughing and talking to each other in Yoruba.

"I can pay you," she said. "Take me to the bank and I will get what you want."

"Ooh," the driver said to his friend. "You hear her, man. Big, rich American lady say she go give what we want." He laughed. "We go take what we want." His voice was hard. "You no worry bout give."

The men exchanged looks again and laughed. They drove in silence until they reached a deserted warehouse near a lot filled with squatters who had erected cardboard canopies against the sun. The man in the passenger seat jumped out, opened the garage door, and the driver pulled in. His friend followed him, slamming the door behind him. The driver turned off the engine, got out, opened the car's back door and climbed in next to Lindsay. She could smell his pungent sweat and edged toward the other door, but his friend got in on that side.

"I'm a reporter for an American newspaper," Lindsay said as assertively as she could. "I have permission to be here. I interviewed General Olumide. He has guaranteed my safety." She was staring straight ahead.

The driver lit a cigarette. The man on her right reached over and put his hand on her thigh, casually, resting it there as he spoke.

"She go know General Olumide. Dat be big man. Big man. He like dem foreign reporters. He like dem when dey tell da trut bout dis place, when dey don' go lookin' for rebel lies." He moved his hand to the inside of her thigh. She tried to close her legs, but he pulled them open.

"You go give da general what he like, lady?"

Lindsay didn't answer. Her mouth was dry.

"You go give da general what he want, lady?" the man repeated, pinching the skin under his hand.

"Yes," she said softly. "What he wants. Like you said."

The man released her inner thigh and put his hand on her knee.

"You give Babatunde what he want too, yes, lady?" the driver said suddenly. He leered. "You like Babatunde, no? He tell you sad story? Poah boy. But he no want you. He beg at end, but no for you. He beg for die." The man sneered.

"We no bad men. We give what he want." Both men laughed again. The driver put his hand on Lindsay's breast.

"Now we go give you what you want and you go give us what we want, yes?"

Lindsay didn't answer. Her mind was racing. She wondered if she could get the attention of the squatters or if they would help if she did. She scanned the garage looking for something that might serve as a weapon.

Suddenly, the driver took his hand off her breast and got out of the car. The second man got out on his side, leaving his door open as he sauntered away to open the garage door. The driver swaggered to the front. She saw him stretch his legs before he got back in with his friend. Lindsay edged closer to the open door of the car.

"Get out," the driver said, over his shoulder. "Dat what you want, yes?"

Lindsay jumped out of the car. She sensed running might trigger a chase response, so she walked quickly, willing herself not to look back. When she got to the corner she turned. The car wasn't following her.

She was not sure if the men had really gone, and she kept looking around nervously, half expecting them to pop out at every street corner. Finally, she found an outdoor market with stalls of wilted lettuce and rotten tomatoes. A truck driver had just delivered cases of beer, and she approached him as he climbed back into his cab.

"Can you give me a ride to Ikoyi?" she asked.

She read on his face what he saw: a dirty, sweating white woman in an unlikely place, sure to bring him trouble. She wasn't surprised when he said no.

"Please," she said. "Don't take me to Ikoyi if it's too far. Just drop me where I can get a cab. I need to get out of here."

"That not my lookout."

"I know. But I have money." She rummaged inside her purse and pulled out two hundred naira, waving them at him.

That stopped him. He reached over and opened the truck door.

"Get in," he said. "Where you go in Ikoyi?"

She gave him the address and climbed in. He didn't speak to her and she didn't try to make conversation. She was badly shaken; her body was trembling as though she had caught a chill, but she was angry too, angrier than she had ever been. That bastard Olumide, she thought, he wants the "truth" about this place. That's exactly what he's going to get. She knew he expected her to be scared and leave. Well, she was scared, but she wasn't going to run away.

She considered informing the embassy, but decided the ambassador would use it to persuade her to leave. James would only point out that he had been afraid this would happen and pressure her to back off. Maureen? Maybe she would tell her, but no, on second thought, she didn't want to worry her. For the moment, she would confide in no one. But she would have to be more careful. She would hold any potentially dangerous story until she was out of the country.

When she got home she went straight to her room. The tremor was worse. She curled up on her side and hugged her pillow. After a while, she felt the trembling subside, and finally, in early evening, she fell asleep.

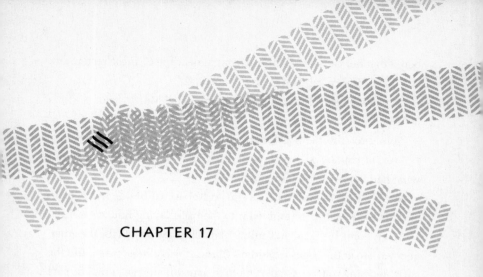

CHAPTER 17

Lindsay tossed and turned, lost in the shadows of restless dream images. A voice was talking to her but she couldn't make out the words. She struggled within the dream to hear better and the voice became clearer. "Madam," she heard. "Please, madam." Someone was speaking to her. She opened her eyes reluctantly and saw Martin standing in her doorway.

"Please, madam," he said again with quiet urgency. "It Eduke; he very sick. You have medicine?"

She got up quickly, wrapped a robe around herself, and hurried next door to see the child. She found him, whimpering and gagging as he retched convulsively, his small body doubled over. His eyes were glazed, his lips chapped, and his skin ashen. Lindsay immediately thought of cholera, knowing that the open sewers and dirty water in Lagos spread the disease that killed thousands of children each year. They had to get to the hospital as fast as they could.

"You have medicine?" Martin asked again.

"My medicine isn't good enough. We must get help." She remembered that her car was still incapacitated near the Chinese restaurant. "We have to get a cab and go to the hospital."

"It will be faster if we take your car, madam," Martin said.

"I know. I don't have it."

"John brought it late last night," Martin said. "You can drive us?"

"Yes, of course," she said, with relief. She would have to find out what had happened to John later.

She climbed in and Martin's cousin Robert sat beside her. Martin and his wife Pauline scrambled into the back, laying Eduke carefully between them, his head on Pauline's lap. Lindsay headed for the emergency room at the Lagos Children's Clinic. It was almost 7 A.M. and the early morning traffic ensnared them in a maddening go-slow. The cars inched along. Occasionally Lindsay heard Martin sigh, a desperate sound of resignation. Eduke whimpered intermittently, but his gagging seemed to subside and he fell, finally, into a deep sleep that was even more frightening.

An hour passed. The traffic moved slowly forward. Lindsay kept straining to hear Eduke's shallow breath, faint but still regular. In the next lane, Lindsay caught sight of a ministerial limousine, a few cars ahead of her. She leaned forward to see the number above the plate. It looked like a four.

Finally, the Peugeot arrived at the clinic, a pathetic three-story structure with peeling white plaster and a tin roof. The limousine pulled in behind them, and a heavyset man in a well-tailored business suit stepped out and headed for the door. Martin carried Eduke, and Lindsay and the others followed them inside. A small waiting area opened onto a large room full of rickety hospital beds. Every bed was occupied. A dozen or so mothers sat with their children on hard-backed chairs against the wall. Some of the mothers slept, their mouths open. Others sat patiently with their sick children, who were wailing or curled listlessly in their laps.

There was a small commotion around the government official. He must indeed be an important minister, Lindsay thought, judging by the sycophantic fanfare that greeted him. Though others had obviously been waiting unattended for a long time, several hospital employees hurried to see what he needed. Lindsay thought he looked familiar, and as she approached the desk to register Eduke, she suddenly recalled where she had seen him: in the parking lot at the hotel in Ibadan. He was Billy Anikulo, the health minister. It crossed her mind to approach him and ask for help—the intervention of a government minister could do wonders for Eduke's chances—but she hesitated. This man worked for Olumide and might well have participated in the decision to kidnap her. Instead she turned away, hoping she wouldn't be noticed. As she turned, she noticed the man who accompanied the official. She was so stunned, she stepped closer and stared. Mike Vale was at the minister's elbow. She quickly stepped behind a pillar and watched as both men were hustled into a back room by a hospital administrator.

Pauline and Martin still sat waiting. Finally, Lindsay understood what was needed. Slipping a fifty-naira bill into a stack of papers on the desk, she told the receptionist that Eduke was dying. The woman didn't look at Lindsay or change her expression but, picking up the bill, walked behind a screen, signaling them to follow her. The woman told Martin to lay Eduke down on a cot and leave. He went out hesitantly. Lindsay didn't move. The woman ignored her and called over a colleague in a white uniform who examined the boy, pressing his stomach brusquely.

"Excuse me," Lindsay said. "Are you a doctor?"

"The boy has gastroenteritis," the woman answered, ignoring the question.

Lindsay was relieved. It didn't sound too serious.

The woman tied a rubber tube around Eduke's arm and looked for a vein to insert an intravenous drip. When she didn't find one, she slapped his arm, to make a vein stand out, but still didn't locate one. She called a nurse who shaved the hair near his temples, looking for a place to insert the needle. Eduke opened his eyes. He looked scared. Lindsay wished Pauline or Martin were there, but didn't want to leave to get them. She held his hand, but he hardly seemed to know her. Meanwhile, the woman was still unable to insert the needle. Eduke's face was contorted.

"We need some morphine," the woman said, "for the pain and to slow down the intestines."

"We don't have it, Doctor," the nurse answered. "We are waiting for a delivery."

"Get some paregoric. Quick."

The nurse disappeared and returned with a syringe. She gave Eduke a shot of something in the stomach. Lindsay started to go out to get Pauline. She heard a small gasp and ducked back inside.

Eduke was lying on the table, totally still. The nurse and doctor had turned away.

"The child is dead," the nurse said coldly. Lindsay called after the doctor, who was already leaving.

"What happened?" she shouted.

"Gastroenteritis," the doctor said.

"But you don't die of gastroenteritis, do you? Not so fast."

"But he had no blood," the nurse said.

"No blood? What do you mean 'no blood'?"

"He was anemic," the doctor said, walking off in Martin's direction. Pauline, seeing the doctor, followed nervously, still not realizing what had happened.

As soon as Martin saw the doctor he jumped up and waited meekly for her to speak.

"How long was he sick?" she barked.

"Since yesterday," Martin answered.

"There, you see. You should have brought him earlier," the doctor said. "It's your fault. You can come tomorrow to take him away."

Martin was confused. "What? Where is he?"

"He's dead." The doctor turned and walked away.

Pauline fell into Martin's arms. Martin pounded the wall just once, hard, with both his fists. Then he walked behind the screen to see his son, followed by his wife. Lindsay could hear Pauline's loud keening and Martin's soft sobbing. Then Martin collected himself, led Pauline from behind the screen, and headed straight for the door. But before he got there, he collapsed onto the floor. Lindsay rushed to help him up. He could barely walk. His cousin supported him, and Lindsay ran back inside and found the doctor.

"Excuse me," she said, "I heard you say you had no morphine." The doctor stopped in her tracks. "Would that have saved him?" Lindsay persisted.

The doctor looked tired and wary. "Maybe."

"But how could you not have morphine? How is that possible?"

"We ordered it. We paid for it. It didn't arrive. That's all I know." The doctor turned and walked away.

Lindsay stood for a moment, trying to understand. An orderly who was wiping the beds with disinfectant watched her.

"Dey go for steal it, madam," he said softly.

"Who? Who steals it?"

But the orderly just shrugged.

All morning, Lindsay couldn't think of anything but Eduke. His three-year-old smile, the shy way he thanked her when she gave him a piece of chocolate, the big wondering brown eyes as he followed his brothers and sisters around the courtyard, his curious questions when she read him books. She remembered taking his family's picture with a Polaroid shortly after she arrived and how he had stared, fascinated, as the image magically took shape. And now he was dead. Why was this country so goddamn cruel?

Every day was hotter than the one before. The humidity was so high it was hard to breathe. But there were worse things than the weather to deal with. She drove Martin and an elder from his home village back to the hospital to retrieve—and bury—Eduke's body. Pauline stayed at home preparing the mourning ceremony.

When they arrived at the hospital, they were directed to the morgue out back. Built of cinder blocks, it was nothing more than a big cold room with a metal table on one wall and a dirty white tiled floor centering on a drain. Lying face-up on the tile, unprotected and uncovered, was Eduke, still wearing his gray cotton pants and blue T-shirt.

Lindsay sucked in her breath. She looked at Martin, who seemed about to faint. As Lindsay reached out to steady him, an orderly entered, blocking the exit. Martin said he had come to collect his child's body for burial. The orderly shrugged and said he didn't know about that. Lindsay stared at him in disbelief. Then she knew. She could hardly believe it, despite everything she had seen in this country, but when she reached into her bag and pulled out a twenty-naira bill, the orderly grabbed it and disappeared. A moment later, he returned carrying a small wooden box that looked like an orange crate. He picked Eduke up and tried to force his body into the too-small crate. Martin turned abruptly and left the room. Outside, he pounded his fists helplessly against the wall, not once, this time, but over and over till his hands were bleeding. Then he walked back into the morgue and collected his son.

At the nearby graveyard, they were denied entry until they handed over another twenty naira. When the grave digger ignored them, Lindsay simply pulled out another twenty, after which he strolled over to dig the shallow grave.

There was no time for the Catholic family to get a priest. Martin and the village elder lowered the small crate into the ground. Martin said something in Igbo that Lindsay didn't understand. He looked at Lindsay, gesturing that it was her turn to speak.

"Sleep well, sweet baby," she mumbled, fighting tears. And so it was over.

They were silent on the way home. When they arrived, Lindsay went inside, turned on the fan, and lay on her bed, watching it turn slowly. She was waiting for James. When he arrived about fifteen minutes later, she poured gin and tonics and told him the story.

"I'm going to write about this," she said. "I want people to know how corrosive corruption can be, how much harder it makes every aspect of life, how much worse the pain is when the system consistently turns against you."

James put his arm around her. "That's always your reaction, write the story, as if telling the story has some healing power. But the medicine only heals you, Lindsay. You feel better once you write it. You even have the illusion that you've done something good. But that's bullshit. It's self-indulgent. What difference will telling this story make to Martin or Pauline or Eduke? Readers will sigh and turn the page."

It was as if he'd hit her. She tried to shield herself and strike back at the same time.

"No, you're wrong, James. I have to believe that people are capable of reacting, of helping, of trying to create change."

She thought of telling him about her terrifying run-in with Olumide's thugs, to show him how strongly she believed in the power of telling the truth. But she decided against it. It wouldn't help and it might complicate things. She sighed and said softly, "You're so cynical. That's the easy way. Your attitude is 'life is terrible, nothing changes.' That's just one more excuse for doing nothing. If people don't know what's going on, they can't protest. Change is prevented by ignorance, not inertia. People do what they can. I try to end the ignorance. It's just a small, not very important kind of help, I know that, but I can do it, and I do it well, and that's better than doing nothing."

"I'm sorry, Lindsay. But I'm afraid I don't believe in changing the world. I don't think it can be done. I want to take care of myself and the people I love. That's hard enough. And I try to be of some help to whoever crosses my path. We should go to the ceremony for Eduke. We should reimburse Martin for any expenses he had. We should help him educate his other children. I don't believe in anything grander than that."

They could hear Martin and Pauline's many friends and relatives arriving at the compound, crowding Martin's quarters and spilling into the garden. The scent of the simmering cassavas and spices was already starting to permeate the air.

"I'm afraid we are going to have to agree to disagree on this for now," Lindsay said, peeking out the window.

Preparations for the gathering in honor of Eduke were well under way. One of Martin's cousins brought a goat to be sacrificed. Others carried crates of beer. Lindsay knew that the party would be given to appease Eduke's ghost so he wouldn't come back to strike down his family. Pauline, Martin, and many guests had rubbed white powder on their faces and marked the doors of their quarters with white paint. It saddened Lindsay to think that little Eduke, having joined the dead, was transformed from a beloved child into a fearsome spirit.

She told James she was exhausted and needed to sleep. She did not add that she wanted to be rested enough to write Eduke's story before going to his mourning ceremony the following night.

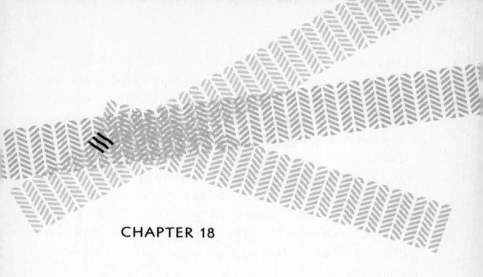

CHAPTER 18

By the next morning, Lindsay recognized that her first
impulse to file a scorching story about Eduke's death was rash. She
would write it now while the details were still sharp and her outrage
white hot, but she wouldn't send it until she was safely out of the
country. She sat at her computer and made a couple of false starts. By
the time she finished it was 12:30, the time the foreign press gathered
at the Ikoyi Club for a weekly session of drinks and gossip. Maureen
had left a few days earlier to do a story about oil production and Lindsay hoped she might come back in time to join her there.

Unsubstantiated gossip in Lagos often turned out to be useful. Brian
Randolph, the London *Times* man, was due back in town after a week's
leave in London. He may have picked up some information from British government sources at home.

Lindsay pulled the Peugeot into the circular driveway of the genteel,
pink stucco Ikoyi Club, a run-down vestige of colonial Africa, comforting somehow in its shabby familiarity. The paint was peeling, the
chintz awning slightly frayed, but out back you could see the swimming pool, the squash and tennis courts, and the field for polo. Such

an African sport, she had thought snidely when she first saw it. Members of the club were expatriates or wealthy Nigerians who somehow had managed to remain anglophiles—so brainwashed that even now, more than three decades after independence, they thought anything British was the height of sophistication.

Lindsay walked past the bulletin board that listed upcoming events—a bingo game, a billiards championship, a table tennis tournament—into the bar. There, at the usual table, she saw Ken Abbot, the *Telegraph* man, the *Guardian*'s Ed Courvet, Brian Randolph, and Mike Vale. Evan Peterson of Reuters, a regular, was nowhere to be seen. Neither was Maureen. A bottle of scotch and several bottles of beer sat on the table

Ken Abbot called, "Hey, Lindsay, I was just wondering when you'd turn up. And here you are. Have you heard what happened to Evan?"

She frowned. "No. What?"

"Kicked out. Probably on his way to the border right now. Picked up in a Black Maria and driven up-country. Orders were to drop him over the border."

Lindsay pulled up a chair and sat down. She was shaken. If they threw Evan out, did that mean she was vulnerable too?

"I don't get it. What'd he do?"

"The stupid bastard wrote there were reports of 'tribal violence' up north. That's a no-no ever since the Biafran war. You never report 'tribal violence' here."

"Especially if it's not true," added Mike Vale.

"Are you sure it's not true?" Lindsay asked. "He's usually pretty careful."

"He believed what he heard," Mike said. "But it was wrong to go with it." He drained his scotch. "Look, there are plenty of other things to worry about. The rumor is there will be a coup. Olumide will make it look like Fakai supporters are rioting and use that as an excuse to arrest him."

"Sounds like there might be a fair chance of tribal and religious violence after all," Lindsay said.

"It all makes sense," Ken agreed. "But it didn't happen—not yet, anyway—and Evan Peterson is in a hot sweaty van on his way to the border. No one ever said it was easy being a hack."

Of course, Lindsay thought, she wasn't the only one on to the Olumide rumor. The hyenas all got there at the same time after all.

Mike Vale, already a little drunk, weighed in again.

"Who the fuck cares? The lucky bastard's out of this shit hole. If he's really out. Remember Colin Packman, who was thrown out a few years ago? The same deal. They drove him to the border, him and his wife and eight-year-old kid. But while they were on the road, there was a coup, so while one group had the order to throw him out, the group at the border was ordered to close it off. Big impasse. Packman and his family are left to sweat in the goddamn car while the Nigerians slug it out. They sleep on it overnight. Next morning, same problem. Finally, the Nigerians drive them way up-country to the river, put them in a canoe and push them toward Benin. No papers, no visas, no local money. Of course, the Packmans know when they get there they'll be arrested for illegal entry, but they don't care. They're so happy to be the hell out of Nigeria. The wife and kid are laughing and waving as the boat drifts away. The wife told me later it took them days to straighten it all out, but it was the highlight of their two years here. Getting out."

Lindsay was only half listening. She'd heard different versions of this story before.

"Any news about Olumide?" she asked. "Is everything quiet?"

"Not sure," Brian Randolph said. "There are rumors that Olumide has started to move against some group called The Next Step, which is a new one to me. Have you heard of it?"

"Yes," Lindsay said. "They support Fakai. I don't know too much about them but I think they're mostly young and poor."

"That's a lethal combination," Ken said. "They say Olumide's men have arrested rural leaders in some of the villages. But it's not confirmed. I'm about to check it out."

"In the villages?" Lindsay asked. "I was under the impression The Next Step was mostly disgruntled city kids."

"It sounds like they may be more widespread."

"It's beginning to sound like the big guy's getting ready to make his move," Lindsay said.

"I'm not so sure," said Brian. "I flew in from London this morning and ran into a delegation of ministers at the airport. I heard they were headed to a meeting in Paris. Even the defense minister and the health minister were on the plane. I don't think all those officials would leave the country if there was about to be a serious move against Fakai."

"The health minister?" Lindsay asked. "I saw him at the hospital yesterday."

"Well, he's on his way to Paris now," said Brian.

"Did he mention anything about leaving?" Lindsay looked at Mike.

"Why would he talk to me?"

"I don't know. I saw you with him at the hospital yesterday."

Mike looked put out. "I didn't see you. Why were you there?"

"That's not the point. What was the health minister doing with you? What story are you on to? Is he ill? Did he go to Paris for treatment? Is he going to be replaced?"

Mike laughed and refilled his glass. "It could be any of the above, Sherlock, and if you had agreed to work with me, as I so gallantly suggested, you'd know, wouldn't you? As it is, I think I'll keep my reporting to myself for the time being."

"Have you filed anything?"

"No. Don't worry, you won't be asked to match it." He paused, clearly enjoying his advantage. "Not yet anyway."

"Well, well," Lindsay murmured. "Never a dull moment, I guess."

"Shit, Lindsay, you know that isn't true," said Mike. "Almost every moment is dull. That's what makes moments like this so much fun."

After lunch, Lindsay headed for the embassy to check in with the ambassador or Dave Goren. She found Goren at his desk, but didn't learn anything. The ambassador, she was told, was busy in meetings all day. On her way out she ran into Vickie, who also didn't offer anything new. Lindsay told her about Eduke's death and Vickie expressed her sympathy. She returned home and was weighing whether she should drive to the Juju House to ask Bayo about the Next Step arrests when Maureen walked in. Maureen was exhausted, but had uncovered a good story—local demonstrations against the international oil companies. Soldiers had broken it up by firing into the crowd, and a dozen people were dead or injured. Lindsay was sure to get a call asking for a follow-up, but there was no way she could leave Lagos at this time.

"There's a lot happening here too," Lindsay said. "Let's fill each other in."

"Fine. But give me half an hour," Maureen said. "I need to take a short nap."

"Go ahead, Maurie. I'll be up in a bit. I'll bring you some tea."

She was in the kitchen boiling water when she heard an urgent knocking at the door. When she opened it, she found J.R. dressed in his usual dashiki. He was out of breath, speaking in such a mix of pidgin and English that she could hardly understand him. But she got his main message: Something had happened at Bayo's compound. The military had come. There was a riot. People were beaten, were still being beaten. The police had thrown one of Bayo's wives from a second-story window. She must write the story. The world must know.

"Hurry, man," he said. "Dey go for kill Bayo dis time."

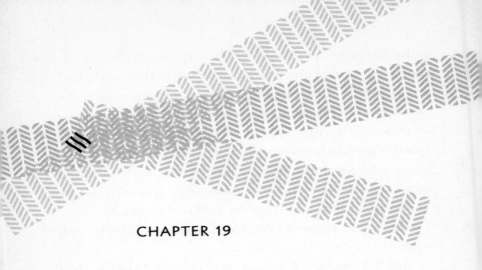

CHAPTER 19

Lindsay saw a crowd and heard the shouting as her Peugeot approached Bayo's street. She parked the car around the corner and walked toward the house. Dozens of men gathered around the front gate shouting insults at the police and heavily armed soldiers who blocked the street. There seemed to be a temporary standoff. The police fidgeted, shifting their batons from hand to hand, but the demonstrators didn't seem intimidated; a group with little to lose: young, poor, and angry. One young man picked up a handful of stones and, quoting a popular Bayo song, screamed, "Da pig is dead," hurling a stone straight at an officer who had turned to talk to someone. The soldier winced, then raised his gun. The crowd started rhythmically chanting, "Da pig is dead, oink oink; da pig is dead," inching menacingly forward. Suddenly, a phalanx of soldiers responded with force, moving on the crowd, swinging clubs. Lindsay, dodging quickly out of the way, could hear a terrible, hollow sound as a baton smashed into a human skull.

As Lindsay slowly worked her way forward, she glimpsed broken furniture that had apparently been thrown from the windows or set up as barricades. Dark stains on the ground looked like blood.

J.R., who had led the way in his own car, gestured for her to move away from the house. They went down the block and stepped into an alley. She asked him what had happened.

Apparently, Bayo himself had been arrested after being badly beaten. He probably didn't feel much, though, J.R. said, because he swallowed all the Nigerian Natural Grass they didn't have time to dispose of before the soldiers burst in. J.R. said the soldiers knew, but had no proof, and the arresting officer proclaimed triumphantly that they would hold him in prison until nature forced him to expel his stash. They would analyze it to prove he had been in possession of an illegal substance.

"You big man, but you go shit sometime, brother," the officer had said.

Bayo announced he was starting a fast as they dragged him away.

This was almost too good to check, Lindsay thought.

"What happened to everyone else in the house?" she asked J.R.

"They go for hide."

J.R. confirmed that two of the women were in the hospital and three others had been badly injured. J.R. had escaped by running to alert Lindsay. The government acted, he said, because of Bayo's diatribe against Olumide. As James had told her, spies had infiltrated the performance at the Juju House.

"I heard members of The Next Step were arrested in some of the villages," Lindsay said. "Do you know anything about that?"

"No," J.R. said, looking worried.

"Are there any organized Next Step groups in the villages?"

"We be everywhere," he answered cryptically.

The crowd was quieter now, watching as the soldiers tossed the ringleaders, beaten and handcuffed, into a van. About two dozen people drifted off grumbling. Lindsay moved through those remaining, stopping to interview some of the protesters. She spotted Dave Goren behind a group of men in T-shirts. He seemed to be taking notes. She waved, but Goren disappeared into the mob. She looked around for Vickie, but didn't see her. A number of men confirmed J.R.'s story about Bayo and the NNG.

Suddenly, from across the street, one of the boys who were leaving threw a large stone at a policeman guarding the front door. It hit him at the base of his skull below his helmet. He fell to the ground and lay there, motionless. The other policemen went wild, swinging their clubs viciously, knocking people down, kicking them in the head and gut. Lindsay tried to back away but she was pushed down. Her head struck a lamppost and when she touched her lip, she saw blood. After a bit she got up and worked her way past the crowd, dabbing her lip with a tissue. She tried to observe unnoticed but was aware that her auburn hair and white skin made her easy to spot. Almost immediately, three soldiers approached her.

"What you want here?" one asked.

"I'm a journalist," Lindsay replied. "I work for a New York newspaper."

"Write about your own country. We don't want you here."

He demanded her name and address. Reluctantly, she gave them. After writing them down laboriously, he ordered her to leave. She was walking to her car when J.R. appeared and motioned her to follow. They climbed into their cars and he led her several blocks away to a small cement-block house.

"This is my home," he said.

"Are you sure you want me to come in?" Lindsay asked. "I may have been followed."

J.R. smiled, showing his pink upper gums. He put his arm around her. "Welcome to de club, sistah," he said, opening the door.

A black and white mongrel barked ferociously until J.R. bent to pet him. Mollified, the dog wagged his tail and licked Lindsay's hand. A young woman in Western dress and two children stood as they entered and came forward to shake her hand. "This is my wife, Margaret," J.R. said, "and my boys." The boys solemnly shook Lindsay's hand and then ran off, followed by the dog.

"They just returned from a visit to their grandparents. They're happy to be back with their friends," said J.R.

"Where do the grandparents live?"

"A small village near Badagry, close to the Benin border."

Margaret returned with several bottles of orange Fanta, then withdrew. J.R. sipped his drink and filled in a few more details about the bust. The commune had been warned to expect trouble, but Bayo hadn't taken it seriously. He was surprised when the police broke into his home—smashing the windows and breaking down the door. J.R. said The Next Step had supporters in the countryside and small villages, but he couldn't estimate how many. Lindsay wrote everything down and got up to leave, but he stopped her.

"There's one more thing you should know," he said. "We've been hearing about something strange—some foreign business group. They make trouble, they even make wars, all for money. We hear they are here, in Lagos. Maybe hired by Olumide. Maybe not."

"Do you have any names, anything I could check out?"

"No. They're very secretive. I'm not even sure they're real. But I hear things."

"Thank you, J.R. I'll see what I can do to find out more."

She drove off, remembering what Vickie had told her about Solutions, Inc. She would definitely try to follow up on it. The traffic was bad, so she decided to file through Reuters, a backup she sometimes utilized, since that office was more centrally located. The manager had recently fixed communication problems, probably by tendering the same bribes she had. She arrived breathless and sat at a desk, wondering if she should call Dodan Barracks for a statement from the government. It would alert them to her story, but she wouldn't be the only correspondent making such a call. Reluctantly, she picked up the receiver. When she reached the Barracks, the secretary refused to put her through. Yes, she thought, gathering official information was as hard as ever.

She had written most of the story when suddenly she remembered Maureen—probably still asleep at the house. She wanted to call her, but before she got to the phone, it rang. It was James saying he'd gotten no answer at her home and guessed she'd be at Reuters. He had something to tell her, but it was too important for the phone. He'd be right there. She hung up and dialed her house. No answer. She tried the AP but didn't find Maureen there either, so she returned to her story. She finished and was about to call the AP again when James walked in.

"James," she began, "something terrible has happened." But he already knew and he had some news that trumped hers: Bayo was dead. The information was not public, he said, but he had been told by a reliable source, a friend of his in the Ministry of Antiquities. The government story was that Bayo died of a heart attack while being taken to prison.

"Jesus," Lindsay said, "they killed him. This could start a civil war."

"I don't think so, Lindsay. They've called the military out in force. There are armed soldiers everywhere."

Lindsay turned on the radio, searching for a local station. There was a lot of static and then an Anglicized voice announced Bayo's death from a heart attack.

Lindsay quickly filed a new lead. Then she tried AP again. No one picked up, so she raced out the door to check out the streets. To her surprise, James followed her.

The streets were eerily empty. The drivers of the few cars on the road looked about nervously.

"It's amazing," Lindsay said. "Word is already out."

As they drove through the deserted streets of Surulere heading for the Juju House, everything was silent; there was not even the twitter of birds settling down for the evening or the high-pitched screech of the bats in the breadfruit trees. But as they got closer, Lindsay heard a distant sound, like water running over rocks. In the distance, she could see flames and smoke. When they turned a corner she saw a mob of angry men chanting "Ba-yo, Ba-yo," throwing bottles, breaking windows, and heaving crates into the air. Six young men had surrounded a Renault and were rocking it back and forth. Inside, the middle-aged driver looked terrified. There were two overturned cars in the street and Lindsay saw a European running away, his coattails flapping.

She and James turned down a side street, circled around, and took another road, this time heading for J.R.'s house. J.R. was out, but his wife wailed that Bayo had been beaten to death by the police. She was frantic, literally wringing her hands. They were rounding up everyone close to him, she said. J.R. was hiding, but she pointedly did not say where. She insisted the military police had burned the Juju House and Bayo's compound to the ground.

James and Lindsay managed to make their way back to Lindsay's house without further trouble. Her phone was working—an oversight on the part of state security, she was sure. James waited as she wrote yet another new lead.

"Riots broke out in this West African city today when the country's foremost musician and political dissident was reported dead after his arrest by government troops." She quickly filled in some details. Then she phoned the *Globe*'s recording room and dictated her story. When she finished, one of the *Globe*'s operators said, "Okay. I've got that. Where can I reach you for questions?" She gave her number and hung up.

She and James walked into the living room, where they heard the high-pitched wail of a goat being slaughtered in Lindsay's garden. It was a terrible, chilling sound, like a child's scream. Looking out the window they saw that the guests for Eduke's memorial service were already starting to arrive.

Lindsay shuddered and James put his arm around her. "It's okay. I know this is hard for you."

Lindsay stiffened. "I'm fine."

James pulled her closer. "I mean it's okay to be upset. You don't have to pretend with me."

"I'm not pretending."

He sighed. "I just want you to feel you can trust me. I won't take advantage of your vulnerability."

"I do trust you, almost in spite of myself."

"I'm glad," he said. "You have this amazing ability to dive in head-first, without checking to see how deep the water is. I've never done that. But you're teaching me how. And that wasn't part of my plan."

She wanted to ask him why not. Instead, she led him into the garden.

It had been transformed—it looked like a taverna, in the center of which was an open space for dancing. Around it were ten bridge tables, each with six chairs. Half a dozen bottles of beer sat on each table. Martin and Pauline's table had a bottle of scotch.

Maureen was sitting with them. Lindsay wondered guiltily if Maureen had awakened on her own and learned about Bayo in time to file. Sitting down, she leaned over and asked.

"Yeah," Maureen replied curtly. "No thanks to you. I woke up and turned on the radio. I managed to get off a piece saying the authorities announced he'd had a heart attack on the way to prison. Then I went to the office and luckily, one of our locals told me that everyone was saying he was killed by the police. I didn't have time to go out and do any reporting, but I put something together. I didn't know about Eduke until I came home."

"I'm sorry you had such a hard time. J.R. came to tell me that Bayo was under attack and I forgot everything and just followed him. I tried to call but no one answered. I'll fill you in on everything else later."

She turned her attention to the other guests. Many were drunk.

Several were dancing, either with partners or by themselves, to a high-life tape, accompanied by one of Martin's cousins on an African drum. Their movements had an evangelical frenzy. The dancers perspired in the humid air. Some had plastered coins to their foreheads. As they danced, some of the coins fell to the ground, but most of them remained stuck to their moist skin. James explained that the coins were meant to discourage the gods from claiming any more family members—to buy the living back from the land of the dead.

Pauline and Martin were dancing fiercely, as though they were weeping with their bodies, which jerked and throbbed in rhythm with the music. Lindsay watched them wordlessly. James moved closer to her. She laid her head on his shoulder for a moment. One of the village elders approached them.

"You must stay far away from this pain," he said to Lindsay, taking her hands in his. "There is nothing you can do."

"Yes. Of course, thank you. I'll be all right. I'm sorry," she mumbled. She was ashamed to have called attention to herself.

One of Martin's cousins urged Lindsay and James to join the dancing. Slightly uncomfortable, they walked toward the other guests. As she moved, at first self-consciously and then with more abandon, Lindsay began to grasp the dance's cathartic power. She closed her eyes and let the beat move through her. Other dancers approached them with coins, plastering them on their foreheads. This frenzy is the point, Lindsay thought, it helps to expiate the grief. But in the end, for her, it was still just dancing.

After about an hour, Pauline and her family brought out steaming platters of Jollof rice with tomato paste and goat meat, and *dodo*, the fried plantains Eduke used to love so much. Pauline's sister passed a bowl of *Bendel gari* and *isu*. Lindsay, James, and Maureen didn't really like the fermented cassava fried in palm oil or the spiced boiled yams, but they ate them out of respect, drank more beer, and then, exhausted, said their farewells.

Back in the house, Maureen went straight to bed. James kissed Lindsay and hugged her for a long time, but didn't suggest going upstairs. After he left, Lindsay made her way to her bedroom. But she couldn't fall asleep. She could hear the music and the drums and the dancing late into the night.

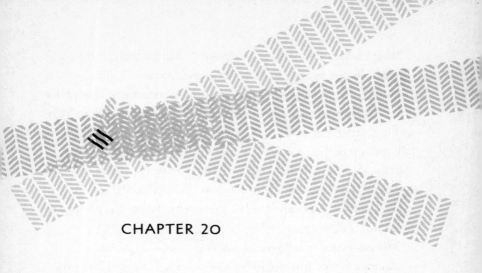

CHAPTER 20

"One of the sad truths about journalists is that everyone else's bad news is good news for us," Lindsay pronounced solemnly. She and Maureen were sitting at the kitchen table drinking coffee. It was two weeks after Eduke's death and Bayo's murder. The riots had been met with force, the opposition routed, the rebel leaders arrested. The spate of headlines had slowed. The events the ambassador predicted—Olumide's plans to arrest Fakai—hadn't occurred. But despite the crackdown, the interview with Fakai, promised by The Next Step, had been scheduled for later that afternoon.

Lindsay opened the *Daily Chronicle*. The front page was unexciting, and she shoved it across the table toward Maureen. It was the first time they were alone together with time to talk, but the mood was tense. Maureen picked up the paper without a word and started to read.

"I mean, when Bayo was killed, I thought the country would plunge into revolution, but now things seem to have settled down."

Maureen looked up. "I guess that's a good thing." She shrugged, returning to her reading.

"That's what I mean," Lindsay replied. "Good for them, bad for us."

Maureen sighed and put down the paper. "Explain."

"Well, for example, you really lucked out. You came to Lagos for a group interview of a famous dissident and wound up covering a high-profile murder and street riots before the interview even took place. Talk about reporter's karma! You couldn't ask for more."

Maureen was silent for a few seconds, stirring her coffee. "I might have asked for a more thoughtful friend," she said softly.

Maureen was angry and Lindsay knew why, though she'd hoped to dodge this confrontation.

"Maurie, I tried to call you. Everything moved so quickly."

Maureen leaned forward in her chair. "Look, Lindsay, I know how you work. When a story breaks, you're all over it, you're competitive as hell and you don't consider anyone else. That's okay—you didn't have to tell me your exclusives. But you could have at least woken me up."

Lindsay couldn't look her best friend in the eye. She felt deeply ashamed. Maureen would never have done this to her. Looking at her friend's hurt and angry face, Lindsay suddenly remembered being fifteen and calling Maureen in the middle of the night when Lindsay's parents told her they were splitting. Maureen had stayed on the phone with her for hours. And afterward, when her mother was bitter and alone, Lindsay's only escape was the many happy weekends and holidays she spent with Maureen's loud, large Irish family.

"You're right, of course. I should have woken you the moment I heard, but I was so overwhelmed by what had happened, I just forgot. Please forgive me." She paused and then added, "But in the end, you were able to file a story, right?"

Maureen didn't answer.

"Are you still mad at me?"

"Not mad. I just wish you'd surprise me sometime."

Something occurred to Lindsay and she jumped up and went into her study. When she returned, she was carrying a bulging file. "I can help you prepare for the Fakai interview today," she said, handing over the file. "We don't have to leave for another hour."

"I've done my preparation, thanks," Maureen said. "But I'll look through these. Why don't you go and get ready?"

Lindsay nodded. It was 12:45, hot and muggy. Soon it would rain, Lindsay knew, hard and long. She could feel it the way her mother always said she knew when one of her migraines was coming, a certainty mixed with dread. Lindsay was adjusting the shower temperature when Maureen knocked on the bathroom door. "I'm off, Linds," she shouted. "I'll meet you at the interview."

"Wait," Lindsay shouted back. She turned off the water, grabbed her terrycloth bathrobe, and walked back into the bedroom. "Where are you going?"

"To the office first."

"Be careful. Go straight there. Don't stop anywhere else."

"What? Why not?"

"I don't know. I'm just nervous about this interview. Olumide is going to be furious that the press corps is listening to Fakai. As long as we're all there and pretty much hear the same thing, we'll probably be all right. But don't try to get anything exclusive. And don't write the piece until you leave."

"What's come over you? Do you have some exclusive you don't want me to get?"

Lindsay looked down. "I guess I deserve that. But there's something I never told you. Two of Olumide's thugs picked me up. John was supposed to meet me with the car but either he wandered off or they scared him away, I'm not sure. They grabbed me. I thought they were going to kill me, but they let me go with a warning to back off on reporting about Olumide."

Maureen frowned. "Why didn't you tell me?"

"I didn't want to worry you. And I guess I just didn't want to think about it."

"Do I need to be worried about you?"

"No, not anymore."

"What happened to John?"

"Nothing. He came back the next day and told me some story about getting a newspaper and coming back to find the tires flat and me gone. I don't blame him. But I don't really trust him anymore either. He's terrified and may even be reporting on my whereabouts. I'll tell you the whole story later. There's no time now."

Maureen nodded.

"I'll do better next time, I promise," Lindsay said.

"I know. Forget it." They hugged.

Maureen started to leave, then paused. "There's something I haven't told you either," she said.

"What?"

"Well, I've discovered what's causing the health problems I've been having." She paused, then smiled. "I'm pregnant."

"Oh my God. That's incredible. Fabulous."

Lindsay ran back and wrapped her arms around Maureen. "How long have you known? Why didn't you tell me? Have you told Mark?"

"Slow down." Maureen laughed. "Believe me, it was hard. I've known for about a week, but I was too mad to tell you. And of course I've told Mark. He's thrilled. I'm going to go home right after I write up today's interview. So if we're going to talk, it will have to be tonight after we file. I'm going to go over now and get a good seat. Do you want me to save a place for you?"

"That would be great. Thanks. I'll just take a quick shower and leave right away. I'm so excited. I feel like an aunt."

"How about a godmother?"

"Really? Oh, Maurie, thank you. I love you."

Lindsay returned to the bathroom and stepped into the shower. She stayed a little longer than she meant to, going over questions for Fakai in her mind. She was just rinsing the shampoo out of her hair when James arrived. She wrapped a towel around herself and went to the bedroom to find something to put on. Finding the pants she wanted, she dropped the towel and reached for her panties and bra. Before she could get them on, James opened the door and walked in.

She instinctively pulled the towel up, assuming he would retreat. But to her surprise, he just stared at her for a few seconds. Then, deliberately, he reached behind him and closed the door.

"Is everything all right?" she asked.

He didn't answer but walked to the windows and pulled the shades down.

Lindsay's lips felt dry. Why now?

"James," she began, wrapping the towel tighter around herself. But her voice betrayed her.

"Why don't you drop that and come over here?" he asked quietly.

She paused and he came to her instead and pulled away the towel.

He looked at her for a moment. Then he moved his hand slowly to her face, tracing each of her features before he moved his hand downward. She knew he could feel her body quiver as his hand touched her soft inner thigh and explored her as she oh so gently opened her legs.

He bent to kiss her. Finally they were back to where they had been on the beach. But this time, she was ready. She kissed him, running her tongue across his lips and pressing herself against him. Her hand softly caressed the back of his neck. After a few minutes, he led her toward the bed.

"James," she whispered. "I want you so much, but not now."

He pulled away from her.

"No," she said. "Don't pull away like that. Did you forget my interview? I can't be late; they won't let me in and I can't miss it. It's at two, remember?" she added, glancing at the clock. It was already almost 1:00 and she wasn't even dressed yet.

"Oh shit," James said. "I forgot that was for today. Of course, go ahead and dress. I'm sorry."

"No, please don't be sorry. The timing is just lousy. We'll have to take a rain check."

"I wouldn't worry about that," he said, pulling her to him and kissing her again. He released her, and as he walked to the door, he called back over his shoulder, "Good luck. I'll drop by later and we can see about dinner."

"I've promised to have dinner with Maureen," she answered. "How about after?"

"Fine. I'll drop by here around ten-thirty."

"That would be wonderful."

He left, closing the door behind him. Lindsay rushed, skipping makeup, throwing on her clothes and grabbing her bag, notebook, tape recorder—Oh God, did she have new batteries? She rummaged through her desk, found a new pack, grabbed a fistful of pens and charged out.

She had asked John to drive her, but the traffic was worse than ever. She fidgeted in her seat, checking her watch every few minutes. Finally, a lane opened on the right and John followed other cars through it. The interview was being held in an office located in a ramshackle brick house in Surulere. She hoped everyone would be on African time and arrive fifteen minutes late.

As she turned into Ogunlana Drive, she saw a mob gathered on the sidewalk a block away. A few people were sitting on the ground and some of the women were crying. Above them, smoke and dust curled into the sky. When she turned the corner, she saw that the office building lay in shambles. Bricks and stones were strewn around the street and the plaster walls were partly blown out. At first, Lindsay couldn't absorb what had happened. Then she realized that this was the building she had been looking for.

Oh my God—Maureen.

She leaped out of the car and ran toward the house. The explosion must have just occurred, because no police were on the scene and she was able to move through the crowds of onlookers into the shell of what had been the hallway.

Smoke and dust were everywhere, making it hard to breathe, let alone see. She heard a low moan and tried to follow the sound. As she searched, the moaning stopped, and she couldn't locate where it had come from. The smoke burned her eyes and she nearly stumbled over a body splayed on the ground, arms akimbo, chest crushed. She bent down and then quickly averted her gaze to keep from being sick. It was a man. His clothes were burned and torn and his body charred. Next to him, she saw a severed leg, its scuffed black shoe still laced on its foot.

She had to find Maureen. She carefully edged her way further inside, holding a handkerchief to her mouth. Suddenly, someone grabbed her arm from behind. The police had arrived.

"Step outside."

Lindsay turned around.

"Please. My friend is in there. I have to find her."

The policeman released her arm and spoke with surprising kindness.

"We'll find her, madam." He put his hand on her elbow to lead her away. "But you can't be in the building. It isn't safe."

"She's the AP reporter. She was here for the Fakai press conference."

"We'll look," he said, ushering her onto the street.

Now there were dozens of people in front of the house. An ambulance pulled up as the police were forcing the crowd back. Lindsay stood there, the only reporter on the scene.

Olumide, she thought. He knew Fakai and most of his top people would be here. He planned this bomb to eliminate Fakai and his party. What was it to him that he killed all the foreign correspondents? He would just claim it was the work of a terrorist group. She felt a rising panic, thinking of her other friends and colleagues. Could anyone have survived this blast? Maybe Maureen hadn't been inside. Maybe she had saved the seats and then waited outside for Lindsay. Please, please God, let Maureen be alive.

Maybe the bomb had gone off early. If that had happened, Maureen wouldn't have waited for Lindsay to arrive—she would already be back at the AP office filing her story.

Automatically, she pulled out her notebook and began recording the scene: "bomb blast shattered building; bricks, mortar everywhere. Bodies litter blown-out hallway. Severed leg."

She stopped, unable to continue. She approached one of the policemen, her notebook out, and asked if the room had been full and if Fakai had begun to speak. But he didn't seem to know anything.

Dazed, she decided to leave, and asked John to drive her to the AP office. After a minute she saw that all the roads were blocked by army tanks. It looked as if everyone in Lagos was on the street. The road to Reuters was clearer, and she told him to turn in there. She arrived at the same time as Mike Vale. Thank God he was all right.

They fell into each other's arms.

"Did you see Maureen?" she asked.

"No. But I think she's okay. The bomb went off early. Most of us hadn't arrived, but Fakai was there with his team."

Lindsay found the Reuters phone was working and tried calling the AP office, but the line was busy. She tried the American embassy. When she finally reached Dave Goren, she knew more than he did. She got back in her car and once again tried to get to the AP office.

She inched along, stuck in the infernal traffic, but the tanks no longer blocked the streets. The heat baked the car and perspiration dripped down her face. She turned on the car radio; there was nothing but static. All Lindsay could think of was getting there and finding Maureen.

The AP office was in chaos. Lindsay looked around desperately. At the back of the room was Maureen's young assistant, a Yoruba woman who had studied in London. She was weeping inconsolably. Lindsay rushed over.

"There was just a news bulletin," the girl gasped between sobs. "They said there were four dead . . . Maureen was one of them."

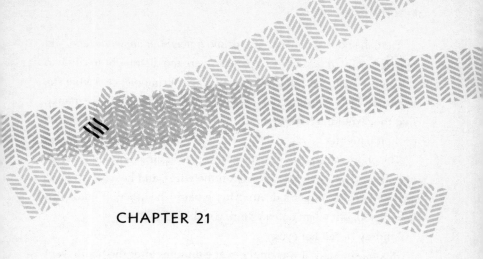

CHAPTER 21

Afterward, when Lindsay tried to remember what had happened in the hours after she learned of Maureen's death, it was a jumble of chaotic images. She must have gotten home somehow because she remembered lying in her bed and weeping. James must have come over because she could call up a picture of him holding her. He had seemed as upset as she was. Who was responsible? he kept asking. Who could have done this?

Eventually, Lindsay had to stop crying and make plans. First, she braced herself and called Maureen's husband, Mark, who had already been notified by AP and whose voice sounded hoarse and barely audible. He didn't mention the pregnancy—maybe he couldn't bear to deal with both losses at the same time—and Lindsay didn't bring it up. James sat next to her, his hand on her back to steady her. He took the phone from her when she couldn't go on, adding a few useless words of comfort of his own and asking about the funeral. Mark said it depended on how long it would take for them to transport Maureen's remains. Then he broke down, said he would get back to them. Lindsay knew she should call Maureen's parents next.

First, she poured herself a stiff drink. A neighbor answered and said apologetically that Maureen's parents were too distraught to come to the phone. Relieved, Lindsay left a message of condolence, saying she would try again. She hoped that they didn't know about the pregnancy, that they wouldn't have to mourn the loss of their grandchild as well as their daughter.

The phone rang as soon as she hung up. Joe Rainey sounded harried and upset. The story was already on the wires, and he expressed his sympathy for Maureen's death. After a pause, he asked, "I know this is hard, kid, but when do you think you'll file?"

Lindsay closed her eyes.

"Soon," she said. "I was on the scene minutes after the bomb went off. Give me an hour."

"Good girl."

She hung up and turned to James.

"Should I go?" he asked.

"I don't want you to, but maybe you should. I have to file."

"I know."

"Maybe you could come back later."

"Of course." He reached out to embrace her. She folded herself into his arms, resting there a moment. Then she pulled away and began to write.

By the time she finished and dictated it to the recording room, the power had gone out. She sat in the growing darkness as Martin walked around silently lighting candles. He looked like he too had been crying.

"I am so sorry, madam," he said gently. "Please, can you eat something? Maybe some soup?"

"No, thank you, Martin. I'm not hungry."

"I know. But it will help you to have something. Maybe some tea and a biscuit? Please?"

She sighed and accepted, more for him than for herself. After he served her, she sat alone in the flickering candlelight thinking about

Maureen, leaving the tea and biscuit untouched. When James returned later, he insisted she lie down, and he lay beside her. She couldn't sleep and finally took a sleeping pill, falling into a deep, dreamless slumber.

She awoke late and groggy. Lying in bed, she struggled to consciousness. For a minute, she didn't remember what had happened. Then the dreadful memory swept over her. She turned toward James, but he had gone. When she went downstairs, Martin was already in the kitchen and he poured her a cup of coffee.

"Mr. James say he will be back later," Martin said. "Please, madam, this morning you must eat." She wanted to hear the BBC broadcast to see how they treated the bombing, but when she looked at the clock she was shocked to discover it was already 9:30—too late for the early broadcast and too early for the next one. She was pouring herself a second cup of coffee when she heard a knock at the door. She motioned to Martin that she didn't want to see anyone. Martin opened the door and there was a small commotion before Vickie pushed her way past him and barged into the kitchen.

"Lindsay, I'm sorry. I know you don't want to see anyone right now, but we've got to talk."

Lindsay was actually glad to see her. Vickie's straightforward personality was just the distraction she needed.

"Sit down, Vickie. Have a cup of coffee."

Instead, Vickie pulled Lindsay out of her chair and hugged her.

"First things first," she said. Then she released her, looked around for a clean cup and poured herself some coffee.

"Have you eaten?"

"No. I'm not hungry."

Vickie turned to Martin.

"What does she usually eat for breakfast?"

"She eats eggs and toast."

"Well, bring her some toast and jam, please."

Relieved, Martin moved quickly to prepare it.

It felt good to be taken care of, and when the toast was ready, Lindsay nibbled it obediently.

"The government is moving faster than I've ever seen it. They're sending Maureen's body back today. The funeral will probably be in a few days in London."

"Thanks for telling me," Lindsay said. "Of course, I'll be there."

"Actually, you can't go," Vickie said.

Lindsay looked up sharply. "What do you mean?"

"Lindsay, if you leave the country, they'll never let you back in. They don't want the bad publicity of throwing you out, but they'll never renew your visa. Not now."

"Then I guess this country will just have to self-destruct without me. I have to be at Maureen's funeral. My priorities aren't so screwed up that I don't know that."

Vickie paused.

"We need your help. What's more important, going to Maureen's funeral or helping us discover who killed her? Sympathy isn't enough. This is a time for revenge."

That stopped Lindsay short. "What could I do that you couldn't do without me?"

"You are the one person with contacts both in the journalistic community and in The Next Step."

Lindsay considered this. "Do you have any idea who was behind the blast?"

"I need to know if you will stay and work with us before I can fill you in."

"I'm still a journalist, Vickie."

"I know, but you'd have to agree that anything I tell you is off the record until I give you the go-ahead."

Lindsay shook her head. "I can't do that."

"Maybe this is the moment to decide whether or not your priorities are screwed up. You have a chance to help us find and punish the people who killed your best friend."

"It's against every principle of my profession."

Vickie's voice softened. "What would Maureen want you to do?"

"Maureen would want me to throw you out. She'd want me to cover the hell out of this story without you. But I'm not Maureen. I want revenge. I need to have time to think."

"How much time?"

"I don't know. My impulse is to refuse. How can I miss Maureen's funeral? What would I say to Mark or to her parents?"

"We could work all that out."

"It's not that easy. And you're asking me to trust you, but you haven't shown that you trust me. Tell me, off the record, what you know. I'll tell you my decision later." She pulled out her notebook. "Do you believe this was engineered by Olumide?"

Vickie seemed to consider her answer. Then she got up and closed the kitchen door.

"Some of us did think that—especially the ambassador and Dave Goren . . . but most of us disagree. Killing Fakai isn't in Olumide's interest; it creates a martyr. We think it was someone who wants to provoke a movement against Olumide. They'd expect Olumide will be brutal putting down protests. He certainly stopped the riots after Bayo's death. To tell you the truth, we're puzzled about who the instigator is. We've been poring over diagrams of the bomb site and the early lab reports on the materials used and they all point to Solutions, Incorporated. But we don't know who hired them or who their point man is here."

"But why kill Maureen? Why target the press?"

"Exactly. That doesn't make sense. They would want the press to cover the event. We think the bomb went off early. They probably just wanted to kill Fakai and his people and timed the bomb to go off just as the press was arriving. That way, they would all write about the blast. Maureen was collateral damage."

Lindsay blanched. If only she had persuaded Maureen to wait for her, Maureen would still be alive.

"Come back in an hour, Vickie. I'll have an answer for you."

After a while, she picked up the phone and called Mark. His voice was still shaky, but he sounded glad to hear from her. They talked for a few minutes before Lindsay broached the reason for her call.

"Mark, I need to ask you something. I can't say too much because you never know who might be listening, but I'm told that if I leave Lagos, I won't get back in, and I want to find the people responsible for Maureen's death. But if I stay, I won't be able to get to the funeral."

"Are you asking me what you should do?"

"Yes. This time I am."

Mark didn't speak for what felt like a long time.

"Stay there, Lindsay. Nail the bastards. And then get the hell out of there and come see me."

As soon as he said it, she knew it was the answer she wanted.

"Will you explain to Maureen's parents?"

"Yes. Don't worry. But be careful."

"I will. Thanks. I'll be in touch soon."

By the time Vickie returned, Lindsay had worked out a compromise on her role as a journalist with ties to the CIA.

"I'll do this much," she announced. "I'll promise to hold back on writing anything you tell me for the time being. I'm not filing from here anyway, and I don't expect to write anything until I leave the country. But then, I'll write what I want. I'm not one of your agents, and I won't follow orders. But I will share what I find on my own with you. You'll have to trust me."

"What about Mark, and Maureen's family?"

"I've taken care of that."

"So we have an understanding. And I don't need to tell you that this arrangement has to be entirely secret, do I? You can't confide in anyone."

Lindsay nodded. Before she left, Vickie impulsively reached out and squeezed Lindsay's shoulder.

"Be careful."

"I'll try."

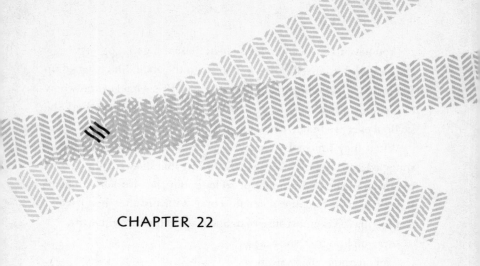

CHAPTER 22

Several days went by before Lindsay was ready to begin her investigations. There was enough daily news to keep her busy, and she needed some time to recover. She only wrote what she had to— Olumide's statement of regret and his promise to find the responsible parties, the public funerals for Fakai and his associates, the few surprisingly mild demonstrations against the government. Maureen's funeral was postponed because despite Vickie's optimism, her remains were not released quickly.

During this time, James treated Lindsay with a level of affection she had not seen before. He seemed shattered by Maureen's death, and they comforted each other. He came over every night and little by little the tender moments of physical comfort began to change into something closer to desire. They both felt the irrepressible yearning of the living even while mourning the dead. It was no surprise to either of them one night when James suggested they skip the meal and go upstairs. She followed him willingly, locking her bedroom door and leading him to her bed. He unbuttoned her linen shirt and threw it on a chair, then fumbled over the clasp on her slacks.

"You have to be an engineer to open these things."

She undid it herself, tossing them onto the chair. She reached up and kissed him, pulling his face toward hers. He seemed to know how to give her pleasure, as if this wasn't their first time together. She savored every moment, every touch.

When they finished, James draped his arm around her and she snuggled into him, luxuriating in the feeling that she was truly desired by this man she had wanted for so long. But she also felt a tinge of guilt that such happiness should come so soon after her friend's death—maybe even because of it. She pushed the thought away.

"Are you hungry?" she asked.

"Not anymore," he answered.

"I mean for food."

He smiled. "I could eat something."

She dressed quickly and went down to the kitchen. Martin looked at her knowingly, but only asked if he should start dinner. She told him that she would cook it herself and that he could take the rest of the night off. She opened the refrigerator and saw what he had been planning: chicken, wine, onions. She rummaged in the cupboard and found a jar of bottled mushrooms and decided that there was enough to put together a passable coq au vin. She bustled about preparing the meal as James came downstairs and watched. When they sat down to eat, he praised it with enthusiasm, marveling at her ability to cook an elegant French meal in Lagos. Later they moved into the living room and put on some music—Miles Davis, James's favorite. They sat close together.

"I've been thinking," she murmured. "You said you'd be ready to leave Lagos soon. I was wondering if you were going to come back after the funeral."

Did she imagine it, or did he stiffen?

"I'm not sure," he answered.

"Well, I need to stay for a while. But at some point, I'll be ready to leave for good. Maybe I could get assigned back to London, if that's where you're going to be."

He didn't answer for a few seconds. Then he got up and walked to the stereo to change the music.

"Let's not talk about future plans right now." He smiled at her. "I want to thank you for the conversation, the music, the great meal. And by the way," he added, sitting down next to her again and replacing his arm around her, "I think that the coq was very well suited to the vin."

Lindsay laughed. "I love you," she said impulsively. He smiled again, but didn't reply. Then, circling his face with her hands, she asked lightly, as if half teasing, "Do you love me?"

"Of course I love you," he said. "What's not to love?"

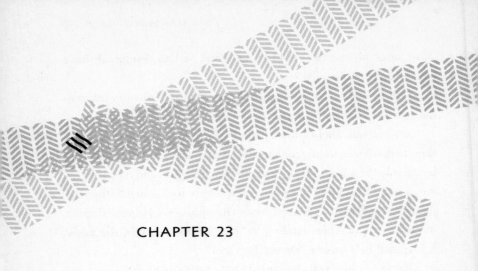

CHAPTER 23

James had already left when Lindsay awoke anxious and sweating under the thin sheets. She knew she had only been dreaming, but it had felt so real. Usually she didn't remember her dreams, but this one was so vivid. She couldn't forget it, and the longer it stayed with her the more vulnerable and frightened she became. Finally she reached over to her night table and pulled out her notebook:

The elephant grass sways on the dry savannah, stirred softly by the breeze. Behind a flat-topped acacia tree the lion crouches, his eyes alert, his body tense, his fur mottled in spots, a tuft torn from his side and clotted with traces of blood. A fight? A battle for a female? The animal's eyes sweep past me and I can feel the terror rise up to my throat. My heart is pounding so hard I fear the lion hears it. I try to silence the beat, to force myself to breathe slowly. I am as alert as he is. But I know that he is dangerous and that I am no match for him.

The lion's attention is diverted, suddenly, by a sound behind him and he whirls his majestic head to find the source. A monkey scampers up a tree behind him, emitting a high-pitched squeal. He waits. Then, slowly, he turns his head again. I feel his yellow eyes on me before I see them. I am mesmerized; I cannot move, I cannot look away. And then he stretches like a lazy house cat waking in the morning sun. Slowly, ever so slowly, he starts to walk toward me. I must run. I must hide. I must stop him. He will kill me, devour me, destroy me. I will myself to break my trance and I turn to run. And then I realize that I can't. I am in a cage in the middle of the savannah. I can't run away, and he can't devour me. I must stay there, watching him looking at me. The cage has wide spaces between bars and his paws can strike through them; if I don't stay alert his claws can rip at my skin. I run to the other side of the cage and huddle against it. I am barely out of his reach. If he moves to the other side, I must make a countermove. Until he tires of me. Oh God, help me. Let me go or let him devour me, but don't let this cage hold me for the rest of my life. . . .

Writing it out had helped dissipate enough of its power to allow her to shake it off and start her day. She showered, had breakfast, and then set out. She hadn't arranged for John to drive her. In some ways, she preferred driving herself. It gave her more independence and she didn't have to worry about John divulging her itinerary to anyone. She climbed into the car and set off to see J.R.

His house looked the same, except that there were more men hanging around. They were young and tough-looking. Their faces registered no interest as they asked her what she wanted. She assumed that they were bodyguards. One disappeared for a few minutes, and then J.R. walked into the room dressed in his usual loose cotton pants and a tie-dyed blue and white dashiki. He greeted Lindsay warmly.

"I'm sorry about your friend," he said, without a trace of pidgin, holding both her hands in his.

He looked at her with concern and her eyes teared up.

"You're one of us now," he said. "You can tell our story from the inside."

She smiled weakly. She was relieved that he seemed to trust her.

He told her The Next Step was devastated by the deaths of Bayo and Fakai. He expressed surprise that so far, the reaction to Fakai's death was more grief than rage. Olumide was more entrenched than ever. Still, the dictator was worried enough about the group to make overtures to their leadership asking for some sort of compromise. In fact, in an attempt to co-opt them—and to show he had nothing to fear—Olumide had given permission for a Next Step rally in the sports stadium. J.R. was worried about possible riots. He had the delicate job of inspiring and solidifying their followers without challenging the government outright. He worried that Olumide could use any lawlessness as an excuse to wipe out hundreds of their people in one place.

"You must come to the rally, Lindsay. You must tell the other journalists. We want this government to know that the world will be watching."

Lindsay promised she would be there. She asked if he had heard anything else about the bombing that killed Maureen. J.R. leaned back in his chair and took a long swig of beer. Finally, he leaned forward, speaking very softly.

"There is something I think you should know. We don't think this bomb came from one of Olumide's people. Why would he want to make Fakai a martyr?"

"But if he didn't do it, who did?"

"There is another group. We don't know much about its members, but it is run by the Hausas in the north."

"Are you thinking the blast was connected to religious extremism?"

"I don't know, but I don't think this has anything to do with religion. These people are like shadows, we never see their faces. But we know they raise money just as Olumide does, trading drugs. Some say that

it is their competition over control of the trade that makes them want
to get rid of Olumide and take power themselves."

"Who says that?"

"Word from the street. That is all I can tell you."

"But why kill Fakai? He was the best bet to get rid of Olumide."

"Yes, but he was a Christian, not a Muslim, so they didn't trust him.
Also, if he ever got power, he would have cracked down on the drug
trade. They needed to get rid of him. They figured that would provoke
massive riots and that would justify another army coup to force Olumide out of power and put their man in. We think this group has a lot
of influence in the military—maybe even one of its leaders is a highly
placed government minister."

J.R. said that the plan had so far fallen short of its goal. There had
been sporadic rebellions, angry crowds, but no real riots. People were
too beaten down by the pressure of their own lives, fear of the police,
and the difficulty of just surviving in Lagos. The Next Step, which
might have been expected to galvanize the protests, was both weakened
and wary of playing into the hands of the northern group.

"They are smart and they are dangerous. They don't only export
illegal drugs to Europe, they also kill us here in the south."

"How do you mean?" Lindsay asked.

"I mean they take medicines that the doctors need for the hospitals
in Lagos and they divert them to the north. We have no morphine, no
antibiotics. They care only about their own."

"Olumide is a Yoruba. He's from the same tribe and the same religion as the people in Lagos. Why doesn't he do something about this?"

"He doesn't care about his people; he cares more for power. But even
if he did, he can't find this group. No one knows who they are."

"So how do you know?"

J.R. laughed harshly and clasped his hands over his head as he
stretched backward. "I don't know," he said. "I just hear things. You
want a beer?"

Lindsay shook her head, thanked him, impulsively kissing him on the cheek, and headed for the car.

She drove back toward Ikoyi, her mind racing. If J.R. was right, then the group that killed Maureen also killed Eduke by stealing the medicine from Lagos that might have saved him. She had to stop them the only way she knew how—by reporting the story as hard as she could and publishing it for the world to see.

James didn't come back that afternoon. He left a message with Martin that he had an urgent meeting about a statue he had bid on and had to leave for Ibadan. He said he'd be back the next day and would stop by in the afternoon. That night, after reading over her notes, she sat alone in her living room, sipping white wine, missing Maureen, and wishing James were with her.

CHAPTER 24

After another restless night, Lindsay decided to pay a visit to Lagos Hospital, this time as a reporter. As she was leaving, Martin stopped her.

"Madam, you go again without a driver?"

"Yes," she said, pushing open the door. She knew Martin thought she'd be safer with John driving, but she knew what he didn't—that the one time she had been kidnapped, John had been driving. Anyway, if they wanted to harm her, John wouldn't be able to stop them. Maureen's murder had scared Lindsay, but it had also freed her. Death could come at any time. She couldn't worry about it or she would be paralyzed.

When she arrived at the hospital, she approached the front desk where a young woman in Western dress was absorbed in listening to music through earphones. The woman neither looked up nor acknowledged Lindsay's presence, but Lindsay could hear the faint strains of a song and noticed that the woman was keeping time with her foot.

"Excuse me," Lindsay said, forcing a smile. "Who are you listening to?"

The woman ignored her. Lindsay spoke louder.

"Is that Papa Wembe?"

The woman looked up.

"Papa Wembe, man? You know for nothing. That be Bayo."

"I know Bayo. I mean I knew him."

The woman turned off her tape recorder and turned to Lindsay, her face showing a hint of animation.

"No lie?"

"No lie. I went to the Juju House. I saw the show. I talked to him. He was great. I wept when he died."

The woman looked at Lindsay, taking in her elegant linen pants and crisp shirt, and, finally, her notebook. Looking suitably impressed, she apparently decided to do her job.

"What you be here for?"

Lindsay told her that she needed to talk to someone in charge of ordering medicine.

"You sit dere," the woman said, gesturing to a molded plastic chair.

Thirty minutes later, a grim-faced woman in a soiled nurse's uniform came out to escort Lindsay to the medical administrator, a distinguished-looking middle-aged woman dressed stylishly in a beige cotton suit. Her hair was braided into a fanciful Lagos style called "Moon/Star," dozens of tiny braids tucked and molded into twists and arches on top of her head. After introducing herself and showing her press credentials, Lindsay said: "I'm writing a story about the Nigerian health service and I'm visiting hospitals in the various regions. One of the things I'm interested in is whether or not medical care is pretty evenly distributed throughout the country or better in cities than in the villages, things like that."

The administrator looked wary, and Lindsay guessed what she would be thinking: that Lindsay's apparent naïveté, her earnestness, the very starch in her crisp blouse were reasons not to trust her. But the administrator answered—albeit with the evasiveness of a true bureaucrat.

"We are a developing country, as you know. You will certainly find unevenness in our medical care. But we are working on bringing better services to the villages and educating our people to use them. We have a vaccination program sponsored by UNICEF that is operating right now in several areas."

"But what about region to region? For example, I recently traveled up north and visited the hospital in Kano, and I was impressed by its facilities and supplies—they seem to have everything they need for now. Is it the same here in Lagos?"

The administrator glared at Lindsay. "Is it the same here?" she echoed. Then, looking as though she was trying to compose herself, she looked at Lindsay almost, but not quite, kindly. "How well do you know Nigeria?" she asked.

"Why do you ask?"

"Because if you knew it at all, you would know that of course it isn't the same here."

She got up to go. "I am busy. You must go now."

Lindsay made no move to get up.

"Look, I know Nigeria better than you think," she said. "I know from good sources that the Hausa gangs supply the Northern Hausa hospitals at your expense. They sell you supplies, which you pay for, and then their gangs steal them before they get here and bring them to the north where they are paid again. What I don't understand is how you let this happen."

The administrator looked at her sharply. "You think we could do something to stop it?"

"I don't know," she said. "But why don't you buy your supplies elsewhere?"

"Believe me, we don't have that choice."

"The government is mostly from the Yoruba tribe and the people in Lagos are mostly Yoruba. How can the authorities allow this to happen to their own people?"

The woman sighed and lowered her voice to a whisper. "This isn't about the government. The drug gangs run this country. But truly," she added, "the government does nothing to stop it." She caught herself and looked down hurriedly. "If you quote me as saying that, I will be in very bad trouble. Do you understand? I spoke in heat. But I ask you to protect me."

"You have my word. Can you tell me when you last got a shipment of painkillers?"

"It is not that we don't get shipments, it is that the shipments are only a fraction of what we ordered and need. A week ago we got a shipment that was entirely inadequate."

"In what way?" Lindsay asked.

"We ordered two hundred boxes of morphine. We received twenty-five. We asked for five hundred boxes of penicillin and erythromycin but received only sixty."

"What did you do?"

"What can we do? We wrote letters to the company. We issued complaints to the government. Nothing will change. We must make do with what we have."

Walking back to the parking lot, she saw a black government limousine pull up. A man she didn't recognize got out, followed by Mike Vale. She watched them enter the hospital. It was strange—this was the second time she had seen him here. Something seemed wrong, and she followed Mike and his companion back inside. The two were walking past the receptionist when she called Mike's name. He whirled around and was clearly annoyed when he saw her. His companion continued on without him.

"I'm busy, Lindsay," he snapped.

"Yes, I see. What are you doing here?"

"The same thing you are."

"Well, not exactly. I'm asking questions about government officials; you seem to hang out with them. Maybe I should just ask you my questions."

"I guess I just have better sources." He turned his back and walked away. When Lindsay tried to follow, the receptionist, apologetically, stopped her.

"Who was the man who went in first?" Lindsay asked.

"He from de health ministry. He come here many time."

Driving home, she noted to herself that J.R.'s information had been confirmed. It was possible Mike was following the same story, but the fact that he arrived by government limo made that unlikely. Since when was Olumide's government so helpful to a journalist? Maybe the officials were giving Mike some whitewashed version of events and he was falling for it.

Lindsay knew that an exposé in an American paper, even an influential one like hers, would not provide a quick fix. But she had to do something, and writing was the one thing she knew how to do. She remembered her promise to Vickie to hold back information on the bombing and wondered if the drugs played a role in it. The administrator had said the medicine was diverted to the north. J.R. had told her of rumors about a radical northern group that wanted to seize power. The two could be connected, but what did Mike Vale have to do with it?

She was approaching the turnoff to her house and signaled right. Before she could turn, another car passed her on the left and cut in front of her. She hit the brake, unsure of what to do. The car was a black Mercedes like the one used to abduct her. She made the turn and saw the sedan parked on the shoulder. As she passed, it began trailing her, so close she feared it would deliberately hit her fender. She pulled up in front of her house, relieved to see James's car parked across the street. She ran to her front door and opened it, taking a deep breath to calm herself. Inside, she peered out the window. The two thugs who had threatened her before were parked in front of her house.

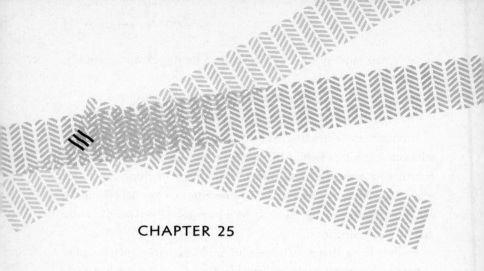

CHAPTER 25

Lindsay gave James a quick peck on the lips. He tried to pull her back for a longer kiss, but she slipped away, walked past him, and sat on the couch. She crossed her legs, tapping her heel on the floor so her knee bobbed up and down. Without asking, he poured her a drink and handed it to her.

"What happened?" he asked.

She tasted it and scowled. She'd expected a gin and tonic but he'd poured her a scotch.

"How do you always know when something is bothering me?"

He smiled. "It's not that hard."

She took another sip of the scotch. She found she liked it. "I had a rough day." Then, fighting back tears, she told him everything that had happened, ending with the two men leering at her from the car in front of her house.

Ignoring her pleas to be careful, he strode to the door and yanked it open.

The car was gone. He walked back and put his arm around her.

"Lindsay, I think your usefulness here has come to an end. You have to leave while you still can."

She remained silent, but her face registered a stubborn resistance.

"What are you waiting for?" he continued. "Do you think Olumide is going to just give up? He knows what you're doing. He knew you were at that hospital today. He has probably arrested the administrator you spoke to. Your investigation is doing more harm than good, and you're risking your own life in the bargain."

She shook her head. "I can't leave yet. I know I have to be careful. I'm not going to write anything provocative until I get out of the country, and I'll try not to cover anything alone. But there's going to be a rally for The Next Step in a few days. I have to be there. I thought I'd see if I can go with some of the people from the embassy."

James looked exasperated and got up and began to pace.

"Exposing Olumide isn't trivial, James," she pleaded. "His policies affect the lives of millions of people. Think of what they do. Think of the depravity of diverting basic medicines from Lagos hospitals to northern gangs."

"And the northern gangs bring the medicines to northern hospitals," he continued. "There are needy children there too who would go without medicine if the gangs didn't exist. The gangs provide a kind of balance to the Yoruba bias toward Lagos, did you ever think of that?"

"I don't think that's a convincing argument. It's so terribly cynical, I find it hard to believe you believe it yourself. And anyway, my job is simply to end the secrecy and let the light in."

He reached out and tenderly touched her hair, running his fingers through it.

"Let the light in on us, Lindsay," he said. "Think about how much longer this kind of life will be meaningful to you. Think about where you'd like to be a year from now, a month from now. And with whom."

She leaned against him. "I have been thinking about that," she said, "and I know with whom. But you have to give me a little more time here. I promise I won't take unnecessary chances."

He nodded thoughtfully. Then he pressed her close to him.

"I'm worried about you," he said. "I have to go up north for a buying trip. I'm supposed to leave for Kano tomorrow, and now I don't know if I should go."

"How long will you be away?"

"A few days. A week at the most." He looked troubled. "Your stubbornness is affecting my business. This is an important trip. I've been working toward it since I arrived. But how can I leave you here now?"

"Of course you can. You couldn't help me if you stayed. What would you do, follow me around like a bodyguard? You need to do what you came here to do and so do I."

"Maybe a bodyguard isn't a bad idea."

"I think that would just draw attention to me. I'll try to keep a low profile. They want to scare me off, not create an international incident. Olumide still wants American support and my paper still matters to him. As long as I don't file, I think they'll leave me alone."

"Up to a point. If he really thinks you're a threat, even a future one, nothing will stop him. People say he had one of his closest advisers killed because he suspected he was working undercover for the Americans."

She perked up. "Where did you hear that?"

"Around. People talk. Even artists."

"Yeah. I know that was the word on the street. And it's probably right. But my case is different. I'll be okay. Go on your trip. Don't worry about me. I can take care of myself."

She smiled, leaning over to kiss him. "But hurry back," she murmured, "because I'll miss you."

He gave in, responding to her kiss, and reached under her blouse to undo her bra.

"Not here," she whispered. "Martin." She led him upstairs.

"When I get back, we'll make some plans to get out of here together," she said.

"First things first," he answered.

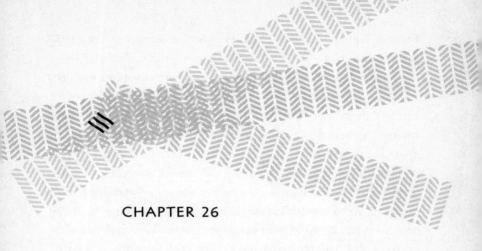

CHAPTER 26

J.R. sent a messenger to tell Lindsay that the rally in the sports stadium would take place the following Thursday morning. Hesitantly—she was not used to sharing her information with government officials—she dropped by the embassy to tell Vickie, who was grateful since Dave Goren didn't know when it would happen. Mindful of her own safety, Lindsay asked if she could accompany them.

"Of course," Vickie said. She leaned over and whispered, "Glad this arrangement is working. It's a big change from the you-can-find-out-what-I-know-by-reading-my-story line."

"Well, I need protection, and I don't think I can get it from that group of miscreants who constitute the press corps," Lindsay said lightly. "Besides, I said I'd cooperate, though don't forget I don't work for you, if you remember."

"I don't know, Linds . . . it's a slippery slope."

"Okay, okay." Lindsay was clearly annoyed. "Will you pick me up or not?"

On Thursday, Vickie and Dave Goren arrived in an embassy car. They had a special pass allowing entry to a VIP section near the exit.

Entering with the diplomats, in full view of her colleagues, made Lindsay uncomfortable. She saw them exchange quizzical looks.

Lindsay noted how potentially explosive the situation was. The stands were jam-packed, as if for a soccer match. Thousands of people, many of them angry, were pushing and shoving to get a seat in the rows of graduated seating encircling the field. Looking around, she appraised the crowd.

At first Lindsay didn't spot any white faces other than the foreign press, but after a few minutes, she noticed some—a Swedish diplomat she knew, and a familiar-looking man two rows below her. He might have been the British Airlines representative, which was strange—unless of course the airline job was a cover. Their presence meant word of the rally had reached the entire foreign community.

Vickie leaned over as though to whisper but then spoke in a loud voice. "This is a good spot. We've heard there may be a provocation."

As if on cue, a group of men walked to the podium. One of them stepped forward. He was dressed in loose, cream-colored flowing pants and a red and yellow dashiki. His face was marked by three parallel scars on each cheek. His deep voice boomed over the microphone.

"Brothers and Sisters," he began, in clear, British-accented English. "Brothers and Sisters," he said again, louder this time to quiet the crowd, "please settle down. I beg for your silence and your understanding. Our enemies are trying to bury us in our tragedies—all the leaders of our struggle have been taken from us."

The audience began to listen—you could feel the shift of attention. Lindsay looked nervously at the various exits guarded by groups of armed military police.

"Bayo is gone," the speaker declared, his voice rising a little, and the crowd stirred. "Fakai is gone," the speaker continued, his voice rising again. A soft sound rose from the crowd as people nodded assent. The police officers shifted restlessly.

"But we still here," the speaker screamed. The crowd roared. "We go stay," he continued. "We go find one more leadah and when dey go shoot him down we go find one moah. And one moah. And one moah. Until we go win!"

Now the crowd was cheering and applauding wildly. The speaker shouted above them, this time returning to flawless English: "So now I give you our next leader. Bayo's best friend. Fakai's trusted aide. I give you the man we call J.R."

The crowd went crazy. People jumped to their feet, screaming and applauding. They chanted: "J.R. You go far. J.R. You go far."

J.R. walked to the mike with a calm authority. He held his hands up for quiet. Lindsay could hear a voice behind her heckling.

"Dey go lie. Dey go bring nothing fo us, dey go bring mo naira for dem, dat all. It nobody lookout who on seat. All dey lookout is deyself."

Lindsay and Vickie turned around, trying to locate the speaker. The sun baked down and they squinted through their sunglasses at the tiers of seats leading to the balcony, but every row was full, and people were standing in the aisles, so their vision was obscured. They heard a commotion above them, but it was not easy to decipher what was being said. Suddenly, they saw a large bundle being passed down, like a sack of potatoes from row to row until it reached the edge of the balcony. At that point it was heaved over the edge. People screamed as it crashed with a loud thud onto the pavement thirty feet below.

"Oh my God," Vickie said, under her breath. "It's a person."

They looked up as another body was handed down, screaming and kicking, and finally hurled onto the cement pavement with that same terrible thud. Vickie grabbed Lindsay's arm.

J.R. began to shout into the mike, "Please, people, you are playing into the hands of our enemies. Control yourselves. This solves nothing. These are your brothers and sisters. Save your anger for our enemies."

Another body crashed onto the pavement, as the crowd roared. Police cars, sirens blaring, surrounded the stadium. The soldiers drew their guns and pointed them at the crowd. They charged up to the balcony and pulled people indiscriminately out of their seats, shoving them down the stairs and into waiting vans.

"We've got to get out of here," Vickie said.

They edged out of their seats and headed for the gate, where Vickie spoke to someone with a walkie-talkie.

The stands started emptying. The rally was aborted, but the violence wasn't. People surged toward the exits in a mad rush to get out. They were elbowing each other, pushing, kicking until, inevitably, some people stumbled and fell and were trampled.

Lindsay, Vickie, and Dave Goren watched from the safety of the gate near the exit. The military police were concentrating on Next Step supporters, rounding up organizers of the rally and ignoring everyone else.

"Do you see what they're doing?" asked Lindsay. "It looks like organized provocation from Olumide's thugs. And they're going to blame it on The Next Step. The evening news will tell how Next Step activists killed innocent bystanders and fomented riots that killed even more."

"I know. But who started it?" Vickie asked. "Olumide's thugs? Or just mob hysteria?"

Lindsay felt sure it wasn't members of The Next Step. She approached several people as they emerged from the stadium. One man just pushed her aside and started running as soon as he passed through the gate, another continued walking without answering her. Lindsay approached a woman who was crying as she staggered out. The woman steadied herself on Lindsay's arm. She was a biology teacher, she said, at a local high school.

"They threw out those people like trash," she moaned. "Like trash. They are animals. No, worse. Animals don't kill for pleasure. Only people do that." Lindsay scribbled the quote in her notebook. A few more people stopped to talk to her. She jotted descriptions to jog her memory, and when she felt she had enough quotes, she looked around for Vickie and Goren to get a ride home. She had promised James she wouldn't write a provocative story, but even he would agree this was an exception. All the other journalists would cover the rally. Olumide and his thugs were unlikely to single her out. Still, she felt nervous. Pushing her way through the crowd, she spotted Vickie and Goren in the distance, near their car. She was about to call out to them when she saw two men advancing toward her. She started to bolt, shouting for her friends, but in the chaos, no one could hear her. The men grabbed her and one crammed a rag into her mouth. Her nostrils filled with a strong chemical odor and she struggled for breath. A moment later, they threw her into the trunk of their car. Before losing consciousness, she had the absurd thought that James had been right and wondered how she would ever be able to tell him.

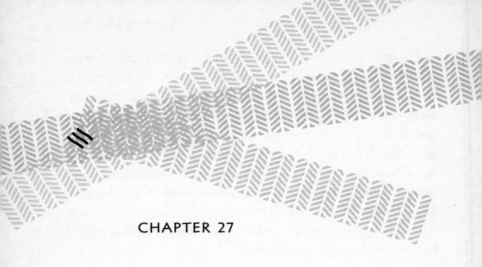

CHAPTER 27

When Lindsay awoke, she was lying on the floor of a large tin shed. She lay very still, struggling against panic and trying to think clearly. She could hear voices and laughter outside and every few minutes something crashed against the wall, emitting a shattering noise that reverberated on the tin. She was still a little drugged and it took her a few minutes to realize that she was not tied up. She got up slowly, painfully stretching her cramped muscles, and attempted to peek out the door. She squinted through a crack and saw the two men who had kidnapped her. They were drinking beer, throwing the empty cans against the shed. She scanned the room, looking for something to use as a weapon. All she saw were cardboard cartons, piled against the far wall. She reached into her pocket and found her keys. The key ring, a present from Maureen, was a tiny sterling silver pocket knife. It made a pathetic weapon but there was nothing else. She heard a radio outside blaring high-life and peeked out again. The taller man threw another beer can and she jumped back. She didn't know if he heard, but he went over to the door and pulled it open. He walked menacingly toward her, drunk, swaggering.

"You no good for be quiet," he said. "Dat no good fo you, but dat be good fo me."

He withdrew a switchblade knife from his pocket, pressed a button and brandished the blade at her. He stood in front of her, so close she could smell his stink, alcohol mixed with sweat. His knife hand darted quickly toward her and, almost playfully, he nicked her shoulder. She jumped back, covering the cut with her hand as a thin trickle of blood seeped through her fingers. Her tormentor laughed. He placed the blade of the knife under her chin.

His partner entered. "Not yet, brother," he said. "We go have fun first, like we say. No one go know. She don be talking no mo."

Lindsay was too stunned to think. She backed away as they moved forward, unable to speak. As they edged her closer to the wall, some instinct for survival broke through her fear.

"I will give you money," she said hoarsely, her mouth dry. "Much money."

The big man shook his head. "Too late, sistah. Dey go for know. Dey wan' you be dead."

The fact that he stopped advancing on her in order to answer gave her hope.

"I could disappear," she said quickly. "Leave the country. You could say I was dead."

The big man laughed. "No for worry. We no be liar. You go be dead. But not yet."

He walked outside and returned with the radio, turning up the volume. As he approached, she tried to dart away, running toward the door. He grabbed her by her hair. She tried to concentrate on the beat of the music, to stare at the wormholes in the floor, to think of anything but what was happening. When the big man pulled her to him, she came alive, screaming, clawing, kicking. She put her hand in her pocket and closed it on the small knife. She withdrew it slowly and jabbed it with all her might into his neck. He jumped back and she could see a trickle of blood ooze down his neck. Enraged, he seized the little knife, threw it across the room, and twisted her arm behind her. The second man held her while the first slapped her hard across the face and then reached over and ran his large, fleshy hand over her body and squeezed her breast so hard she cried out. He tore open her slacks, pulled them to her ankles and undid his belt. His pants slid down. He breathed heavily.

Suddenly, the music stopped and a military march blared from the radio. The men released their hold on Lindsay and exchanged worried glances. The big man hesitated, his pants down at his ankles, unsure what to do. They heard an excited voice announce that rebels had seized control of the government and taken over the radio station. "This is Army Colonel Abdul Murtalla of the Northern Alliance. I bring you great tidings. The oppressive Olumide government is overthrown. We have secured the government. We will apprehend and execute the criminal Olumide and his henchmen. Stay in your homes. We will broadcast further information and instructions later." More military music followed.

The big man backed off, pulled up his pants and buckled his belt. He grabbed Lindsay's bag and rummaged through it, finding her money, which he stuffed in his pocket. He threw her wallet with her identification across the room, and then ran off, followed by his partner, leaving her lying on the ground.

She could not seem to move or feel anything and she wondered, without emotion, if she was paralyzed. She didn't know how long she lay there—fifteen minutes, maybe longer—but finally, she moved her hands and her legs and, after what felt like a long time, she managed to get up, her whole body shaking, and slowly pull her torn pants back up. The button was gone, but she rolled up the top until it felt relatively secure.

Dazed, she retrieved her bag, found her key ring and started to look around for her wallet. She didn't see it. Warily, she approached the packing crates that were stacked in the far corner. The topmost carton was open, and she rifled through stacks of blank paper. Then she saw something red that had fallen behind the box. She moved the carton to pick up her wallet. As she turned to walk away, she noticed another open carton filled with small statues. She picked one up and saw that it was an exact replica of the one Mike Vale had in his apartment. Looking further, she saw that all the statues were alike. She was confused. The statues suddenly assumed a new importance. They were clues, but pointing to what? She couldn't make sense of them in her current state, but she slipped one of them into her bag.

She left the shed and looked around. She was in a semi-industrial area. There was a warehouse across the street, some empty lots, a garage with several beat-up cars and an old truck. She started to walk, hoping to find someone to ask for help. A few cars passed, but she didn't hail them, and they didn't stop. After about twenty minutes she reached a sparsely populated neighborhood. She saw a woman selling beer and cigarettes and stopped to ask for some water. She had no money, but the woman, surprised to see a disheveled white foreigner without a car or cash, understood that she was in trouble. The woman reached under her table and brought up a coconut, which she split in half with a large knife. She kept half for herself and, silently, handed the other half to Lindsay, who received it gratefully and gulped down the tepid milk. The woman asked no questions. She turned up her radio, which was still blaring out military music. Just then a middle-aged man and woman in a Peugeot pulled up to the curb to buy a pack of cigarettes. Impulsively, Lindsay asked them if they were going downtown and if they would be kind enough to take her home.

The couple hesitated briefly—Lindsay knew they were wondering whether befriending her might be dangerous—but they reluctantly agreed and she climbed into the backseat.

"Are you all right?" the woman asked kindly. "Are you in trouble?"

"I was attacked by two men," Lindsay answered. "They stole my money and ran away when they heard about the coup. I'm an American journalist and I need to get back to my house in Ikoyi."

The woman reached over and squeezed Lindsay's hand. Her face registered concern and sympathy.

"Oh my dear, did they . . ." She stopped, looking for a delicate way to ask.

"No," Lindsay said abruptly. "The coup saved me."

"It may have saved all of us," the woman said, but her husband frowned and interrupted her.

"We don't know what is next," he said, angrily. "It is not wise to talk rashly."

As they approached the center of the city, they noticed how quiet it was. There was no one on the streets and very few cars. She knew this was the moment every journalist in Africa hoped for and feared, a coup that would change the government and propel the story, usually of only minimal interest to most Americans, to the front page. But Lindsay didn't care. Something was broken inside her. She just wanted to go home and sleep. Still, she was enough of a professional to know that she had a job to do and asked her new friends to drop her at the Reuters office.

Richard McManus, the new Reuters man, was running out the door as she came in. He said he was heading for the airport to see if it was closed and barked at Lindsay that she ought to try calling the British High Commission. She saw how Richard looked at her and knew what he must be thinking. Her pants were torn, her face smudged with dirt, her hair wild.

"Are you okay?"

"I'll be okay," Lindsay answered slowly. "I'll explain later. Let's just get something on this story. I don't have a car. Can I use one of yours and take one of your staff with me?"

"Yeah, sure. Take Joseph. We'll share on this one. I'll meet you back here to file."

Richard rushed out the door. Lindsay stopped in the restroom. She felt sick and heaved into the toilet. Then she rinsed her mouth and washed her face, running her fingers through her hair to get out the

tangles. She smoothed her clothes as best she could and breathed
deeply. Then, motioning for Joseph, she set out for the High Commission. The mood there was grim. Henry Bryan, the press attaché, a timid,
narrow-boned man with wire-rimmed glasses, told Lindsay that the
Brits had no knowledge of either the Northern Alliance or Colonel
Abdul Murtalla. They were checking their files. In the meantime, he
said, they had reports of tanks moving into central Lagos, probably
from the barracks stationed about ten miles north of the airport. Roadblocks were being set up at all the arteries entering and leaving the city
and at the airport. Bryan offered to check to see if he could turn up any
new information about Murtalla. While he was gone, Richard showed
up, announcing that the airport had indeed been closed. He was followed soon after by the *Guardian*'s Ed Courvet, and Lindsay briefed
them as best she could. Lindsay borrowed a notebook and pen from
Richard, but her hands shook too much to write. Her script was illeg-
ible, even to her. Henry returned in about half an hour with some news.
Murtalla was indeed a Hausa who was camped near the airport, at the
head of a company with a high number of Hausa soldiers. He was
thought to be leading an armored brigade taking control of the airport.
His barracks were believed to be the center of the rebellion.

As they were talking, Mike Vale rushed in. "Sorry I'm late," he mumbled. "What've you got?"

Lindsay gave him a hard look, but said nothing. She turned back to
Henry.

"I wonder how many soldiers are loyal to the government," she said.
"Is it still possible this rebellion will be put down? Is there any news
on what happened to Olumide?"

"We don't have anything official," said Henry, nervously. Quick to
pick up the scent of blood, all the reporters closed in.

"But you do know something," said Mike Vale. "Don't you?"

"Come on, Henry, just blurt it out," said Ed Courvet.

"Don't worry if you're wrong," Lindsay said. "No one will attribute
it to you."

"Nor to anyone from the High Commission," Henry insisted.

"Right. Just a Western diplomat."

"No. Not even a Western diplomat."

"Okay," said Mike Vale. "How about 'a local observer'?"

"I suppose that will do," he said.

"So," said Richard McManus impatiently. "What have you observed?"

"Okay," said Henry, looking down and lowering his voice. "I heard that Olumide is dead. I heard his body is lying in a ditch on the Ikoyi Road."

They were out the door before he raised his eyes.

On their way to their cars, Mike turned to Lindsay. "What the hell happened to you? You look terrible."

"Don't worry about me." She turned to the other reporters. "If this information is true, Olumide was probably on his way to Dodan Barracks when he was attacked."

"The area around military headquarters will be blocked by now," Ed said. "Let's go in one car and take the Ikoyi Road, heading toward his home."

They all piled into Ed's car. The streets became more active as they neared Olumide's house. Crowds were forming and skittish police officers were holding them back, demanding papers and bribes at makeshift roadblocks. As they got closer, the police became more aggressive. At the last roadblock two officers approached. Their AK-47s were slung loosely over their shoulders and swung as they moved. One walked to the driver's side of their car, while the other moved to the passenger side. The first indicated that he wanted the window rolled down. Ed swiftly complied.

"Papers," the officer demanded.

He was staring at Ed's gold wristwatch. Lindsay noticed and quietly removed her own watch and slipped it into her pocket. Ed handed over his press credentials and passport. The passport was stuffed so full of bills that it couldn't close, but the officer continued to stare at Ed's watch. "Give him the watch," Lindsay whispered. Ed unbuckled it and handed it over. The officer slipped it into his pocket and deftly removed the bills from the passport. He returned all the papers without looking at them, nodded at his colleague, and motioned the car forward. Ed drove slowly. A few hundred feet from the roadblock, the flashing lights of police cars and ambulances told them they were getting close.

The reporters found the wrecked car about three miles from Olumide's house. They got out of their car and walked as close as they were permitted. As they approached, they could see the bullet holes. One of the doors was open. Blood was splattered on the dashboard and the upholstery. Olumide's body was missing, but his driver and one of his bodyguards lay dead in the front seat. A few feet farther on, they saw the remains of the car carrying the rest of his security team, its charred metal hulk still smoldering.

They dashed back to their car. On her way back to Reuters, Lindsay switched on the radio. At first all she heard was the same repetitive military music, but after a few minutes Colonel Murtalla's voice addressed the nation.

"The revolution is triumphant," he announced. "The oppressive and corrupt former president has been executed by the people's army. We pledge to carry out free elections as soon as order is restored."

There was nothing for Lindsay to do now but file.

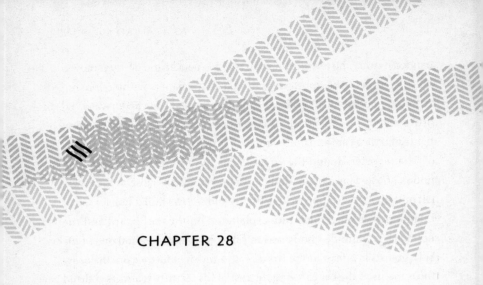

CHAPTER 28

It was midnight and Lindsay, finally, was in bed. She was severely shaken, but she knew that despite everything, she couldn't leave Lagos yet. Even when the borders reopened, the new government wouldn't issue any journalist a visa for a long time. The paper wouldn't be able to replace her and the story was growing in importance every day.

She worried about James and wondered when he would return. He hadn't called, and she always felt uneasy and insecure when he wasn't in touch. She had tried his cell phone, but the calls went straight to message. That could mean no service was available, or he turned it off, or it needed to be charged. It left her frustrated, and she finally dialed his apartment in the Victoria Hotel.

She listened to the repetitive ring and finally hung up. Where was he? She frowned and tried shifting to a more comfortable position, but she couldn't doze off and trudged into the bathroom for her sleeping pills. There was something about James—a kind of distance even when he was closest to her—that kept her on edge. She returned to bed and struggled to find a comfortable position, turning onto her back and then her side before the fog thickened, her mind let go, and she finally drifted into a drug-induced sleep.

She was awakened the next morning by the phone. She grabbed it eagerly, hoping it was James, but instead she heard Vickie's voice, too strong and energetic for such an early call, saying she urgently needed to see her.

"Sure," Lindsay said, masking her disappointment. "Come over in half an hour."

Lindsay needed to talk too. She had kept her first kidnapping a secret for too long and it had contributed to the distance between her and Maureen before she died. She was determined to talk her recent trauma through. Maybe that would help put it to rest. By the time Vickie arrived exactly half an hour later, Lindsay was dressed, coffee was brewing, and toast was ready.

She placed a cup in front of Vickie and, as calmly as she could, brought her up to date on everything. When she finished detailing the second kidnapping, Vickie enveloped her in a protective hug.

Embarrassed, Lindsay tried to squirm away, saying, "The point is, I'm not sure I can do this anymore."

"I know how you feel. You're scared and that's nothing to be ashamed of. But listen, Olumide is gone. His thugs are gone. The new government might not be any better but they have nothing against you."

"Not yet," Lindsay said.

"And you have to stay here, right?" Vickie asked. "At least until your paper can replace you. And you still want to help find Maureen's murderer." Vickie didn't wait for an answer. "So you are going to have to keep going, like the pro I know you are."

Lindsay took a deep breath. She was starting to feel better.

"You sound like my editor."

"I wish I could give you a few days to adjust to all this, but I have something else we need to discuss."

"Fine," Lindsay answered. "But I have to tell you something first. I'm worried about James."

Vickie took a sip of her coffee and said, "What are you worried about?"

"He's somewhere in the north, and he hasn't called or contacted me," Lindsay said. "I thought maybe the embassy has a representative there who could check up on him. You know, make sure he's all right."

"Well, you know how bad the phones are," Vickie said lightly. "Where in the north is he?"

"He was starting out in Kano," Lindsay answered. "I would have thought he'd have tried to contact me to see if I was all right after the coup. He has a cell phone and he manages to get reception some of the time, but I haven't been able to reach him."

"No one is getting any cell service because the circuits are overloaded. He knows you're all right. He knows how strong you are. He saw you after Maureen died, remember?"

"Well, I haven't been feeling so strong lately," she murmured.

Vickie's voice became businesslike. "I know. But I have some information that may lead us closer to the people who set off the bomb."

This got Lindsay's attention. "Okay. Shoot."

"As I told you, we are pretty sure the operation was carried out by Solutions, Incorporated. We think they were also responsible for the Agapo hit. If they followed their usual protocol, it was carried out by one of their senior operatives, most likely a foreigner—they don't trust the locals. He may have already left town, but we have reason to think that didn't happen."

"What do you have? And why do you assume it's a man?"

"They don't use women. This is strictly a macho operation. And if the operative is still here, we have to find him. We think his job isn't finished."

"You're talking in riddles. What job?"

"I'm not authorized to tell you more, Lindsay. We talked about trusting each other. Now it's your turn."

Lindsay nodded. After a pause, she said, almost to herself: "There's someone I'd like to check out."

"Who?"

"I'm not ready to give you his name yet. I may be way off base. But if I turn up anything, I'll definitely fill you in."

"Lindsay, if you happen to be right, then you shouldn't investigate it alone. These people are extremely dangerous."

"Don't worry. I won't do anything foolish."

Vickie grabbed a piece of toast and took a bite as she walked out the door. As soon as her car pulled away, Lindsay climbed into the Peugeot and drove to Mike Vale's house.

Mike was drinking his coffee when she arrived. She knocked and then pushed the door open.

"Don't you lock up?" she asked, as he ushered her into his kitchen.

"Usually not. I think most robberies of expats are inside jobs and I have a very good relationship with my steward. I pay him well and don't ask him to do too much work. He's off today—went to visit his village—otherwise I'd offer you some breakfast. Please, sit down."

"Look, Mike," she began, taking a seat at the table, "I know we've been at each other recently and I don't see any point in it. Covering this story has become more difficult. We each have our own sources. Maybe we would do better to combine them?"

Mike looked at her quizzically. "Where have I heard that before?"

"I know. It's exactly what you suggested and I turned you down. But I've changed my mind. Now, do you want to make me grovel, or do you still want a partner?"

He grinned. "I want a partner. Where should we begin?"

"I was thinking we might start with Lagos Hospital."

"Why?"

"I have a source there who told me that their drugs are being stolen and sent to the north. They buy and pay for morphine, paregoric, antibiotics, and then get only a fraction of their order."

"I'd heard that too, which is why I was at the hospital with Billy Anikulo. I had gone straight to the government spokesman to ask what the government was doing about it. It surprised me, but they decided to give me access to the health minister himself."

"It's amazing he spoke to you."

"Yeah. But they wanted to put their spin on it. It was a policy decision. He claimed the drug shortage was about too little foreign aid. He was making a bid for more."

"Right. I guess he hadn't put enough away in Switzerland yet."

"The thing is, Lindsay, Olumide didn't instigate the theft. He didn't crack down on it—his people were probably paid off—but he didn't order it. Now those same northerners who must have arranged these thefts are running the show. Writing about it could be very dangerous."

"I know that. We'd have to agree not to file until we're out of here."

"Even asking too many questions could be risky."

"Do you want to try?"

Mike paused. "I guess so," he said without enthusiasm.

"Maybe we could start with the health minister," Lindsay said. "Now that he's out of power he might be willing to talk."

"I doubt it. He's probably running scared. The new government had Olumide killed. I don't think they're going to be too cozy with his ministers, and Billy Anikulo had a high profile."

"Maybe he'll want to ingratiate himself by showing that he helped the northern hospitals even when he was part of the Yoruba government. Maybe you can go back to the hospital and see if anyone else there will confirm that the medicine disappeared. While you do that, I will check my sources at The Next Step."

"I've got a few things to do here first," Mike said. "I should be ready to go in about two hours." They agreed they'd meet again at his place at nine the next morning.

CHAPTER 29

Back home, Lindsay went straight upstairs and opened her safe. She removed the statue she had found in the shed and put it in her bag, accidentally knocking down one of the antique ibejis James had given her. It was beautiful and evocative and she looked at it again before carefully returning it to its place. Passing the phone, she called James again, but there was still no answer.

Martin was ironing her T-shirts and underwear—a practice she no longer questioned. Clothing was hung outside to dry, exposing it to the tumbu fly, which often laid its eggs on the cloth. If not killed by the heat of the iron, the tiny insect burrowed into people's skin where it would mature and form a lump like a cyst. Martin had told her that the insect could be killed by covering it with Vaseline so that it couldn't breathe—it would then poke its head out and could be removed with a pair of tweezers—a prospect she'd just as soon avoid.

"I can get you something, madam?"

"No, thank you." She sat at the kitchen table. "I'm just resting for a bit."

She took the statue out of her bag and examined it. It was made of wood and carefully detailed. Its carved crown was rimmed with a deep indigo stain. It was well done, Lindsay thought.

The phone rang, startling her. She picked it up in the living room and was relieved to hear James's voice on the other end.

"James, I'm so glad. I've been worried."

"I couldn't get a line. I'm sorry. How are you?"

"I'm fine. It's been a hell of a story."

"I know. There are roadblocks everywhere and it's been hard to get back, but I think I'll make it through today."

She glanced at the statue and wondered if she should tell him where she found it. She decided against alarming him. She'd wait until he returned.

"I hope you get here soon. I miss you," she said.

"I'll come over as soon as I'm back."

"Good." She paused. "I love you."

But he'd already hung up.

The house was hot and still and she was surprised because they had installed a generator just a few days ago to power the air conditioner. She walked back into the kitchen to ask Martin what had happened.

"I turned it off, madam."

"But why?"

"It is too dangerous, madam. My friend bought one and it blow up. His girl was alone in the house. She died."

Lindsay had heard such stories before. Most local people could only afford second- or thirdhand generators. But she'd bought an expensive new one after waiting her turn on a long list.

"Ours is safe, Martin. It is brand new and made by a good company."

Martin looked down skeptically; he spoke softly but resolutely.

"My children, madam, they are at home."

She understood. After Eduke's death, he wanted some control over his children's safety. He was willing to run the generator when the children were at school but not when they were home. She didn't feel she could force him. She sat in her hot living room, reading the paper.

She checked her watch. An hour and forty-five minutes had passed since she'd left Mike's, so he should be leaving for the hospital soon if he was going to check her story as he'd promised. She got in her car and drove to his house, parking half a block away. She left the car and hid behind some bushes where she had a clear view of his house.

She didn't have to wait long before she saw him walk down the driveway, climb into his car, and drive away. As soon as his car turned the corner, she approached his front door. Much to her surprise, it was locked. She went down an alleyway to the back, climbed over a low fence into his garden, and tried the glass door there. It slid open. Inside, she walked directly to the shelf where she had seen the ibeji. It wasn't there; she searched the room but didn't find it. She climbed the stairs and entered his study. Opening a filing cabinet, she found the statue lying facedown in the bottom drawer. It was an exact duplicate of the one she had found in the shed, but she noticed that it felt much heavier. She removed hers from her bag and held it in her right hand, comparing the weight. His weighed at least five pounds more.

After a minute, she put Mike's statue in her purse, replacing it with the lighter one she had found in the shed. She looked around to be sure she had left everything else the way she'd found it. She hesitated at the door—had it been open or closed? She decided on closed and then hastily made her exit. She drove home and walked purposefully into the kitchen, where she took out a hammer from her tool box. She placed some newspaper on the kitchen table and laid the statue on top of it. Then she swung the hammer down. The blow caused the statue to fly off the table, but aside from a few splinters, it remained intact. She replaced it on the table and swung again, this time holding it steady at the edge with her left hand. A crack appeared near the bottom and she could make out a seam that ran straight down the side. She swung again. This time the statue cracked wide open. A glassine bag of a white powdery substance was tucked into a hollow in the head. She stared at it for a long time.

If Mike Vale was the Solutions, Inc. operative, she had to tell Vickie right away. But then she remembered James had ordered the statues for export. She knew they had been stolen and had even mentioned as much to Vickie, but the agency might still believe he was implicated. She had to warn him. Maybe they could bring the evidence to the embassy together.

Waiting for James to stop by, her mind returned to Mike Vale. Solutions, Inc. had no ideology other than greed. He could have been paid by Olumide to get rid of William Agapo and then paid by the Northern Alliance to get rid of Fakai and finally Olumide. He'd been in Washington before he came to Lagos, and she couldn't figure out what use the Americans might have for him, unless he was working for them too. Her mind was racing.

She put the glassine bag back into the statue and swept up the splinters. She wrapped the statue in newspaper and as she was carefully placing the package into her bag, she looked up and saw Martin standing quietly in the doorway. She was furious with herself for not having told him to go home.

"Martin, I don't know how much you've seen, but you must forget it, do you understand?"

"I understand, madam. But I think you too must forget it. You must not follow it. You will be in much danger."

"We will both be in danger if this gets out. No one must know. I will take this to the American embassy."

"No, madam. Tell no one here. I think it is time for you to go home. Please."

"I can't, Martin. Not yet. Will you help me? Will you keep this secret?"

"I saw nothing. But that may not be enough to save you." He paused. "Or me either." He turned slowly and walked away. "I go for my break now, madam."

"Don't come back today, Martin," she called after him. "Take a few days off. Take your family and go to your village."

He turned slowly. "No, madam. I will stay here."

"Martin," she said firmly. "Don't make me fire you." Then her voice softened. "Don't you think that Pauline has suffered enough? Just for a few days. Come back next week."

Martin sighed but finally agreed. "I will go, madam. But please take care."

She would, but in case anything happened to her, she wrote down everything that had happened and all that she suspected. When she was done, she put the package and the pages in her safe. She wrote the combination to her safe on a piece of paper, put it in an envelope, and wrote Vickie's name on the front. She would deliver it to her at the embassy to ensure that the statue would be found. She walked to the intersection and hailed a taxi—she was too shaken to drive—and told the driver to take her to the American embassy. The go-slow was particularly bad and the heat stifling. The driver seemed unaccountably nervous. "No good stop heah . . ." he muttered, almost to himself. Soon a small group gathered, peering into the car. Sweating profusely, he reached over to make sure the doors were locked. Outside, a mob was growing. Lindsay became seriously alarmed when the crowd started to rock the car, yelling something in Yoruba.

Suddenly, someone smashed a brick through the window and an arm reached in, released the lock, yanked open the door, hauled out the driver and carried him away. Lindsay sat dumbfounded as the crowd dispersed as quickly as it had formed. She climbed out of the cab and noticed an old woman who had been watching from behind a stack of canned goods.

"What was that? What happened?"

"Ayah. He no pay his union dues."

Lindsay sighed. She scanned the street and saw another taxi pulled over on the side of the road, the driver asleep in the front seat. She woke him and told him she needed him to take her to the American embassy and then wait for her.

"I go take you, but you need buy petrol."

"If you don't have petrol it will take hours to wait at the station. I can't wait." She started looking for another cab.

"I got petrol."

"I thought you wanted me to buy it."

"From me. It take me half day-o. You go pay meter plus fifty naira for wait."

It was outrageous but she agreed. On the long hot ride, she tried to calm down. Once there, she got out, walked up to the marine guard, and handed him the envelope, telling him to be sure it was delivered to Vickie Grebow. Then she got back in the cab and steeled herself for the trip home. Now she'd have time to warn James before Vickie saw the statue, and if Mike or his cohorts hurt her, Vickie would know how to get into her safe.

She saw James's car in her driveway as the taxi pulled up and felt a surge of relief. She rushed into the house, flung her arms around him, and held him close. He pulled back, smiling uneasily.

"Hey, hold on. I was only gone for a few days."

"I know. I'm sorry, but wait until you hear what has happened."

She made him sit down. Then she told him about Mike, being kidnapped, and finding the statue in the shed. James took in the information about Mike with restraint. He just nodded, his mouth set tightly. When she finished, she asked him if he wanted to go to the embassy with her. He seemed to think about it for a long time.

"No," he said, finally. "I'll take care of this myself."

"But they might suspect you were involved."

"I wasn't, so I don't have to worry. I need to check with my supplier to see how many of the statues have disappeared. Can you hold off for a little?"

"No. I sent a note to Vickie. If I know her, she'll be here first thing in the morning, if not in the middle of the night."

He was quiet. "All right," he said. "Don't worry. I'll figure something out."

He bent down to kiss her and she pulled him closer. They had the house to themselves. He lay on the couch and she lay on top of him; a few minutes later they moved to the floor. He was less controlled, more passionate and impulsive in his lovemaking than ever before. For a little while her anxiety lifted. She almost felt happy.

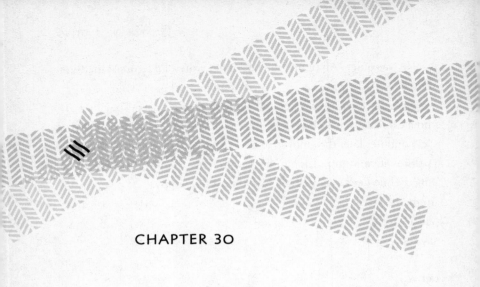

CHAPTER 30

Vickie didn't come over that night. She didn't appear the next morning either, and Lindsay slept late, waking up with a start at 8:30. She had to be at Mike's in half an hour. James had begged her not to keep the date. He thought it would be too dangerous. But Lindsay was determined to see this through and feared that Mike would be suspicious if she didn't turn up. Afterward, she planned to go straight to the embassy.

When she reached Mike's house, it was dark. Since no one answered, she tried the door and found it unlocked. Going in, she called Mike's name several times, but didn't get a response. She figured he was still asleep and decided to go upstairs to wake him. She knocked on his bedroom door and when he didn't answer, she barged right in.

"Hey, Mike, get up. We have a date, remember? It's past nine . . ."

She stopped suddenly. Mike was in bed lying on his back in a pool of blood. An ugly gash slashed his throat from ear to ear, the blood coagulated in a thick black band. Blood also stained the sheets and had dripped onto the floor near the bed in thick, rust-colored puddles. Mike's eyes were open, staring and glassy, as though surprised. She backed into the hallway, horrified. As she passed the spare bedroom, she heard a rustling sound. She froze. Her eyes glued to the door, she saw Billy Anikulo standing there, unshaven, dressed in wrinkled pants and a dirty shirt. She started to run down the stairs.

"Wait," he shouted. "It wasn't me. I couldn't stop them. I hid."

She charged out the front door and into her car and drove to the American embassy. After she told Vickie the whole story, Vickie picked up the phone and asked Dave Goren to join them. Goren entered and Vickie quickly brought him up to date. Before he could respond, Lindsay turned to Vickie.

"Why didn't you come to my house this morning? Didn't you wonder why I left you the combination to my safe?"

"What are you talking about?"

"I gave a letter to a marine at the gate and told him to get it to you."

"I never saw it. Anything hand delivered that isn't expected is sent to security first."

Dave Goren looked impatient. "Lindsay, we need to talk. First of all, we've got to pick up Anikulo. You say he's still at Vale's house?"

"He was when I left. I think Mike was the Solutions operative. Maybe Anikulo killed him."

"Was anyone else there? The steward?"

"No."

"Good. We can pick up Anikulo, clean up, and take the body without being seen. I'll make the arrangements." He walked out. Lindsay looked quizzically at Vickie, who was visibly upset.

"Okay. I'm going to try to fill you in," Vickie said. She got up and locked her door. "I'd appreciate it if you'd hear me out without interrupting. You can ask whatever questions you have after I'm done."

Lindsay nodded.

"Mike Vale was not the Solutions operative. He worked for us."

Shocked, Lindsay started to say something, but Vickie stopped her.

"Let me finish. Mike managed to get a lot of information about what's going on. The operative we're looking for works with the northerners. They're narco-terrorists. They bring in drugs from Colombia and Mexico and smuggle them to the Canary Islands and from there to Europe. They have ties to the new government and can operate with impunity. But Mike uncovered a second operation. Hired thugs are stealing important life-saving medicines from Lagos hospitals and sending them up north. The leader of the operation, who uses Solutions to pull it off, is a guy named Abdul Abdeka. He's becoming a major player in the new government. He sees himself as some kind of Robin Hood, but the Solutions operative who worked with him was only interested in the cash."

"What about Billy Anikulo?" Lindsay asked.

"Mike was offering him asylum in exchange for information. The new government is arresting all of Olumide's ministers."

"But what does he know?"

"He knows about Solutions, Inc. As I said, they work for cash and they work for anyone. They have no ideology and no loyalty. Olumide used them—probably for the Agapo killings among others—and Anikulo might know the name of the man on the ground here." Lindsay was silent, worrying about James.

"When did you find out that Mike had the statue?" Vickie asked.

"I saw it a while ago, but I only found out it was stuffed with drugs yesterday."

"Did you tell anybody?"

"No."

"Didn't you tell me James was exporting statues and that Mike had bought one from a trader?"

"I thought so, but I was mistaken."

"How?"

"It was a different statue, a different style."

"And are you sure you didn't mention anything to James?"

"James was in Kano. Remember, Vickie, I was worried that he hadn't called me."

Vickie looked skeptical. "So you didn't see James last night?"

"I'm beginning to feel like you're interrogating me, Vickie, and I don't like it."

Lindsay got up to leave. "James's statues were stolen. He had nothing to do with this."

"Maybe not. But we ought to talk to him."

"Do what you have to do, Vickie. I've got to go." She pushed past her and walked out the door.

She was scared. She had lied to protect James and even though she was certain he wasn't guilty, she knew it looked bad for him. If they learned she had told him about finding the drug-filled statue at Mike's house before she had evidence to clear him, he would be their prime suspect. She knew Vickie suspected she was lying, but Lindsay honestly believed the statues had been stolen from James. It could be anyone. Still, for the moment, she decided not to tell James anything more. Just in case.

It occurred to her that J.R. had been amassing information about the Northern Alliance. Maybe he had some useful intelligence about the possible thief.

She walked to her car, climbed in, and started the slow hot drive to J.R.'s house. She let her mind wander and, resisting at first, eventually allowed herself to consider a possibility that had been lurking for some time, one she had been reluctant to examine: James might actually be guilty. She had told him about Mike and the drugs, after all, and Mike lay dead less than twelve hours later. The thought upset her and she shook it off. She made a sharp left turn onto J.R.'s street.

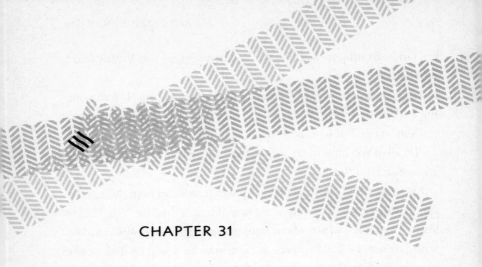

CHAPTER 31

The first thing she noticed was an army van parked in front of J.R.'s house and three soldiers standing guard. The sight unnerved her. As she drove closer she noted that the shades were drawn. She wondered if she should leave, but the decision was taken from her when one of the soldiers started to walk toward her.

"What you want?" he asked.

Lindsay pulled out her press credential, given, she realized after she showed it, by the overthrown government. But that didn't seem to matter. The soldier was predictably impressed by the officially stamped document. He lowered his rifle slightly.

"This place off-limits," he said. "Government order."

"But where is the family?"

"No family here," the soldier answered. "This rebel cell. Terrorists."

"But there was a family who lived here. J.R. and his wife and children. Can you tell me where I can find them?"

"No."

"Well, is that because you don't know or because you can't say?"

The soldier was losing his patience.

"Nobody here. Nobody go be here. You not allow here. Go." He stepped forward, shouldering her back.

"Could I speak to your supervisor?" asked Lindsay.

The soldier walked away, sulking, and after a few minutes, an officer walked over. "You wanted to speak to me?"

"Yes," Lindsay said. "I'm a journalist. From America. I need some information."

"I'm sorry; you will have to go to the ministry for that. We are not permitted to talk to the press."

She didn't know what instinct prompted her, but she blurted out, "I think you can talk to me. I was sent by Abdul Abdeka."

"I received no order about this," he said nervously.

"I think your commanding officer must have," she said, counting on the officer's fear of making a mistake. "Mr. Abdeka wanted me to write a story detailing how the new government controlled the violence," she bluffed. The officer didn't respond. "Of course, if you'd rather I didn't, I can leave and tell him I tried. Could you tell me your name?"

The officer hesitated.

"You will wait," he said, finally, walking away.

"Of course. Thank you."

Lindsay knew this could end badly and wondered who he was consulting with. A small boy from a neighboring house ran in front of her, chased by his mother, who caught him by the arm. Lindsay stopped her.

"Please," she said. "I'm looking for J.R. and his family. Do you know where they are?"

The woman glanced apprehensively at the soldiers standing nearby.

"You tell dem I don' know you," the woman said anxiously.

Lindsay nodded. "But J.R.? Where is he?"

"J.R. be dead. He be shot right here."

Lindsay closed her eyes.

"Who shot him?" she asked.

"Who you tink? Dey." She gestured with her head toward the soldiers.

"And his family? His wife? His children?"

"Don' know. Dey take dem way in Black Maria car."

The woman noticed the soldiers were watching her. "You go now. Don' come here more."

She picked up her son and walked quickly away.

J.R. was dead—what a goddamned tragedy. In spite of everything that had happened, she could hardly believe it. She started to walk toward her car. Before she reached it, the officer approached her respectfully.

"I've checked, madam. My senior officer hadn't received the order, but if you have cleared it with Mr. Abdeka then, of course, I am authorized to talk to you."

"Good," she said carefully. "As I said, he told me to report on the progress of the new government in controlling the opposition. Can I have a look inside?"

The soldier hesitated. "I have orders not to let anyone in."

"But I need to see for myself. Maybe you should ask again."

He looked uncomfortable. "No," he said. "Go inside, but be quick."

He stood in the doorway and allowed her to inspect the room.

It was in shambles. Drawers were emptied on the floor, an opened can of Carnation condensed milk had been thrown off a table, its thick, sticky contents mixed with papers and files that had been tossed in all directions. Lindsay walked into the back room where she had talked to J.R. and his colleagues, peeking into the bedroom where the children had slept. She saw blood stains on the wall near the bed and, unwillingly drawn toward it, she approached. On the bed was the family dog, a black and white mongrel, shot dead. At first she felt a wave of relief that it was not the children's blood, but when she bent down and saw the dog's mottled fur she gasped and struggled to control herself, choking back her tears. Then she walked out of the room.

"When did this happen?"

"Yesterday, madam. During the rebellion."

"What rebellion?"

"There was a terrorist rebellion against the new government," the officer said. "The group they called The Next Step."

Ah, Lindsay thought, this is how this massacre will be explained.

"But where are the residents?" she asked.

"I don't know."

"I know that J.R. is dead," she answered, trying to encourage the soldier to confirm it. "He was killed by soldiers defending the government, is that right?"

The officer sounded relieved. "Yes," he answered, "the terrorist known as J.R. was killed in the gun battle. We arrested his family and they have been taken to preventive detention."

"The children too?"

"They are with their mother. They have been sent to their home village."

"Do you know where that is?"

"No."

"And J.R. was firing at you?"

"From this room. Near the bed."

Lindsay walked down the hallway. There were no bullet holes in the walls, no evidence of shots fired from the room, only shots into the room. But she knew enough about Africa to know that you don't contradict the soldier with the gun.

"And the dog? Why did you kill the dog?"

Her composure was threatening to give way again. The dog, the only physical evidence that remained of the murder, had become a symbol of the utter madness of the whole business.

The officer shrugged. "It got in the way."

He walked out to his men and left Lindsay alone. She stepped into the sitting room, where she had once sipped orange Fanta and listened to J.R. explain Nigerian politics, where she had met his friends and heard their brave vision for their country's future. Sitting on the worn armchair, she knew that the depth of her grief went beyond the current tragedy. She was grieving for the agony of the country, the everyday brutality of life here.

She knew she had to get to J.R.'s village to find his wife and children. Acting as though she were in a rush, she mouthed a thank-you to the officer and walked directly to her car. The man looked after her, probably glad she was going to relieve him of any decision. Aware she had cut this much too close, she drove away.

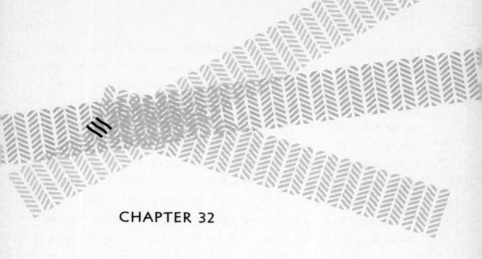

CHAPTER 32

Back home, Lindsay flipped through her notebooks until she found the name of the village. It was on the outskirts of Badagry, a few miles from the Nigeria-Benin border.

She locked the notebooks in the cabinet and carefully zipped the key into a side pocket of her purse. Feeling hungry, she found some eggs and made herself an omelet. Just as she finished, the lights went out and the air-conditioning shut down. The generator was supposed to kick in during blackouts, but she remembered that Martin had turned it off. She lit a candle and went to the basement where she fumbled around until she found the switch. When she pressed it, nothing happened.

"We must be out of propane," she thought, irritably. She looked around for a canister, but didn't see one. Upstairs in her study, she sat at her desk, lit a candle, and wrote a piece about J.R.'s death on an old Olivetti manual typewriter, a necessary tool for any reporter in Nigeria. If they wanted to expel her once it appeared, so be it. Her phone line was still working, so she called New York and read the piece to the recording room. Then, exhausted, she washed up and climbed into bed. But it was too hot to sleep, so she withdrew a pad and pencil from the drawer. She listed everything she knew about Solutions, Inc. and everything she had observed or discovered about James. On another page, she wrote down everything that Vickie had told her. Then she put the pad aside and lay on her back, staring at the ceiling. Tomorrow, she thought, a heavy rain would bring relief.

The next morning she was up early. Still no rain, and the air was so thick it was hard to breathe. She made herself a sandwich, filled a large thermos with filtered water, and took some cash from her safe.

The Lagos-Badagry Expressway was notoriously dangerous. Bandits often robbed and killed drivers, sometimes leaving their bodies on the roadside with their arms propped up as if to wave at passersby. Shortly before the coup, a newspaper article detailed a horrendous case of an ambushed bus—everyone on it had been hacked to death with machetes. The case had heightened outrage against the Olumide regime.

Lindsay found the road littered with potholes. A car ahead of her suddenly bucked as it hit a deep hole at too high a speed and then stopped, its wheels stuck. The driver gunned the motor, but the car didn't move. Lindsay hit the brake and turned the wheel, just avoiding a collision. A few miles after leaving Lagos, she came to a blockade. Two small fires burned on both sides of a makeshift booth. About ten cars had come to a standstill in front of it. She stopped, waiting her turn. When she reached the booth, a soldier demanded her passport. He looked at it for an exasperatingly long time before she realized what he was waiting for. She handed him fifty naira, at which point he returned her passport and waved her on. Similar checkpoints materialized every five miles, and she knew that the sooner she handed over the money, the faster she'd be on her way.

Eventually, she saw the sign for Badagry. She drove through the town and into the bush on roads that skirted dense rainforest. Soon she saw a cluster of mud houses with palm frond roofs and a few larger homes topped with tin. Chickens wandered freely pecking in the dirt, and toddlers, some of them wearing only a bead necklace, played next to them. A girl of about six swept one of the yards with a straw broom, a baby strapped to her back. She stopped and stared as Lindsay approached.

"Hi."

The girl smiled shyly and looked down. Lindsay reached into her purse and offered her a peppermint, which she accepted quickly. Four more children ran over and Lindsay managed to dig out and distribute several more pieces of candy. One of the boys carried a toy car made of elaborately strung and twisted strands of steel wire. "That's beautiful," Lindsay said. The boy didn't answer, but proceeded to show her how it worked, kneeling and placing it on the ground and pushing it forward on its rubber wheels. "Did you make that?" Lindsay asked. The boy shrugged and nodded proudly.

Lindsay asked them if they knew Margaret, but the children looked confused and she realized that she didn't know Margaret's last name. But J.R. was well known, so she asked if they knew who he was. This time they looked scared and the older ones ran away.

"I'm Margaret's friend," she said. But the little ones just stared at her. A man came over and asked why she was there and she explained that she was a journalist, a friend of J.R.'s.

"I heard what happened to him," she said. "I've come to pay my respects to his family."

The man hesitated. "Wait here," he said, at last.

She moved to the shade of a nearby walnut tree. More children surrounded her, begging for candy, but she had run out.

She heard a voice behind her speak harshly in Yoruba and the children scattered. Lindsay turned and saw Margaret.

"Margaret, I just heard. I am so sorry. Are you all right?"

"Yes. We are safe here." She led Lindsay to one of the round mud houses. It was surprisingly cool. Lindsay sat on a mat on the floor and Margaret offered her a beer and then sat down next to her.

"Now tell me," Margaret said. "Why did you come?"

"I wanted to tell you how sorry I am for your loss," she said. "But, I also came to ask something of you."

"If I can help you, I will," Margaret said softly.

Lindsay told her about the statues and the murder of Mike Vale. Finally, she confided her suspicions. Lowering her voice to a whisper, she said, "J.R. told me before the coup that he had heard rumors of a shady foreign organization that helped the northern radicals organize the coup. I was hoping that he had told you something more. Did he ever mention James, for instance?"

Margaret looked thoughtful. "No. I never heard names. But I have something that might be useful." She got up and fetched a carton from the far side of the room. "After Bayo was killed, J.R. persuaded me to take the children and come here," she said carefully, in flawless English. "He gave me this for safekeeping. I haven't even looked at it. If he had kept out of this, his children would still have their father. But he was a good man. I could not persuade him to stand back."

Lindsay thanked her and opened the box. It was filled with photographs, memos, and newspaper clippings. She glanced quickly through the written material but couldn't make much sense of it: names she had never heard of, memos from people she didn't know. She skimmed the reports for any evidence that James had been involved but found nothing, so she turned to the photographs. She rifled through them but recognized no one.

She asked Margaret if she could take the carton with her.

"Yes. Keep it. I don't ever want to see it again."

"Maybe there are still friends of J.R. who would want it."

Margaret gave a weary sigh. "They are all dead or in jail." She got up and walked outside, making it clear it was time for Lindsay to go.

Lindsay drove even more slowly on the way back, fearing that she might hit one of the potholes and damage her car, or worse, expose her cargo. At the checkpoints, she was polite and generous knowing that she was walking a thin line. If she gave too little, it would be resented as stingy. If she gave too much, she would probably be robbed. At one roadblock, she saw a man bleeding on the ground while his family stared, frightened.

The two-hour trip took her close to four, but she managed to get home without mishap. She carried the carton up to her bedroom and locked the door. Then she sat on the floor and went through it, item by item. She couldn't make much sense of the written material, though it was clear that The Next Step had an informant up north. She pulled out the stack of photographs. She still recognized no one. Her eyes were getting bleary and she felt discouraged, but she kept going. Toward the end of the stack, a small color snapshot grabbed her attention. She saw three men. Two of them were dressed in the elegant long white robes of the north. The third wore a stylish beige tailored jacket, a striped shirt with a white collar that looked like it was made by Turnbull & Asser, and neat brown slacks. He was carrying a black cane. When she looked closely, she could see that the cane's white handle was carved in the shape of a dragon's head. Lindsay had no doubt—this was the man she'd seen James talking to in Oshogbo. The picture had a piece of paper attached to it with a pin. An arrow pointed to the man in Western dress, identifying him. "Abdul Abdeka," it said.

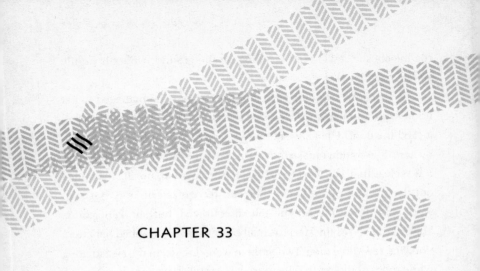

CHAPTER 33

The next day, Lindsay brought the carton to the embassy. Vickie plopped it on her office table and the two women pored over the contents. Vickie scrutinized the picture of Abdul Abdeka.

"I'd like to know who took this," she said. "And how it came to J.R."

"I'm guessing it was taken by someone undercover for The Next Step," Lindsay said carefully.

Vickie looked up sharply.

"I think the picture might have been taken by James," Lindsay said.

"I don't think so," Vickie said abruptly.

"Why not?" Lindsay challenged.

"Because I think it's more likely that James was less innocently involved."

Lindsay stiffened. "What are you saying, Vickie?"

Vickie sighed and reached for Lindsay's hand. "I think you know what I'm going to say."

Lindsay pulled away. "Stop playing games, Vickie. Tell me what you want me to know."

"There's no way to say this gently. It's James. He isn't who you think he is."

"You have no idea who I think he is."

"Do you know, for example," Vickie said evenly, "that his art gallery is a cover for discreet mercenary activity?"

"What do you mean by 'discreet mercenary activity'? Are you saying he's an assassin?"

"Not directly. But he hires the people who are."

"And how do you know this?"

"Because he's worked for us on occasion."

Lindsay stared at her.

"I'm sorry. I wasn't authorized to tell you."

Lindsay felt a jolt of hope. "Is he working for you now?"

"No. He worked with us to bolster Olumide, but this time, he acted as a double agent. We believe the Northern Alliance employed Solutions, which must have paid him a lot of money to double-cross us. We think this means he's getting ready to retire and he wanted a big cash-out. The pension plan for mercenary assassins isn't what it used to be."

Lindsay was taken aback by Vickie's contempt for James.

"You despise him," she said coldly. She felt surprisingly calm, almost detached. "But you admit you've worked with him, he's done some dirty work for you. You just don't like it when he does it for someone else. How dare you pose as a moralist. Why are you any better than he is?"

Vickie started to answer, but Lindsay cut her off. "Oh, you're going to tell me you do it for your country, but that really means you do it for the oil companies, doesn't it? You're government mercenaries instead of individual ones, that's all. You don't care how corrupt these governments are as long as you have oil rights. You don't care how many people smuggle heroin as long as it's not to the U.S. Maybe James got tired of seeing the locals screwed. Maybe he thought this new government would be better for the country. Maybe he got fed up with your hypocrisy."

Vickie withstood the onslaught until it ended. When she spoke, her voice was soft but firm. "People who are in love can invent anything, Lindsay—including the person they love. You can make him into anything you want in your imagination, but you're a journalist and you know better. The only thing his group stands for is greed, death, and deceit. The leaders of the Northern Alliance lied to their own people to get their cooperation. They financed their movement with drug sales and now they will continue to line their own pockets in the same way. He doesn't care, Lindsay. He is a truly amoral man. We work with people like him because fighting terrorism and drug smuggling is a dirty business, and the people who help us in that struggle are usually not the nicest people in the world, but that's who we need to work with to keep the rest of us safe."

Lindsay was tired and confused.

"What do you want me to do?"

"We need your help. He trusts you."

Lindsay was silent.

"Look, he killed Maureen. We recognized his signature on the bomb."

Lindsay whirled around. "Now you've gone too far. He would never have killed Maureen. He cared about her and her husband. What motive would he have?"

"I don't think he did it deliberately. I think he planned the bombing but he didn't expect Maureen to get there so early. She was the only journalist killed." Vickie paused. "Why didn't you come with her, by the way?"

Doubt crossed Lindsay's face.

"I was held up," she said softly.

"Where?"

Lindsay hesitated.

"At home." She resisted saying it, resisted thinking it, a cherished memory suddenly seen in a terrible new context. "James came over. I was taking a shower. He walked into my bedroom. We started to make love—"

"And it delayed you."

"Yes. It saved my life."

"I think he delayed you on purpose." She paused a moment. "At least you have that."

Lindsay still wasn't sure. She had to give him a chance to answer these charges. Surely she owed him that.

"I think I should go now, Vickie. I can't think straight. If what you say is true, I'll want to get out of the country as soon as I can. I certainly don't want to get involved in spying on him for you, if that's what you have in mind. If it isn't true—and I still hope to prove it isn't—then obviously I'm going to fight you as hard as I can."

Vickie reached into her briefcase, withdrew some papers, and tossed them on the table.

"You might want to take a look at these. They track the pharmaceutical shipments to Lagos Hospital. You can see how much quinine, antibiotics, morphine, and paregoric were ordered and paid for and then what they received."

Lindsay bent forward to see the figures.

Vickie continued. "The hospital received only a third of what they paid for."

"What has that got to do with James?"

"It's all handled by Solutions, Inc. They arrange for the drugs to be stolen and diverted to the northern hospitals."

Lindsay looked at the figures. One of the expected deliveries, a shipment of quinine, morphine, and paregoric, was scheduled for receipt four days before Eduke died.

She sat down heavily. She didn't want to hear any more.

"You're proving that Solutions, Inc. is evil," Lindsay said sullenly. "You haven't proved that James works for them."

"He's responsible, Lindsay. He's responsible for Maureen's death and he's responsible for Eduke's death. And who knows how many more if you don't help us stop him."

All business now, Vickie began to explain what she wanted Lindsay to do. The Americans needed to know when James planned to leave and where he was going. They needed the distribution list showing how the drugs are smuggled out and to whom they are delivered. U.S. agents couldn't pick James up in Lagos, she explained, because he was protected by the new Nigerian government. They needed to arrest him in a friendly country. And James must not suspect that the Americans knew about his double cross.

Lindsay listened in a kind of dazed disbelief. Vickie removed a small glass vial from her drawer and placed it on the desk. "If you decide to help us, you may need this. Three drops will put him to sleep for two to three hours. You could slip into his apartment at the Victoria and look through his papers."

"Why don't you just get one of your guys to break in?"

"We can't risk being connected to this."

"Jesus, what next? You want me to wear a wire?"

"It may come to that."

"I'm afraid our relationship isn't chaste enough to get away with that anymore. I'm leaving, Vickie. You can keep your magic drops. I don't want them."

"I'm sorry, Lindsay. I am really so sorry. But I think when you've had time to assimilate this you'll be back in touch. Please, at least agree not to tell him about this conversation. Even if you won't help us, don't help him escape."

Lindsay got into her car and drove home. She had a headache and rooted around in her bag for her aspirin. She couldn't find them. Instead, near the bottom, she found the bottle of drops, right where Vickie must have placed it.

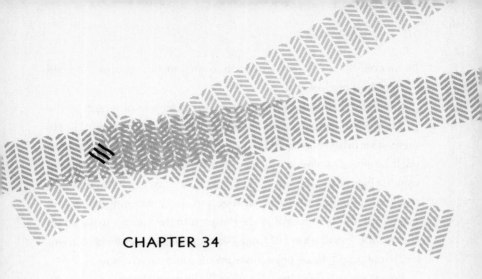

CHAPTER 34

By the time Lindsay got home, a torrential rain had begun. She was aware that the case against James was mostly circumstantial, but she found it hard to still believe in him. She hadn't seen James since she'd told him about the drugs in Mike's statue. He had dropped off a note saying he'd arrive at around 4 P.M.—"happy hour"—a custom that had survived in the former colonies long after independence.

He arrived a few minutes late, dripping wet. Grinning, he shook himself off and headed for the kitchen, where he fetched a dish towel and dried his face and hair. He was wearing a lightweight khaki safari suit and had a day's growth of beard—an effect Lindsay had always found particularly attractive. Looking at him, she found it nearly impossible to believe this man who stirred her so deeply was the same person Vickie had described.

His face lit up when he saw her, and he pulled her into a strong embrace, his wet clothes cooling her body. She responded involuntarily, at the same time, wondering if his greeting was part of an act and if he tailored his method of seduction to each victim. Victim? She had to stop thinking like that.

She didn't want him to notice that anything was different, so she gently pushed him away on the pretext of telling him about J.R. He seemed surprised and sorry, but not really distressed, and she couldn't tell if he already knew. His reaction intensified her suspicions and she couldn't help stiffening when he sat next to her. She began to talk about trivialities, jumped up to get drinks, and then, changing her mind, asked him to mix them while she darted into the kitchen to get some cheese. She was in a kind of frenzy, as though her heightened activity had some prophylactic power to ward off more catastrophe.

"What are you drinking?" he asked, as he poured himself a scotch.

"I guess I'll have a scotch too," she said. "With soda, and make it light."

She sat on the couch and sipped the drink, which was very strong. Then she got up again and moved to the chair across from him.

"Lindsay, what's wrong?"

"Everything, James. I'm having trouble dealing with everything that's happened."

He didn't answer for a few seconds. Then he patted the seat next to him invitingly.

"Why are you trying to do it alone? Let me help you."

Lindsay didn't move. "I'm just so upset," she said. "Everything's happened so fast I haven't had time to process it. I think I need a little time to myself. Do you mind?"

He said no, he was exhausted too. He would go back to his hotel and return later to take her out for dinner.

"See you later," he said.

She nodded and squeezed his hand.

After he was gone, Lindsay tried to figure out her next move. She knew she needed proof, either to clear or convict him.

She decided to go to his apartment to look around. But how? It was nearly five and he would be back at eight. Maybe she should surprise him, show up at his place. She'd never done that before, and he'd made it clear he liked to keep his hotel apartment exclusively for business meetings, but she could say she was disturbed by their visit. That would explain her strange mood and allay his suspicions.

She walked into her garden to collect herself. She stood on the stone patio under the roof's overhang, watching as the torrential rain flooded the cobbled pathways. Impulsively, she walked into the center of the garden and let the water pour over her, plaster her hair into her eyes, smash her clothes against her body. After a few minutes, she went back inside, leaving puddles wherever she stepped, and climbed the stairs to her bedroom to change.

She drove to Victoria Island, pulled up at the hotel, walked past the front desk, bypassed the elevator, and climbed the stairs to the sixth floor. She knocked on James's door and waited, but there was no answer. She could hear the air-conditioning unit and someone moving inside.

"James, it's Lindsay. Please open up. I really have to talk to you."

She could hear water running. She knocked again.

"I'll be right there. Hang on."

The water stopped and a few minutes later James opened the door. He was naked, except for a towel wrapped around his waist. He looked alarmed.

"Are you all right? What's happened?"

Lindsay knew that barging in saying she was worried about their relationship would strike him as foolish but would be effective. He would put it down to "woman behavior," which meant, in his view, emotional, irrational, insecure, and needy.

"James, I have to talk to you, now, while I have the courage to say it." He looked puzzled.

"Come in," he said. "What's happened?"

"Nothing new," Lindsay said. "I'm just shaken by everything that's happened and everything that hasn't happened. I feel so alone. And I started thinking that I always am alone, even when I'm with you. These last awful days, you didn't even call."

"Call? You know how difficult that is. I didn't think you'd expect it."

"Well, maybe it's my fault if you don't think I expect anything, because I do."

James looked irritated.

"Maybe you ought to tell me what's really bothering you," he said, leading her into his sitting room. "But give me a minute, will you?"

She sat on the couch to wait for him. Oh, if only she could tell him what was really bothering her. If only she could be sure that he would erase her doubts with the truth.

She noticed his khaki safari jacket thrown over a chair. She got up and went through the pockets. She found a gum wrapper, a cough drop, and a crumpled piece of paper. She opened it and saw a handwritten receipt for N270,000, marked paid from an airline she'd never heard of named "Fly Right." No destination was listed, but the flight was scheduled to leave in three days. She quickly slipped the receipt back into his pocket and was about to sit down when he walked back in.

"I can't sit down, I'm too nervous," she said. "I'll probably be expelled from here in a few days."

"Why?"

"I filed a story about J.R.'s murder."

"I thought you said you wouldn't file anything until after you left?" His voice was cold.

"I did. But I can't let J.R. disappear without anyone being held to account. If they want to expel me from the country, I'm ready to go."

James didn't answer.

"I was also thinking, given the political situation, you'll probably be leaving soon too."

When he nodded, she said, "Well, do you know when you'll be leaving yet?"

"No," he said. "I still have some work to do here. But I think I'll probably go in a few weeks."

She didn't respond.

"Our leaving won't make any difference between us, you know. Is that what you've been worrying about?"

"Well, yes," she said, nervously. He strode over and pulled her to her feet.

"I love you, Lindsay, don't you know that? It will be easier once we leave." He took her in his arms. "I know we need to talk," he said, "and you'll want to make plans for the future. But we don't need to make them right this minute, do we? I thought we'd talk about it later, over dinner."

Only a day ago, those words would have made her very happy. Now they weren't important anymore, not if her suspicions were true.

"You're right," she said, "I'm sorry. We can talk later."

They moved to the couch and he started to unbutton her blouse. "So," he said, "if we're not going to talk, I wonder if we can think of anything else we can do."

He was going to make love to her and, in spite of everything, she wanted him to.

CHAPTER 35

It dismayed Lindsay that she could make love to him, and mean it, while plotting to deceive him. She had climbed onto his lap, straddling him, deliberately teasing and arousing him. She felt his body stir under her as she pressed against him.

She was more excited than she had ever been. For the first time she was taking what she wanted from him, not worried about what he wanted. But she realized too that the other aphrodisiac was the deception itself. It was exciting. It was dangerous. This is what he feels, she realized. This is how he lives. It had taken this for her to understand something deep and distasteful about him—and about herself.

When they finished and he got up to go to the bathroom, she walked directly to the door, releasing the button on the knob to ensure that it didn't automatically lock when closed. Then she dressed and waited for him to return.

"I'm starving," she said, when he appeared.

"Sex always makes you hungry," he smiled. "Like dope."

She grabbed his hand and pulled him toward the door. "Who you callin' a dope?"

He rolled his eyes indulgently.

Just as he was closing the door, he automatically jiggled the handle to be sure the door was locked, and when he found that it wasn't, a puzzled look crossed his face, but he simply pressed the button to set the lock. He dropped his keys in his pocket as they walked to the elevator.

"Where do you want to dine, madam?" he asked.

"Let's go back to my place," Lindsay said. "We'll eat, we'll drink . . ."

"And be merry?" he finished.

"I'm always merry when I'm with you."

"Not true. But well said."

Lindsay arrived home first, and went to the kitchen to see what she could cook, but when James arrived a few minutes later, she met him at the door saying, "New plan. Let's get some Chinese food and bring it home. Martin's taking a few days off and I don't have any food in the fridge."

It was odd, she reflected, that the circumstances that should have poisoned their relationship heightened the electricity between them.

They stopped at the Chinese restaurant, ordered shrimp and lobster sauce and chicken with snow peas, and brought the meal back to Lindsay's place. Asking him to choose the music while she laid out the food, she went into the kitchen. She took a bottle of Chardonnay from the fridge and poured the drinks. Then, as if it were the most natural thing in the world, she opened the spice cabinet and reached for the bottle she had hidden there. Glancing over her shoulder, she put three drops into James's glass.

He had chosen one of her favorite songs—Otis Redding:

I've been loving you
A little too long . . .

"Good choice," she said, carefully carrying his glass and a plate heaped with Chinese food to the dining table and putting it in front of him before returning to the kitchen for her own plate. She placed her food and wine on the table, sat down, and lifted her glass for a toast.

Lindsay had never done anything like this before but she knew everything that might go wrong. "To us," she said, taking a long sip of wine.

"To us," James repeated. He raised the glass to his lips and drank.

She suddenly felt scared. She didn't know how long it would take for the drug to work or how much he had to drink for it to be effective. She wasn't even sure what to do if he actually passed out. Right now he was showing no signs of slowing down. Maybe she hadn't put in enough drops. In any case, the important thing was to keep talking, to keep the conversation going, keep him believing nothing had changed.

"I'm worried about J.R.'s family," she said. "The police said they were back in their home village, but they could be lying. I should try to see them."

"The police had no reason to lie. It was him they wanted. Now that he's dead, his family is no use to them."

James finished his wine and poured himself another glass. Lindsay wondered if she should try to add more drops, but decided she couldn't pull it off.

"You're probably right," she answered. "It's weird, you know. J.R. is dead. His home is wrecked, his family has disappeared, and I have fixated on a dead dog. I can't get it out of my mind. I keep tearing up when I think about it."

"I know what you mean," James said. His eyes looked tired, suddenly heavy, and his words slurred. He started to get up, but rose only halfway and then sat down again heavily.

"Whoa," Lindsay said. "I guess you had a bit too much wine."

"I didn't think so," James answered groggily. "I hope I didn't pick up some . . ."

He stopped mid-sentence and pitched forward, his head on the table, out cold.

Lindsay called his name, softly at first, then louder. When he didn't respond, she slipped her hand in his pocket and took his key. Vickie had said she had two, maybe three hours. She'd better count on two.

Traffic was unaccountably light, and she arrived at James's hotel in less than fifteen minutes. She entered the lobby, looking around quickly to be sure she didn't see anyone who knew her, skirted the front desk and the elevator, and climbed the stairs. When she reached his floor, she saw a group of businessmen emerging from the elevator. She darted back into the stairwell until the coast was clear. At James's door she pulled out the keys. She tried a few before finding the right one. But there were two locks and she had to repeat the process. Finally, she opened the door and slipped inside.

She checked her watch, determined not to spend more than an hour searching the suite. Vickie had said she wanted papers, lists of contacts in Europe, maybe a ticket that specified his destination. He'd had this suite reconstructed to his own specifications. Would he feel safe enough here to just keep everything in his desk? She walked over and opened the drawer. Inside was a neat arrangement of pens, stationery, envelopes, and an engagement calendar. She leafed through the date book and saw a record of his buying trips to Ibadan, his Oshogbo purchases, his lunch and dinner dates, including those with her. She closed the book and put it back in the drawer. Across the room was a chest of drawers and, next to that, a bookshelf unit with four drawers. She noticed a cup that said CIA across its top. Below the first line, **SPECIAL AGINT** was written and crossed out. Below that, **SECRIT OPERATIVE**— also crossed out. And finally, in all capital letters, the word **SPY**. She could imagine him thinking that was funny. She pulled open the drawers, one at a time, and carefully looked through each. They were all neatly organized and sparsely filled, so it was easy to see what was in them. In the top one, she found another set of keys, loose change, a cigarette lighter, a Mark Cross fountain pen still in its black leather box, and a Swiss Army pocketknife. She held the keys next to the ones she took from his pocket and satisfied herself that they were copies. In the next drawer was a neat pile of leather-bound pocket diaries, each marked with the name of a different country: Spain, Italy, England, U.S. She rifled through them and found what appeared to be client lists and orders from each country. But there was no way to tell who the people were. Besides, she couldn't take the books with her and she had no time to copy them. She jotted down some of the names and numbers and then moved on. The other drawers contained more notebooks, a box of candles, spare batteries, tubes of toothpaste, and cans of shaving cream, all packed away so neatly that it unnerved her. It was almost as though he didn't really live here.

It was getting late and she still hadn't checked out the bedroom. She moved to the bookcase and started going through the drawers under it. The first drawer was full of neatly stacked shirts, still in their cellophane wrappers. The second drawer was hard to open; it seemed to be off its track and she had to jiggle it out. There were more client files but she decided to skip them. As she tried to close it, the drawer fell off its track completely. She reached her hand in to lift the drawer back and felt a small lever. She pulled it.

A book on the shelf above trembled and then fell off, revealing a small trapdoor that had swung open. Behind the door was a cabinet about the size of a small safe. Excited, she reached up and inserted her hand, withdrawing the items one by one.

When she found the money, she gasped. She removed stacks and stacks of hundred-dollar bills. Her heart sank as her last hope for his innocence faded. Behind the cash she found a folder. Leafing through it, she scanned a note from Roxanne Reinstadler, decorated with an ink drawing of one of her sculptures. "Special Order," it said. "Hollow Oshogbo dolls for immediate delivery 8/16." Behind Roxanne's note was a receipt from "Fly Right: African Airlines: private flights." It was stamped 8/17 and confirmed a flight and delivery of freight from Kaduna airport to Paris. She pulled out another receipt for carrying freight from Oshogbo to Kaduna. On the bottom were some numbers jotted in James's handwriting. It looked like he was figuring out costs. They were very high.

Folded into an envelope was a list of names, addresses, and phone numbers in Paris, London, and New York. Many were Russian, and next to each, someone had jotted down what Lindsay assumed was the territory of the person receiving the shipment as well as the price for each delivery: "Maxim Stepanovich, 50 kilo. New York. Payment on delivery." Payments were each in the hundreds of thousands of dollars. This was about drugs, Lindsay realized, her heart sinking; this was his contact sheet for the drug cartel. Last, she found a leather case containing several passports under different names and photos: James with a mustache, James with his head shaved, James with blond hair and glasses, as well as one as she knew him. Tucked inside were two tickets to Paris on a Fly Right charter leaving from a small airport outside Lagos in three days' time. Attached to the tickets was a copy of the receipt she had found in his jacket pocket.

She swallowed hard as the pieces fell into place. The statues at Roxanne's, that's where he stashed the drugs. What a perfect foil— delivering African art for sale in the West. Mike must have been on to them—that's why he held one of the contraband statues. But she was confused by having found the carton of statues in the shed used by Olumide's thugs. If Olumide was involved, why was James dealing with Abdul Abdeka, Olumide's enemy? Was he a double agent, working for both of them? The two tickets to Paris simply said "one-way passage to Paris," and she wondered who was going with him. She pulled out her notebook and copied as much information as she could before realizing that an hour and a quarter had passed since she'd left James. She wrote faster, gripping her pen so tightly that her third finger hurt and she could see a small indentation where the pen pressed tightly against it.

She carefully put everything back in the safe, closed it, and put the drawer back in place, taking care to leave it slightly off-track as before.

Then, as she was replacing the fallen book, she heard a murmur outside the door followed by a knock. She didn't move, tried not to breathe.

"James, open the door," said a man urgently. "We need to talk." The accent was British, but tinged with the musical lilt of an Oxbridge-educated Nigerian.

"Let's open up and let us wait for him inside," said another voice.

Lindsay froze. She looked around for a hiding place, her eyes darting from the closet to the bedroom. Someone was fiddling with the doorknob.

"I'm sorry, sir," said a third voice. "Mr. Duncan doesn't allow anyone else to hold his key. Perhaps you can wait downstairs."

More mumbling, and then footsteps receded down the hall. Lindsay waited a few more minutes, knowing she had to leave quickly. She cautiously cracked the door open and peered out. No one. She stepped into the hall, closing the door and making sure it was locked. She darted down the stairs and hurried into the parking lot.

The traffic was moving slowly, but it was not at a standstill. Thinking she'd get home with time to spare, Lindsay crossed the bridge onto Ikoyi only to be forced to stop by a massive go-slow. She got out of her car to peer down the line of cars, but saw nothing to explain the sudden traffic jam. She sat at the wheel, checking her watch every minute or so, desperately trying to think of what to say to James if he were awake when she got home. Finally, she pulled over and drove on the shoulder—a violation punished by a police whipping in Lagos. She drove freely for about half a mile until she saw a police car ahead of her and signaled one of the cars to let her back in line. Luckily, a woman complied and Lindsay avoided being seen by the authorities. Gratefully, she waved at the woman, who waved back. The police were letting the cars through a makeshift barricade, checking identity cards. Almost two hours had passed since James fell asleep when finally her turn came. She nervously showed her passport, unsure whether or not to offer a dash. This time a bribe wasn't necessary. The officer abruptly waved her on. The road cleared and she stepped on the gas.

James was still asleep when she tiptoed in. Greatly relieved, Lindsay gently put his keys back in his pocket. He stirred and she withdrew her hand as if burned. She bent down and tentatively kissed his cheek to see if there was any reaction. Nothing. He sank back down into a deep sleep.

She poured herself a scotch, her hand shaking. Then, quietly, she opened her filing cabinet and placed the notes in the file titled "J.R. GOVT. OPPOSITION." As she locked the drawer, she noticed James had opened his eyes. He appeared dazed but she wasn't sure if he had seen her at the filing cabinet. Suddenly, he sat bolt upright and looked at his watch.

"What happened?" he asked, sounding angry.

"You were so exhausted you fell asleep." Lindsay moved toward him and hugged him from behind. "I didn't have the heart to wake you."

He didn't respond, but he stared at her in a way that made her nervous. When he stood up, he was clearly still disoriented and he held on to the table for support. Lindsay couldn't tell if he was confused or suspicious. He looked at her for a long moment and she felt her heart pounding.

"James," she said softly. "Are you okay?"

"I really have to go," he mumbled.

Before she could answer, he left.

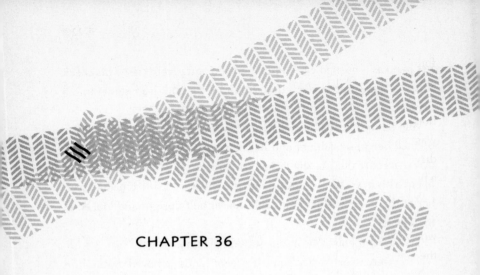

CHAPTER 36

Lindsay was dry-eyed as she arrived at the embassy the next morning. When Vickie saw her, she leaped up to greet her, but Lindsay waved her back. This was not a social call.

Lindsay opened her notebook, tore out the pages that recorded her espionage work, and tossed them onto Vickie's desk. Sitting down, she told Vickie what she had discovered.

Vickie's manner was professional, for which Lindsay was grateful. After answering a few questions, Lindsay knew it was time to go, but she just sat staring at the floor. Vickie was silent. Finally, Lindsay rose and reached over awkwardly to shake Vickie's hand.

"I'll be leaving soon," she said. "After my story on J.R.'s murder, I'm pretty sure my credentials will be lifted. In any case, after working with you, I'm through as a journalist anyway—"

"Not necessarily," Vickie started to interrupt.

"Forget it, Vickie." She gave a small, tight smile, turned, and walked out.

"One more thing," Vickie called after her. "You didn't say if you found out his plans. We need to know when he's leaving the country and where he plans to go."

Lindsay had deliberately left the page with his escape plan in her notebook, and she hesitated before answering. She knew that his plane was not leaving from Lagos but from a small airport about an hour's drive away. Even if he was being followed, James was adept at shaking a tail. Vickie would be unlikely to find out if Lindsay didn't tell her.

Vickie seemed to understand.

"Jesus, I know what you're feeling. You think you can stop his network but let him get away. But remember what he's done. Stopping the network isn't enough because he can always build another."

Vickie was talking so loudly that Lindsay was alarmed. "Please keep your voice down," she said icily. She knew that Vickie was right. She knew what she had to do. Still, she hesitated.

"He's used you," Vickie said, in a near stage whisper. "He used you from the beginning. Are you going to let him continue?"

"You used me too," Lindsay said.

Vickie couldn't answer that.

"And I used him too," Lindsay continued. "I owe him something for that."

"That's bullshit, Lindsay. How can you compare it? How did you 'use' him? By loving him?"

Lindsay looked down in frustration. "Being with him changed me."

"He changed you the way love changes you, the way pain changes you. So what do you mean? That you used him to open something inside you, to help you feel? Okay. Maybe that's true. But he used you in a more callous way. He used you to help him achieve terrible goals."

Lindsay was silent.

Vickie continued, speaking urgently. "Look, Lindsay, if you won't think of all the anonymous people he's hurt, just remember Maureen."

Furious at Vickie for manipulating her, Lindsay couldn't help thinking of her funny, ambitious, loyal friend, whose body was blown to bits. Then she thought of Eduke, of Martin banging his fist against the wall, of J.R., and finally, the bloodstained couch, the dead dog, its fur sticky with its own blood.

"Paris," she said at last. "Thursday night, six o'clock from a private charter airline. The flight leaves from a small airport outside of Lagos. Two tickets. I think one is meant for me."

Vickie released her breath. "Thanks, Lindsay." She scribbled the information onto a pad. "Believe me, you did the right thing."

Before leaving, Lindsay stopped in the women's bathroom across the hall. As she opened the door to leave, she saw Dave Goren and the ambassador go into Vickie's office, followed by the ambassador's secretary, pad in hand. They didn't see her and they left the door partly open—she could hear the murmur of their voices in the hall. Stealthily, she moved closer to listen. She couldn't hear every word, but caught snippets of conversation.

"Good work," a man's voice said. She identified it as Goren's. ". . . never thought . . . Lindsay." Then a laugh.

Vickie's voice was louder and easier to make out. "It was painful for her. She's full of guilt and anger."

Goren spoke louder this time. "Right. But her psychology isn't my concern."

"Her psychology may become all of our concern," the ambassador said in a sharp voice.

"We have to get him before we move on the others. We can't let him escape."

"Hell no," Goren said. "This time we've got the bastard cold."

"Well, he's got tickets for them to go to Paris," Vickie said. "The French will cooperate as long as we're not going to charge him with a capital crime. We can extradite him."

Lindsay couldn't hear a response. She moved slightly closer to the door.

"Extradite him?" she heard Goren say contemptuously. "Vickie, get real. We can't extradite him."

Vickie's voice was louder this time. "Why not? We have good relations with the French secret service and plenty of evidence against him."

Goren laughed. "Evidence only matters if you are going to trial."

Lindsay heard a sound in the corridor and turned quickly. A young man pushing a cart laden with packages was walking toward her. She ducked into the bathroom again and waited a minute or two. When she came out, she caught part of Goren's sentence: ". . . embarrassing to us and worse." Then something she couldn't make out before he said, "He'll compromise all our other operations. There will be investigations, congressional committees."

Vickie spoke softly now, but Lindsay could still make out her words: "You want him to disappear without a trial, do I understand you correctly?"

"Without a public trial, Vickie. That's all," said the ambassador.

A woman from a neighboring office opened her door and headed for the ladies' room. Lindsay hastily moved away from the door and walked down the hallway toward the front exit.

She could hardly believe what she had overheard. Goren wasn't talking about a private trial. He was talking about a disappearance, an assassination. She was sure that Peter Bresson wouldn't sanction Goren's plan, but she was still disturbed that Goren would suggest it and that Peter listened without throwing him out of his office. She knew that there were undercover CIA operations in which people "disappeared," but they were not, to her knowledge, aimed at Americans.

She had decided she would leave Lagos as soon as possible. She'd quit her job, go back home to New York, and start to think about what she should do with the rest of her life. She'd have to see James again before he left or he would know something was wrong. He might even invite her to come to Paris with him, but she'd come up with some excuse and pretend to make plans to meet him there. She rooted around in her bag for her keys as she approached her door. Just as she found them, the door opened.

"I'm back, madam." Martin beamed at her. "Are you well?"

"No, Martin. Not at all well. But I'm very glad to see you." Then, suddenly, she burst into tears.

"I'll make you some tea," he said, embarrassed. "And I baked some banana bread. Would you like some?"

"Yes," she said, wiping her eyes. "Thank you."

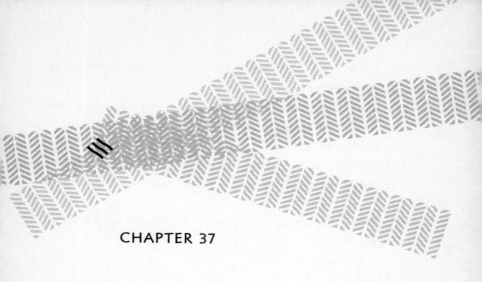

CHAPTER 37

It was time to pack. Lindsay moved around the room, picking out her most treasured possessions.

She chose the items that mattered to her. Picking up two small statues dressed in cowry shells, and wrapping them carefully in tissue paper, she remembered her first conversation with James about ibejis. She packed the Shango staff she bought the day they went to Ibadan, the day she bought the fertility statue and lied to him about it, saying she'd paid less than she did. She opened her safe and removed the fine antique ibejis James had given her. She looked at them for a long time, then put them back in place. Every item held a memory; every memory was painful. She went into her bedroom for her clothes.

What a nightmare. She returned to the safe, pulled out the ibejis again, and went in search of Martin. She found him in the laundry room and handed him the statues.

"These are very good sculptures, Martin. You can sell them for a lot of money. I'd like to give them to you as a good-bye present."

Martin held them and said shyly, "These are too good, madam. You keep them."

"No. I don't want them. They're for you." She walked away before he could say another word.

She went upstairs, undressed, and stepped into the shower. The phone rang but she ignored it, listening for the machine.

"Hi, sweetheart."

His voice sounded so cheerful, so dissonant. "It's me. Let's have dinner tonight. There's something I need to talk to you about. I'll drop by at eight."

She stood in the shower and let the water wash over her for a long, long time.

≡

At 6 P.M., Vickie knocked on the door. When no one answered, she walked in and found Lindsay in the living room, packing. Otis Redding blasted on the stereo.

Don't know much about history.
Don't know much biology . . .

Vickie was the last person Lindsay wanted to see. She blamed her even though she knew she was misdirecting her anger.

"What did you forget?" she asked dryly. "Do you want me to shoot him?"

For just a second, before she realized that Lindsay was being sarcastic, Vickie was startled. Then she smiled.

"No. But there is something else we would like you to do."

"What a surprise. And I thought this was a social call."

"Come on, Lindsay. I'm just doing what I have to do—like you, actually. I don't like it either."

"Yeah. Right. So what did you and the boys forget?"

"We need to get James to Athens instead of Paris."

"So?"

"So, you're the only one who can do that."

Lindsay shook her head. "Look, I'm through, understand? Don't come to me again. I simply can't do more," she said, wrapping another set of ibejis and putting them into the carton. "I'm not trained in your special brand of deception."

"You mean you're not as good as James is."

Lindsay suddenly felt very tired. She sat down on the sofa and closed her eyes briefly. When was this going to end? And then she knew that like all stories, it would end only when it was over and it would be over only when these people had James.

"Why Athens?"

"Because it's a looser airport. We can operate without being watched. We want to pick this guy up quietly and get him home without a lot of questions and official forms."

Lindsay had not lost all her reporter's instincts.

"You mean without resorting to legal means?"

"I just know they want to pick him up in Athens," Vickie said, shrugging helplessly.

Lindsay smiled in spite of herself. The idea of Vickie helpless was amusing. She didn't care how they got him to trial, she thought, as long as they did, and she trusted Vickie to make sure that happened. The idea of justice, however painful, was comforting.

"I need to know something, Vickie," she said. "After you get him, will I have to testify at his trial?"

Vickie didn't miss a beat.

"No. We have enough evidence against him that we can spare you that. Do this last thing for us and we will never contact you again."

"How am I supposed to get him to go to Athens?" Lindsay asked wearily.

"Tell him you need a few days of vacation. Tell him you always wanted to see the Parthenon. Tell him you just have to stop there to do an important interview. Tell him anything that works."

Lindsay sighed.

"Okay. I'll do what I can."

"Good. Now listen. When you exit the plane at Athens, he will be picked up by local agents as he goes through customs. They have very few pictures of him, and it's remarkable how bad they are. I don't want the local agents to miss him. They have good pictures of you. Take his arm at the customs check. That's how our guys will be sure they have the right man."

"Why can't someone from here be sent to identify him?"

"Too risky. We don't want him to recognize us and we don't want to be connected to his arrest. He'll be brought to the U.S. without formal extradition to save time."

Lindsay sighed. "I'm not sure I can get him to do this. I just said I'd try."

"Fine," Vickie said. "That's all we're asking."

After Vickie left, Lindsay looked around at the mess in her living room and realized that she couldn't let James see it if she didn't want him to know she was planning to leave. She started to clean up, putting the boxes in closets, stashing the pile of newspapers inside them. She unwrapped some of the statues, placing them in their old positions.

She decided to dress well—James would definitely notice if she didn't. He knew she always fussed over her clothes, makeup, and perfume when she prepared for a date with him. Even though she'd already showered, she bathed, shaved her legs, and smoothed almond lotion all over her body. She dried her long hair so that it flowed, silky and shiny, straight down past her shoulders.

She hurriedly put on cream-colored linen slacks and a green silk top that set off her auburn hair. She slipped into sling-back sandals and, taking a quick appraising look at herself, walked into the living room. She thought about what music to put on, and finally settled on Mozart's *Requiem*. Not cheerful, but appropriate. This wasn't going to be easy.

James bounded in at 8:10. By that time, Lindsay was calmer. He was carrying red roses that were wilting, like most picked flowers in the heat. She kissed him quickly and walked to the kitchen to put them in a vase. She cut the stems at an angle and added a little sugar to the water, taking longer than necessary to arrange the flowers. Then she carefully placed the vase on a side table and sat down next to him.

"I don't think you've ever brought me flowers before."

James smiled and switched off the music. Then he came back to the couch and, with a touch of self-mockery, got down on one knee in front of her.

"I don't think I've ever proposed to you before."

Lindsay froze. Was this a joke? She smiled tentatively.

"Well, that's certainly true. And you still haven't."

"No. But I'm about to."

She didn't know how to react.

"Lindsay, my work here is finished. I think yours is too. Isn't it time for someone else to pick up this story? I've got two tickets to Paris. Come with me."

For just a moment, Lindsay allowed herself a surge of excitement. "I think I missed the will-you-marry-me part."

He laughed. "Will you marry me?"

"Where, when?"

"Anywhere you want. Anytime you want."

Lindsay paused. This was her chance. Suddenly she remembered a story she had heard as a little girl in summer camp. It was called "The Monkey's Paw," and it was about a man and his wife who were given a monkey's paw that had the power to grant any wish. But it came with a warning. There were often terrible consequences. The couple ignored the warning and wished for a great deal of money. Two days later, they got word that their beloved son had died. He left behind an insurance policy for the exact sum for which they had wished.

"I always wanted to get married in Greece," she murmured.

"Greece? Why?"

"I don't know. I visited there with my family and fell in love with it." She put her hands in his, flushed with excitement, as if the scene were real. "James, are you really serious?"

"I've never been more serious."

Lindsay threw her arms around him and kissed him. "Could we change the tickets? Could we go to Athens instead of Paris and get married there?"

James paused. He seemed, for a moment, slightly uncomfortable. Then he smiled.

"Athens it is," he said. "You drive a hard bargain."

So it was settled. It was terrifyingly easy to lie, Lindsay realized. You just had to believe, on some level, that the lie was real. James must have realized this early in life and made use of it. She wondered if something terrible had happened to him to turn him into a criminal or if it was never a clear choice. Maybe he'd gotten lost little by little. But what central moral decency was absent that allowed him to keep doing it? She didn't understand. And she realized that she would have to accept the likelihood that she never would.

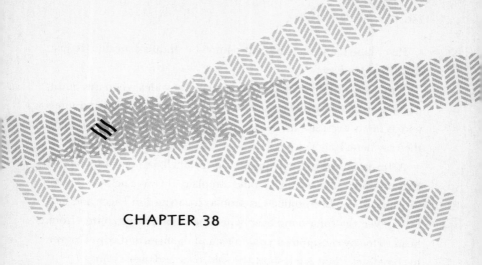

CHAPTER 38

The plane to Athens departed a day after the Paris flight, from the same small airport outside Lagos. Lindsay had alerted Vickie and had been informed that there was a change of plans. Vickie herself would be in Athens to make sure everything went smoothly. They weren't taking any chances, Lindsay thought, and wondered if Vickie didn't trust her, or if she didn't have confidence in her CIA colleagues.

She had assumed the charter was an illegal operation run by the drug cartels, but if true, she wouldn't have known it from the other passengers waiting to board at the ramshackle airstrip. Many of them worked in Nigeria's oil fields, fresh-faced young men out to make some money to take back to the States. Others were weary-looking business-men, mid-level oil executives who flew in to check productivity and then flew out again as fast as they could.

One man just ahead of Lindsay and James in line began chatting as soon as he realized they were Americans.

"Well, it's good to see a friendly face," he said. "Dan Ryan's my name."

He grabbed James's hand and pumped it enthusiastically. He just nodded at Lindsay.

"I'm really glad to meet you. Do you have any idea when this outfit is going to get started? I've already been on line for twenty minutes and as far as I can see, no one is up there taking tickets. 'Not on seat,' they say here. Hell, I've got to get out of here."

A Texan businessman who worked for Shell, he was desperate to find an American to whom he could complain. He was a nervous wreck, he said. He had been robbed as soon as he arrived in Lagos and had been given the runaround everywhere he went. He was bitten from head to toe by mosquitoes, couldn't stand the heat, and vowed never to come back. "Life is too short," he said, over and over again.

Lindsay noted unsympathetically the profusion of sweat around his temples and above his lip and the stain on his wilting white shirt. She was offended by his assumption that because they were white and American they would share his opinions. James, however, seemed amused. When Dan said he needed sleep more than anything, James pulled a sleeping pill out of his pocket and offered it to him.

"It works for about five hours," James said. "Just take it after the plane takes off and you'll be sure to nap."

After fifteen more minutes, an airline clerk arrived and, as if on signal, the line, which up until then had been orderly, was suddenly thrust into chaos by dozens of people pushing to secure seats on the plane. James plowed his way successfully through the crowd, pulling Lindsay along with him. Dan stuck close behind and all three secured boarding passes. They elbowed their way to the front of the line and finally, sweaty and exhausted, they boarded the plane. Another small victory in survival. In a funny way, Lindsay thought, she'd miss this daily struggle that allowed you to feel proud when you accomplished tasks that were simple in other countries. They waved at their new friend, who sat several rows in front of them.

Lindsay looked around the plane. Did the CIA send an agent to travel with them? Several people looked suspicious, but maybe she was just paranoid. It was even possible that Dan was an agent. After they took their seats, James leaned over and squeezed her hand.

"You're not having second thoughts, are you?" he asked.

"No, of course not," she answered. "I'm just excited. This is a big day for me. Leaving one life and starting another."

They settled in for the trip, James reading a book about Leni Riefenstahl's African photography and Lindsay reading an old *Newsweek*. One flight attendant pulled out the serving cart to offer the passengers coffee and another followed, distributing landing cards. Lindsay put hers in the seat pocket—it would be several hours before it would be needed—but James, with his characteristic orderliness, started to fill his out. His pen ran out of ink and he asked Lindsay for one. Preoccupied with the story she was reading, she told him to look in her bag. He picked it up and rooted around, past a lipstick, a powder brush, a hairbrush, gum, candy, an eyebrow pencil, and two pairs of glasses before he found a Bic ballpoint pen stashed underneath her reporter's notebook. He pulled out the notebook and began looking through it. Lindsay saw him but wasn't concerned—she knew she'd given the incriminating pages to Vickie. Suddenly she noticed that the spiral notebook still had thin strips of paper caught in its coil and one page remained. Before she could grab it, he read, "James departure: private charter, Thursday—Lagos–Paris, leaves one P.M. Two tickets in safe."

He looked surprised at first, then thoughtful. Then his face set in a way that frightened her. He grabbed her arm, so hard it hurt. She thought fast, trying to come up with a story to throw him off the track, but drew a blank.

"Well, now I know," he said, his voice threatening.

"James, you're hurting me. What are you talking about?"

He kept his grip on her arm. "I know that you are not what you appear to be. I know that you think you know things about me that make you willing to betray me, even going so far as to pretend you want to marry me. I know that you sneaked into my room and gave my private information to people who want to hurt me. What I don't know is whether they are waiting for me in Athens, and that's what you're going to tell me right now."

She pulled her arm away. It was bruised where he had been gripping it and she rubbed it as she spoke.

"I am not what I appear to be? You dare to say that to me?"

"Oh, of course, you did everything in the name of justice and the American way. It must be nice to be so self-righteous."

"It's not so nice when you're the one being deceived, is it, James? You usually play the other role, don't you? Only you don't just deceive, do you? Deception, that's just one baby step for you, you must have learned that in your first week at this. It's nothing compared to planting bombs and killing your old friends or stealing medicine from children."

She watched his expression change from rage to surprise. He was realizing the breadth of her knowledge of his activities and the depth of her hurt and disgust.

"Listen, Lindsay, you have to let me explain. You know I didn't do all those things. They have their own reasons for blaming me."

Lindsay's eyes filled. Then, collecting herself, she said, "I didn't believe them at first. But we both know what you did. What I don't know is why. I thought I knew you. I thought I sensed a strength and decency. I actually believed you were honest, at least with me. And I believed that you loved me. Now, I don't even know why you asked me to marry you, but I doubt it was because you wanted to be with me for the rest of your life."

James sighed. "I want to be with you for the rest of my life. I do love you. Look, Lindsay, I'm not going to pretend I'm an innocent man or a good one, we both know better. But I'm not a monster, though it's easy for your friend Vickie to demonize me now that we don't work together anymore. I didn't seem so bad to her when I was carrying out CIA orders. But I didn't kill Maureen. I knew about the bomb—you might remember that I delayed you that day—but I never thought Maureen would get there early. Shit, she was never early. I thought she'd wait for you. It was meant as a warning, set to go off before any-one came. I cared about Maureen too. I swear it."

Lindsay was a trained reporter. She often had to intuit who was telling the truth and who was lying. She saw how James looked down as he talked as if he was trying to convince himself rather than her. She heard the tone of despair in his voice, and she believed him. She didn't forgive him, but she believed he didn't know that Maureen would be killed.

"But you live a life of such corruption and violence that terrible things happen because of you whether you want them to or not," she said. "You helped people steal medicine that might have saved the lives of hundreds of children. I knew one of those children and so did you. You say you're not a monster. What does it take to be a monster if that doesn't qualify?"

Lindsay's face was flushed with emotion and she turned away, fight-ing tears.

James regained his composure. "Look, I'm not going to try to excuse myself to you, that would be impossible. But, for the record, that medi-cine saved the lives of children in the northern hospitals. It's all corrupt. People like us, outsiders, we can't stop it. We can't even understand it. I just found a way to profit from it. If it hadn't been me, it would have been someone else. The only reason those southern hospitals could order medicine in the first place is that there was a southern president in power who took care of his own tribe. We just tried to even the score."

"You betrayed him too, didn't you?"

"Are you going to tell me he didn't deserve it?"

"That's not the point, James." She simply couldn't bear to continue the conversation. "I can't argue anymore. It's over. You're neutralized. They have the list of all your couriers. You won't be able to hurt anyone ever again."

"Okay," he said. "So it's over. Maybe that's a good thing for you."

It was the worst thing that had ever happened to her. Even now, as she berated and condemned him, she loved him, though she was no longer sure what that word meant. She was horrified by his actions and the justifications he used to salve whatever conscience he had, but she was still drawn to him.

"No," she said, her voice and manner softer than before. "It's not a good thing for me. I think you know that."

As if he sensed her weakness, he said, "So what's the plan? Will they pick me up at customs?"

"Yes," she said, looking away.

"Is that your goal? What do you want to come of all this?"

She didn't hesitate. "To stop you."

"You've already stopped me. I assume they will arrest all the people in my network. I'm through. I'd have to start all over again, and that's the last thing I'd want to do even if I could. This deal was planned to be my last, to free me, to buy me the rest of my life to forget all this. I'd hoped to do that with you . . ."

He seemed to choke up for a second and looked away, but not before she saw his eyes misting. Then he turned back to her.

"You should know that even if my network is busted, that won't stop the drug trade. Another network will rise up. It always does."

Lindsay wavered for a second. He was right. He was no longer a danger. But that didn't satisfy her.

"Don't you think you should pay for what you've done?" she asked. This time her voice held neither anger nor reproach. She really wanted to know what he thought.

James gently took her hand. She didn't withdraw it, and he went on. "So, stopping me is not the issue. You want to punish me."

She started to withdraw her hand, but he held it tighter. "I can understand that. That's fair, right? That's the American way."

She relaxed her hand and let it rest in his.

"Only just make sure you know what the punishment will be, Lindsay, and take responsibility for it. You'll be a part of it. You won't just be writing about it this time. Do you know what they are planning?"

Now Lindsay withdrew her hand from his. There was something disturbing in his tone.

"They're going to put you on trial. You'll get a fair hearing. How will you like it, actually dealing in truth for a change?"

"Lindsay, you don't understand. They can't put me on trial. I know too much and they know I'll use it. They can deal with me or kill me, those are their only choices, and they've decided not to deal with me."

She remembered Goren and the ambassador discussing just this possibility. She'd trusted Vickie, but maybe that was a mistake. She didn't know whether to believe him. Suddenly she was furious. How dare he put her in this position, hurt her so badly, then force her to make these impossible choices?

"It was you who decided not to deal with them when you joined the other side. And why? Because they paid more. Jesus. I still can't believe it. How could I have been so wrong about you? Are you that good at this, really, or was I just such an easy mark? And how did you know I would be? Can people like you just smell it, the weakness, the need?"

"Lindsay, please. Don't do that to yourself. Don't do that to us." He reached for her hand again but she pulled it away violently.

"Us? There was never an 'us,' James. You used me, that's all. And you underestimated me from the beginning. I don't even know if your name is James."

He gave a weak smile. "It is."

"Well, good. You told me one truth anyway."

"I told you more truths than I ever told anyone else."

She turned away from him. He tried to put his hand on her shoulder, to turn her toward him, but she threw it off and refused to look at him.

"Lindsay," he began, "I know I hurt you. I'm sorry."

She faced him. He looked her straight in the eye, the way he used to, the way that threw her off balance with desire. This time she met his gaze evenly.

"Did I use you?" he asked rhetorically. "Yes."

She sat unmoving, her face revealing no emotion.

"Did I love you?" he continued. "Yes. Can you understand that? Must you believe only the version that makes me into a monster?"

"You are a monster," she blurted. "How can you live with yourself?"

He showed a quick flash of anger. "What do you hate me more for? Your list of the atrocities I supposedly committed or the fact that you think I deceived you? Is it your conscience or your pride I'm hearing?"

"I hate you for all of it. I don't need to qualify my hatred. And what do you mean 'supposedly'? The atrocities are well documented and very reliably sourced."

"Stop talking like a journalist."

"What is it you really hate about journalism, James? Is it the search for objective truth? Is that what bothers you?"

"It's the mistaken idea that there is objective truth. And that journalists think they're on the moral high ground."

"No objective truth. No objective morality. No code, no rules, no right, no wrong. You developed this rationale as a way to live with your greed. You disgust me."

She had spit it all out, finally, and it ought to have felt good, but she just felt tired and sullied and sad. She stared out the window at the same clear blue sky. The same white cotton-candy clouds. But everything else was different. She didn't want it to end this way.

She touched his arm and said softly, "Can you try to explain, James? Can you help me try to see this from your point of view?"

James put both hands over his face, rubbing his forehead.

"What do you want me to tell you, Lindsay? That I was abused when I was a child? That I was abandoned? Rejected by my mother? Beaten by her alcoholic husband? I wasn't. I don't know what happened. I liked adventure. I started out within the law. I worked as an operative for these people you trust so much now. A lot of what I did wasn't much different from what I do now. That's where I learned to lie and manipulate and strategize, but it was supposedly for the good of my country, and they didn't pay much, so I must have been doing it for good reasons, isn't that how it goes? Then, after a while, I started seeing how hopeless everything was. When the first offer came to work for profit, I took it. After that, I kind of slid into what I do now, little by little, inch by inch." He paused and looked at her. "I'm not proud of it, Lindsay. I'm trying to get out of it. I was going to Tahiti, I'm planning on building a house there. Come with me."

Lindsay shook her head. "I can't, James. You crossed a line I could never cross."

"And you don't see that by helping them kill me, you are crossing that same line?"

"Kill you? I don't believe it," she said brusquely. "Vickie wouldn't be involved in murder."

"Maybe not," James said, "but Goren would. I've been wondering about him." He turned toward the window and stared out. They sat in silence. James seemed to have given up trying to persuade her.

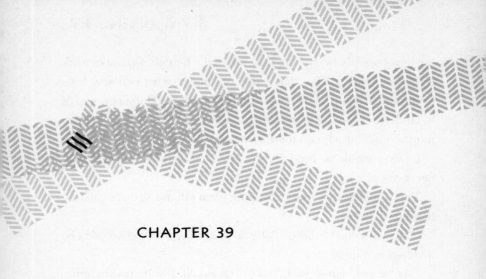

CHAPTER 39

They were two hours from Athens and there was nothing left to say. The flight attendant wheeled a drinks cart slowly down the aisle, stopping at each row. Lindsay asked for scotch and James did the same. She stole a glance at him but could read nothing in his face. She pulled the flight magazine from the seat pocket in front of her and pretended to read it, then gave that up and placed it back where she had found it. Time passed, and she dimly heard an announcement that they would land in Athens in about forty-five minutes.

Signs of life on the ground began to appear through the clouds; first green and brown patches, looking from that distance like a flat, one-dimensional grid, and then slowly, as the plane decreased in altitude, taking shape, turning into fields and trees and hills and sea. Soon she would see houses and swimming pools and cars. Soon they would be on the ground and she would have to do what she had to do.

This last part would be the hardest. He seemed calm and resigned. He had said that they were planning to kill him—was there any chance that was true? How would they bring him to trial? Maybe some kind of court-martial, but she wondered under what pretense. Would they claim national security and close the trial? It would probably seem so much easier to just make him disappear.

The voice of the captain came over the loudspeaker. "Ladies and gentlemen, due to bad weather conditions in Athens, we are diverting to Crete. A local flight to Athens will be available later in the day. Please fasten your safety belts and remain seated for the remainder of the journey. We should be landing in approximately an hour." The passengers groaned.

Outside her window, the sky was bright blue. She felt James's eyes on her, and turned to face him.

"Does it look like bad weather to you?" he asked.

Lindsay looked puzzled.

"This is Dave Goren. He or someone he trusts will be waiting on the tarmac in Crete. But Vickie will be waiting in Athens. When she figures out what's happening, it will be too late."

Lindsay got up and walked briskly to the back of the plane. She picked up the onboard telephone and, using her credit card to pay, dialed Vickie's cell. She listened as the phone rang, slowly losing hope until, finally, she heard the recorded message. She hissed into the phone:

"Vickie, we've been diverted to Crete. I don't know what to do. It's three P.M., we land in about an hour. James says it's a—" and then the line went dead. She walked slowly back to her seat. James was staring at her.

"Even if I wanted to stop this, I couldn't," she said.

"I'm not so sure," he said. Without another word, he stood up, slipped past Lindsay, and opened the overhead bin, taking out a small black leather carry-on bag. Then he strolled toward the front of the plane, past the row where Dan Ryan, out cold from the sleeping pill, was snoring lightly. Dan had filled out his landing card before he fell asleep, and his passport and card were on his dinner tray. James brushed by Dan's seat; the passport now in James's pocket, he continued on to the men's room.

About fifteen minutes passed before the lavatory door reopened and a bald man with a black mustache and bushy eyebrows emerged. Lindsay watched as he walked back down the aisle, casually dropping Dan Ryan's passport back on his tray. She was sure that if the Texan took the trouble to look, he would see that though his photo appeared unchanged, his passport now identified him as James Duncan. She was equally sure that James's passport displayed Dan Ryan's name with a photo of this bald stranger attached to it.

Barely recognizable, even to her, James returned to his seat.

"They will be looking for you and your traveling companion. Goren knows me but he can't be everywhere at once, and he won't expect a disguise. I'll try to get to the front of the line. You need to take the Texan's arm so they see you together. In the confusion, I'll get away."

Lindsay didn't answer, and the two sat in silence as they began their descent. The airport came into sight as the plane sank lower and lower. The wheels hit the ground with a light thud and the passengers broke into enthusiastic applause. As the plane stopped, people rose and began to collect their belongings. James moved quickly. She turned to look at him and their eyes met, both serious, both sad. He reached out and briefly touched her face with his fingers, tucking a stray lock of hair behind her ears. Then he made his way to the front of the line. Lindsay grabbed her bag and pushed her way forward. She spotted James ahead of her, weaving in and out of a group of determined tourists.

There was the usual chaos in the arrival area but she managed to keep James in sight, edging closer. She was nearly paralyzed with indecision. If she helped him, he would get away with everything. She scanned passport control and saw no one she recognized. Why should she believe that this was a trap? This was more likely just another of James's tricks.

She made her decision. She would not let him get away. She would take his arm as he passed through passport control. He stood ahead of her in a long line parallel to hers, looking straight ahead. She hung back, waiting for him to be called forward.

Suddenly, she saw something alarming. A man walked out of a closed office and briefly scanned the crowd before disappearing again behind the heavy door. She only got a brief glimpse, but she was sure it was Dave Goren. She quickly reviewed her discussion with James, trying to decide if he had been right in his prediction. Certainly he had foreseen Goren's presence at the airport, but did that fact have the sinister implications James suggested?

She watched as the person in front of James stepped forward. A middle-aged man in a cotton shirt and linen suit, he had the rumpled look of the British upper class. It didn't take long for the guard to stamp his passport and let him through. As James moved to the control booth, she stood perfectly still, never taking her eyes off him. She made no move to take his arm. Just as it seemed as though the officer might stamp his passport and let him through, Dave Goren walked briskly over, accompanied by two heavyset men in black leather jackets. They roughly pulled James out of the line and started to walk away with him. Lindsay leaped forward, but it wasn't her turn and the guards held her back. She could see James, Goren, and the two men ahead of her.

"Dave!" she called out.

Goren turned toward her.

"I saw you with him!" she shouted. "Remember that!"

Goren whispered something to one of the policemen and the officer darted past the immigration counter and pulled Lindsay out of line. One of the thugs with Goren grabbed her arm and twisted it hard before Goren signaled him to let go.

"I thought you were here just to identify him," Goren said. "You didn't. Someone might think you decided to help him escape."

"Someone might think you planned—" Lindsay started to answer, but he cut her off.

"Luckily, we had an agent on the plane who saw him disguise himself. Did you meet our friend Dan? Friendly Texan, isn't he?"

"He was sound asleep."

"Was he? I don't think so. In any case, I am putting an embargo on everything to do with this situation. I suggest you forget what you saw, Lindsay. If you write about this, I will have you arrested for aiding a terrorist."

"Aiding a terrorist? More like preventing an illegal assassination! You'd have to prove your charge in court and I don't think you'd want to do that."

"We have special courts for terrorists, haven't you heard? And for those who help them."

"I think Vickie might have something to say about that."

"I wouldn't count on her." Goren smiled coldly. "She approves of everything that is happening."

He walked through the airport to the outside curb, accompanied by the police officer and the two men marching James between them. Lindsay followed as they approached two parked black Fiats. She tried to check the license plates but there were none. James caught her eye. "I'm sorry," he mouthed before one of the thugs shoved him into the vehicle.

Goren turned to Lindsay. He seemed to hesitate a few seconds before he came over and put his hand on her back. "I think you'd better come with us for the time being," he said, leading her toward the second car. Lindsay shrugged off his hand, but he forced her into the car.

"Be careful, Dave," she said icily. "I'm not so easy to dispose of."

She watched as the first car pulled away from the curb. When they started to follow, she pleaded. "This is crazy, Dave. I know what you're planning. You can't get away with this."

"I think you'll see reason, once you realize the alternatives," Dave answered. "And what do you mean? We're planning to arrest him, that's all."

The car continued to move forward. Just then, another car sped down the ramp and cut it off, parking horizontally in front of it. Three marked police cars and a police van followed, sirens screaming. A line of other drivers held up behind blared their horns. Two police officers jumped out of their car, guns drawn. They yanked open James's door and transferred him into the van. His captors were quickly handcuffed and deposited in the same van. Another policeman pulled a protesting Goren out of the second car and Lindsay climbed out after him. Relieved but confused, she looked on in wonder as her friend Vickie, cramped in the back of the last police car, got out, stretching her long legs. Smiling broadly, she ordered Goren handcuffed and arrested.

"What do you think you're doing?" he shouted. "You are interfering in an authorized operation. Tell this idiot to let me go."

"I'm interfering with an illegal operation on the direct orders of Bob Albright," Vickie said evenly. Goren continued to shout threats and objections, but she ignored him and enveloped Lindsay in a crushing hug.

"Are you okay?"

"Yes. I'm fine. But what happened? How did you get here?"

"I got your phone call and heard 'Crete.' I had to act fast, but I had suspected Goren might try to pull something and had already contacted Washington. It turns out that Goren was running a rogue operation—ignoring regulations, making arrests, breaking the law, even ordering assassinations, all in the name of fighting terrorism. He even tried to co-opt the ambassador."

Lindsay took a deep breath. "I always thought Goren was only out for himself. I wouldn't have thought he'd take risks like that, even to fight terrorism."

"I haven't finished. It gets worse. He doesn't care about terrorism."

"What?"

"He's worked out a deal to represent a consortium of American oil companies. They want to divest Shell of its exclusive drilling rights. He's been secretly working with the northerners to pull off their coup in exchange for an arrangement with the new government. They'll drop Shell and award all drilling rights to Goren's clients."

"How much does he get for this?"

"Millions and millions of dollars."

"But I thought he was supporting Olumide."

"He was. But Olumide wouldn't give him exclusive rights."

"How do you know all this?"

"Mike had been on to him for a while. He'd talked to people like Billy Anikulo and others in Olumide's government who had dealt with Goren. They agreed to talk in exchange for U.S. citizenship. Mike took notes and left his files at the embassy for safekeeping."

"So Goren—"

"Got wise to Mike and had him killed. And there's something else you should know. Goren was behind the bomb that killed Maureen— the Northern Alliance had to get rid of Fakai and create unrest in preparation for the coup."

"And Agapo?"

"That was set up by Goren too."

"So James—"

"James is a criminal and a drug smuggler, but he's not a murderer. Not directly, anyway. His helping divert the drugs to the north probably killed Eduke, and God knows how many people's lives are ruined by the drugs he exports. Or exported. We've stopped that now."

"What about Solutions, Inc.? Does this mean they didn't arrange any murders?"

"They have. They would. But they didn't this time. James does work for them and that's why Goren thought it would be easy to pin all the murders on him."

Lindsay was silent, thinking. She was relieved to know that James, for all the harm that he'd caused, hadn't been responsible for Maureen's death. But something was nagging at her. She looked accusingly at Vickie.

"You told me James was responsible for the bomb. That's how you convinced me to get on that plane with him."

"I know. I believed that. I had my suspicions about Goren, but I never guessed the extent of his activities. Mike never told us what he'd found—he was waiting to nail down a few more facts before he filed his report. I didn't even know about his files. But after you left, I was putting together his personal effects and found the key to his filing cabinet. I looked in it and found the Goren file. That's when I called Washington for authorization to arrest Goren. When I got your message from the plane, the rest of his plan became clear."

Lindsay was puzzled. "But how? I still don't see why he wanted to kill James."

"James knew about him—don't forget he was working with the northerners too. Goren knew that James would use what he knew to get himself a better deal."

Lindsay looked at her friend with admiration.

"I hope you get a promotion out of this. As for me, I've never been so happy to see anyone in my life. But now I've got to find a hotel and a computer right away."

"Why?"

"I've got a story to write," Lindsay answered, looking around for a cab.

"I thought you'd given that up."

"I know I'm compromised, but I came to Africa to investigate corruption and stayed to find out who was responsible for killing Maureen. Now I know both answers. I'm going to write that story and admit my part in it. After that, I'll have time to figure out what to do."

"Why can't you just go on as you were?"

"I crossed the line. I don't regret it, but I'll have to resign."

"No one needs to know the whole story."

"I know," Lindsay said.

Vickie didn't answer.

"I feel so empty," Lindsay said.

Vickie brightened. "Listen, I think you're just hungry. And I know just where to go to fix that."

She put her arm around Lindsay and led her toward the taxi stand.

"The Casa Leone," Vicky told the driver as she settled into the seat. It was one of the best hotels on the island.

"I need to file first," Lindsay said. "Just drop me off at the hotel. I'll meet you later."

"Fine. But you know there are certain details you can't put in your story. National security."

"If you mean your name, I'll leave it out. Everything else goes. Nothing was off the record."

"We'll talk about it."

"I don't think so."

Vickie was silent for a moment. Then she leaned close to Lindsay and said, "Look, Linds. We're a great team. Maybe we can work together. James isn't the only operative in Solutions, Inc. They're all over the world."

Lindsay laughed. "Just what I need. Another James. Thanks, Vickie, but I don't think the CIA is my kind of place."

"What is your kind of place?"

"I don't know. Maybe I'll retire to a Greek island."

"Somehow I don't think so."

Lindsay turned toward her friend. "Well, what should we do when I finish my piece?"

"Get drunk," Vickie shot back.

Lindsay smiled. "I like the way you think."

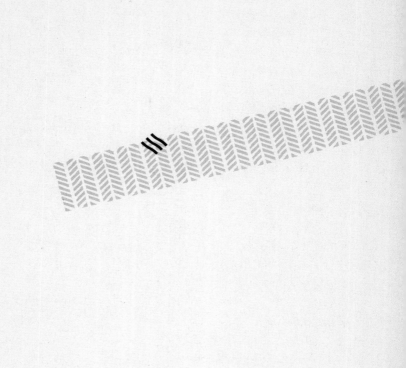

ACKNOWLEDGMENTS

In writing this novel I have benefited from the wisdom and generosity of many people. I would like to thank Susan Tarr, who saved the long descriptive letters I wrote to her when I lived in Lagos. They were an important guide and prod to both my memory and my imagination. I thank Evie Lieberman, Julie Appel, Maggie Cammer, Joan Snyder, Leslie Garis, Elena Delbanco, and my daughter Liza Darnton for their perceptive and intelligent suggestions. Rachelle Bergstein at The Robbins Office gave excellent editorial comments and helped shape the novel. Thanks also to Richard Cohen, who provided the title.

To my agent and dear friend Kathy Robbins I offer my deepest gratitude and affection. Her support and encouragement, her careful reading and editorial comments before, during, and after the initial manuscript was written, and her belief in me were invaluable. I also thank Clare Ferraro for taking a chance on a first-time novelist, Liz Van Hoose and Amanda Brower for their help in turning the manuscript into a book, and all the people at Viking who made this experience so pleasant and rewarding.

I send my love and gratitude to my daughter Kyra Darnton, with thanks for marrying David Grann and bringing the amazing Phyllis Grann into my life. I can't thank Phyllis enough. Her editorial comments and suggestions were pivotal and taught me lessons I hope to use in future books. I also thank my son, Jamie Darnton, and his bride, Blythe Vaccaro Darnton, for their unending encouragement and support.

And last, I want to thank my wonderful husband, John Darnton, for his love and support, his tireless reading and rereading of the manuscript, and his advice and guidance at every stage of its development.